IN IT
T'WIN

A UNIQUE POKER NOVEL

J. MICHAEL BEAL

ACTION
FLOP
PUBLISHING

Se De'charger sa Reponsabilite'

This is a fictional book. Some characters are loosely to tightly-based on real people or a combination of real people. Their actions and personalities have been altered to make for a better story. The use of real people is either authorized or unauthorized because the author is intrigued with or inspired by their 'bigger than life' reputations, accomplishments and personas.

In any case, everything that happens in the book possibly could have; under the same, unlikely conditions, would have; or, for the benefit of the audience, should have happened in real life.

Copyright © 2015 by J. Michael Beal.
All rights reserved.
Published by Action Flop Publishing, Temecula, California, USA
ISBN: 978-0-9964100-0-7

To My Wife

I wrote this before we were engaged and long before our recent 40 year anniversary but it is even stronger now than it was then:

> *Our love is sunshine, bright and new each day*
> *Constantly revolving in a never-ending circle of warmth;*
> *Covering the earth with its life-giving soul;*
> *Reflecting its goodness upon itself,*
> *As we mirror each other… Always!*

When you have that kind of brightness around you, you are never in a shadow, never cold, always filled with energy and you walk around in a glow. Thank You.

Table of Contents

1. The Barnes Door Opens 1
2. The Dirty Dozen 9
3. Wyllie Twins 24
4. Best of the Rest 28
5. Open Seats 33
6. Dealers 37
7. The Pay Outs 42
8. The Home Tournament 44
9. WSOP Registration 55
10. Day One: Chips, Chairs, Champs, Chumps 62
11. The Magician's Story 72
12. The Fable of the Giant on an Outer Table 78
13. The Raise'n Asian 82
14. Playing in the Zone 88
15. Double Bubble, Toil and Trouble 95
16. Angel in the Wings 106
17. Delta Force 111
18. Hawaiian Cruise and Curse 117
19. Delta Force Two: The Rake 129
20. The Homecoming 134
21. Heads Up: The Showdown! 140
22. The Looking Glass Funeral 153
23. The Shark Tank 160

24. Check/Raise: The Media 164
25. In the Court of Public Opinion 171
26. Slow Play on a Break In 177
27. I'll Cut; You Deal 181
28. Media Circus and Paparazzi Parade 186
29. The Envelope, Please! 194
30. Binding Arbitration 205
31. Leading Out/First to Act 211
32. When You Know It All: Start Learning 216
33. A Wild Card Missing 222
34. On Tilt: Moral/Ethical/Religious Dilemmas 229
35. The Antes are Up 233
36. Beat the Bullies; Share the Wealth 239
37. Aces Cracked 243
38. Plan B 249
39. The Final Table 258
40. Under the Gun 269
41. Mo Power to You 278
42. The Pack is Back! 284
43. Back on the Meadow 296

Postscript 300

CHAPTER ONE

The Barnes Door Opens

"Dinner's served, Mr. Barnes," announced the jailer. "You better keep your strength up," the guard added. "Somebody has a pretty visitor waiting outside when he's finished dinner."

Mack Barnes was not your typical criminal. He was a clean cut, six foot tall, near 60 year old. He had the body of a retired athlete and the mind a Cheshire Cat. His eyes and ears caught everything and was hyper active even when sitting motionless on the couch. ADHD is a medical condition that results in distractions, ideas, misadventures and a mind in constant 'search' mode. Mack was delighted when people asked for I.D. when he ordered the senior citizen breakfast at Denny's. In 59 years on this planet, he had managed a couple of speeding tickets, a few parking citations, and one 'failure to smog' fine. Put aside his vehicular rap sheet and he was a model citizen. He wasn't sure how so many parts of those incredible nine months had come together the way they had. He certainly couldn't have foreseen how so many of them had fallen apart. He spooned through a sauce the county had dubbed 'mashed potatoes'. He tried to make what should have been an easy cut in something called a cutlet. Mack couldn't help but wonder what combination of who's, what's, where's or why's made the biggest difference in his latest misadventures and subsequent criminal charges.

Barnes leaned over and made another scratch on the wall. That made an even dozen and he realized he was half way through his sentence. When the judge had asked him if he had any requests on how he wanted to serve his time, Mack should have kept his mouth shut and refrained from including any of his quick repartees. He was never disciplined enough to keep his sarcastic wit out of the equation. Now he was paying for his lack of self control.

Mack had looked up at Judge Jamison and quipped, "I'm really just here for playing a card game. Maybe I should get *solitary*."

"So be it, Mr. Barnes," the elderly man in the black robe replied soberly, "Solitary it is!"

Now it was New Year's Eve and he was going to start a new year in jail. Mack leaned against the bars that made up one side of his mostly brick cell. He slowly and somberly reflected on how imagination, divergent thought and a series of incredibly good and bad luck stories had resulted in a most improbable string of outrageous scenarios. Would he do it again, knowing how so many lives were changed or even ended? Mack had to admit he would. Now he'd just serve his time and move on with his life. How could one little social, I'm sorry, the legal term Mack had learned when charged, was *'Private'* poker tournament have gone so wrong. He was trying to understand how a simple game of poker among friends could result in death, television shows, meltdowns, etc. The legal problems at the local, state and federal levels made this journey one neither he nor his assembled cast of characters would ever forget. Mack had plenty of time to reflect on his own decisions. He learned the hard way. He spat in the face of logic to follow his dreams and a few, unexpected nightmares decided to spit back. Now, as his stomach fought to win a war of digestion versus indigestion, Mack remembered that moment as if it were happening all over again.

Everything started so innocently one lazy retirement afternoon on the back porch overlooking a 400 acre meadow behind his California ranch style home.

"Sherri, get me a beer," Mack called, "make it one of those *Longboard beers* Randy Halemano brought from Hawaii. Randy claims that brew has 'Island Magic' in the bubbles. Sounds more like a bad Don Ho song to me." Barnes slowly leaned his head back and took a long sipping taste and swallow as he looked out over the Temecula Valley. For 180 degrees, he could see a poor man's forever. His eyes scanned beyond the sagebrush and dry river bed. He spotted Lake Elsinore in the distance to his left and continued north past the two well-shaped raised mounds the locals had nicknamed the *Dolly Partons*. Directly in front of him, two hours away, was Big Bear Mountain where he and Sherri had a trailer on the lake. Just to the right of that was the peak of Mt. San Jacinto where an aerial tramway ran down the other side to the desert floor of Palm Springs.

"Mack, you need to find a project," Sherri observed, "something that would keep you busy and get those nonsensical organization skills going again. You need to do something 'stupid' again." The couple had both been local high school teachers. Mack was one of those classroom leaders who had a story or an explanation for everything. He would tell his special education students to ask stupid questions. "STUPID," Barnes would advise his young charges, "just stood for '**S**omething **T**hat **U**nleashes **P**otentially **I**ntelligent **D**iscussions," One of the new kids would invariably ask, "What about DUMB?"

"DUMB," Mack would reply, "stands for **D**idn't **U**nderstand **M**r. **B**arnes."

Barnes knew his wife was just politely telling him to get off his butt and think 'stupid'. He needed to get creative juices flowing again. The couple had put on 10K runs, giant costume car rallies, Kentucky Derby Parties, Murder Mysteries, and even formed a NASTY Bear softball team. The NASTY stood for **N**ot **A** **S**oftball **T**eam **Y**et. They'd just put on their uniforms; grab their hats and gloves; throw on a little dirt for affect, and meet once a week for pizza and beer. The 'players' drew out of a hat to find out how they had performed. The team was undefeated for four years.

"Sherri's right," he said to himself, "I need to initiate, create, collaborate and manipulate."

Mack didn't have the energy he once had but he was about to act on an idea that, once set in motion, would captivate a huge following and exhaust everyone in its path.

"You know, Sherri, I've always wanted to put together a poker tournament here at home with the winner representing the whole group in the Main Event at the World Series of Poker, the WSOP, in Las Vegas!"

Sherri was a heck of a poker player, herself. She had never been the frilly female type. She was more athletic. At one time she could start her day bench pressing well over 200 lbs; paint a mural in the school wrestling room in the afternoon; and, in the evening, slip into a slinky dress for a night on the town. She had several outfits in those days that featured necklines that not only plunged; they made a splash when she entered the room. She didn't look 55 and made Mack feel younger than his AARP card would indicate. Anyone who knew the two instantly realized they were in love as much today as the day they were married over 30 years ago.

"People," Barnes would say, "age suddenly the day they fall out of love with life." Sherri added, "That will never happen in this house."

As far as marriage, Mack always advised those about to tie knots, "Don't waste your time looking for that perfect mate. Find someone who has at least 75% of what you want and can provide you with at least 25% of what you never knew you needed. Sherri and I got more than the minimum on both counts." Barnes considered himself a 'hopeful romantic'.

In the game of Poker, Mack didn't want to admit it but he might have tutored Sherri too well. She had probably won more at the poker tables in the past few years than her mentor husband. Barnes was proud of his wife's talents. In fact, on Mother's Day, Mack had melted down her broken gold jewelry and had it made into a bracelet that read WSOP as though she had won a big tournament.

It actually read dOSM when you turned it upside down. Engraved on the back was 'dream On Super Mom'! Sherri loved the fact that men at the poker table saw the bracelet. The male ego notices enough to wonder but is a little too intimidated to ask. In poker jargon, that's called an 'edge' and she used it beautifully.

"I think you *should* put on your tournament and I'll help with the set up," Sherri added, "but you'd better count on paying for my entry as well. How many more do you think we'll need?"

"I worked it out years ago, honey," Mack replied, energized. "We just have to find 18 more people as crazy as we are and all they need to put up is $600 as a buy-in. Each player would get a percentage of any winnings based on how they did in our little home tourney. The winner would get an expense paid trip to Vegas and a $10,000 entry into the Main Event.

"I know hundreds of people," Mack surmised, "but most of them are just too frugal or intelligent to put up $600 on what amounts to not much more than a low percentage pipe dream. On the other hand, I know quite a few characters that might."

Mack went on, "On a sliding scale, and considering the economic strata in this country, the decision to gamble $600 varies in importance from the wealthiest to the poorest. Starting with the rich, it's a 'drop in the bucket' or a couple of green fees." Mack would start with the few he knew. "The moderately wealthy," He went on, "might see it as a quirky adventure that displayed their ability to flaunt their indulgences." He knew a couple of those, too. "The upper middle class," he continued, "might see it as an escape from the sensible financial strategies that guide their investments toward an insured future." (Sherri and Mack fell into this category, at least for the time being.) "To any of the middle class," Mack added, "especially those who might admit to membership, $600 would be 10 full tanks on a truck or minivan. They would have to see an angle or be addicted to poker. They'd still call it an extravagance but the true strength of the 'middies' is their ability to rationalize poor decisions. Finally, for people immersed in poverty, or barely keeping their heads above water for whatever reason, the entry money would be hard to fathom. It would be a month's rent or two weeks of groceries."

Surprisingly, according to his wife, some people in that final category used a different barometer when measuring gambling and money. They had a much different standard to evaluate worth and value. According to Sherri, her cousin Chloe, "had fallen on, been pushed to, and even dragged down to hard times." Her day-to-day existence was understandably consumed with survival.

"I just hope your husband knows I wouldn't blow that kind of money on one night of poker," Chloe later told Sherri, "$600 would pay for a whole weekend at the slots in Vegas. Now, that's what I'm talking about." Mack realized that it was just a matter of perspective.

Barnes figured he could find his players among the rich and poor; the dreamers and schemers; the gamblers and the desperate; and those who had just come into money or just picked up their pay check. "For a true gambler," Barnes observed, "being part of the action was the lure, the prize potential was the hook, and the tournament would be his net." After thirty years of teaching, following his own analogy, Mack knew how to cast into the waters and 'reel 'em in'.

"Poker isn't gambling," Barnes always educated the uninformed, "The lottery is gambling. I'll believe in the lottery when somebody wins and wants to be paid off with scratcher cards."

Barnes would have to be part P.T. Barnum and part Donald Trump. He'd also be required to tempt like that little red guy with a pitchfork who perches himself on people's left shoulders. Mack hoped he didn't have to rely on playing Satan to get the job done.

"I look horrible in red," Barnes said to himself, "Sherri, on the other hand, might wear it well."

It was a hard sell but Mack, as mentioned earlier, had taught Special Ed in high school. "This," he calculated with undaunted optimism, was doable!"

CHAPTER TWO

The Dirty Dozen

The city of Temecula has a built-in poker connection. From Pechanga, the largest casino in California, to Harrah's Rincon in Northern San Diego County, there are a half dozen or more gambling venues. Pechanga is a Vegas style casino with a huge poker room, hundreds and hundreds of slot machines and tables of all kinds. It's clean, well-run and exceptionally inviting. It is absolutely the friendliest place in the world to play the game of Poker. From the dealers to the servers to the players themselves, it has all the charm of a local watering hole like the TV show, *Cheers*. Mack describes it that way, "When I walk in there, I fully expect everyone to yell, Norm!" According to the commercials, "Pechanga has first class entertainment and dining; is located 'just off Interstate 15; with plenty of parking, and adventure at every turn." The promo entices even further, "Enjoy the thrill and excitement of winning while experiencing the alluring element of fun with friends."

The name Temecula comes from *Temeku*, an Indian word

meaning, "sunlight through the morning mist." Along with its neighbor, Murrieta, well over a quarter million people call the valley home. Last year, on one survey, it replaced long running Irvine, California as the 'safest city in the United States.' We'll just agree to call it an upper middle class community. The valley has over 42 wineries and some appear to be functioning on steroids based on size and scope alone. They are proud of comparisons to the Napa, Sonoma, and Mendocino 'wine country' up north. 'Old Town' has been so built up that it's practically 'new' town. Barnes balances his praises, "Good schools, tour guides and a few politicians all provide their shares of the 'hot air' that helps to elevate the city like its world famous balloons."

Mack targeted a dozen gamblers in this picture post card town. He reasoned each would find the idea intriguing. As it turned out, the survivors would have their worlds turned upside down and inside out. Some, in fact, wouldn't live to see the ultimate outcome. Barnes knew he would recruit religiously. In fact, Mack set the date for the tournament as Friday, the 13th. He knew it would attract his parish priest, Father Patrick Jinks, who considered that day his unofficial 'feast day', of sorts. Jinks had the map of Ireland for a face. His rosy red cheeks and a heavy brogue belied the fact that he'd been in this country most of his 50 years. Jinks wore a black cord sash with strings that hung from his waist like spaghetti down his cassock. He had a tremendous love for life. Regrettably, most of his naivety had been shattered by the scandals in his own Church. He was personally blessed with an innocence that would be valued, tried and altered in the months to come. On his days off, he often found his way to Del Mar Race Track, where he loved to play the daily double and a trifecta box or two. On a weekly basis he was a pillar of the church. Father Jinks had, typically, presided over two funerals, a wedding and hosted four counseling sessions. In the months that followed the home poker game, this group wouldn't hurt his average. In addition to his official duties, he dealt with a daily barrage of crises from his many parishioners. To lighten his load, Mack and Sherri took charge of the yearly parish carnival and Fish Fry Fridays in Lent.

The good padre had tucked away $1000 for an adventure like this and he was the first invitee to accept a seat. Jinks decided to play sans collar so that everyone could relax around him, share some their off-color stories, and allow them to curse openly in his presence. He would soon realize that his unique capabilities and confidentiality would provide a valuable conscience and a moral gauge for one major player. When times got tough, in the not too distant future, Jinks would be a friend first, a priest second, and, if need be, a third party who was not afraid to come *forth*. This man of the cloth could hardly wait to hear Mack shout out the traditional "Shuffle up and deal. Put the cards in the air."

"The ponies," Father Pat announced, "can wait a year. Put my name on the board for Friday, the 13th. I'm in!" Mack was not surprised.

Speaking of horse lovers, Jonny Collison, was raised a track fanatic. Jonny was a former student of Mack's and life long friend. He lived each day paralyzed from the chest down. Shortly after birth, doctors discovered a large tumor on his spine. Subsequently, a pair of day long surgeries removed the growth but, unfortunately, severed the cord. People, on more than one occasion, observed, "He's Michael J. Fox in a wheelchair." Jonny loved the thoroughbreds. Not surprisingly, he had saved his money from his own computer spreadsheet company and planned to buy a racehorse someday. A more practical plan might have targeted personal ease of transportation. He could use any winnings to design a more accessible van. As Mack would say, "One man's nest egg, however, is another man's omelet. Jonny kept both in the same basket. Some metaphors get mixed and others get scrambled in the process." In this case, as it turned out, he would have the luxury of trying both without risking either. The equine dream kept him energized, alive, and full of hope. A poker tournament gave Jonny a chance to play on equal footing with the able bodied. The young man loved and respected the game of poker too. He trusted Barnes to put on a unique experience. Mack told his former student, "The tournament presents better odds than the 'sport of kings' you love at Del Mar." He knew that Jonny played well and could perhaps make enough to buy a good horse or a better van. He was a definite 'yes' for the tourney and had an outside chance of winning. Jonny liked to mess around with people about his wheelchair, "Save me a seat," he dryly told Mack. Barnes was used to former student's sense of humor and was tempted to engage but he resisted making puns that referred to 'wheels' or 'on a roll' comebacks. Mack let Jonny have this round. He had earned it.

Ahmed Kahlid was a retired school administer turned real estate agent. He had the money and he had the swagger. That's a dangerous combination for a gambler. Kahlid tried, unsuccessfully, to sell Mack and Sherri's house during the economic downturn. Mack felt like he had to do something as a sign of appreciation for Ahmed's effort. He decided to share a 'tell' with Ahmed that he had picked up on over the years. A 'tell' is something someone does at the table during a hand that gives away information to those who notice it. For example, rubbing your neck might show weakness for one person or strength for another.

"Ahmed," Mack said seriously, "when you're bluffing on the turn (the fourth common card), you always throw your chips into the pot with your left hand and palm down. When you have a good hand, you slide the chips along the felt backhanded from the right."

It was the truth but it only served to play with Kahlid's decision making when the two of them sat down at the table together.

"Should I do the opposite?" Ahmed would ask himself or should I do it when I have a hand. Does he know I'm compensating because he knows?" It's the typical mind game poker players depend on at a cerebral level when someone else gets inside their head. Ahmed would buy in just to finish higher than Mack.

One of the names that Mack and Sherri agreed belonged on the lists of 'well to do' and 'poker players' was Ruby Boudreau. More importantly, she also showed up on the lists marked 'what the hell' and 'count me in!'

The silver-haired Boudreau had once played poker with a crowd that included hall of famer, Linda Johnson. Ruby and her husband, Doc, used to fly from California to Vegas in his private plane for the weekends. They weren't there for Liberace or Frank Sinatra. They were there for the action in the card rooms. Not many women played poker in the casinos in those days. They weren't really welcome when they sat down with the boys. When they won a pot, it was luck. When they lost a pot, it was inability. The ladies were only reluctantly taken somewhat seriously when they managed to string together some unbelievable luck and 'hid their inabilities' with consistent winnings. Ruby was on that short list. All of this was not only 'back in the day', it was many, many days prior. No one could even imagine how many birthdays Ruby had celebrated. Her dignity, grace, and confidence made her ageless. Her responses to the actions of other players at the table were sharp and spot on. When someone came up with a great line or an entertaining story, her infectious laughter radiated warmth and put her sense of humor on display for all to enjoy. However, when another player, particularly an obnoxious man, threw out a rude, crude, inappropriate, or insensitive comment, Ruby's typical response was somewhat dismissively poetic. Sherri told the story about a fellow poker pal who wrote a limerick about Boudreau and gave it to her for her 80th birthday:

> *First, her closest eyebrow is raised with a twitch*
> *Then her hand rises slowly to her nose and an itch*
> *A short scratch without linger*
> *Using just middle finger*
> *Subtly tells the offender, "Don't mess with this bitch!"*

Ruby loved the poem and posted it on face book. Sherri always shared, "Yeah, she's been around." Boudreau's sharp enough. She starts every day with the New York Times crossword puzzle. In younger days, Ruby played volleyball well enough in the 1950's to be on the women's national team and travel the world playing against the best. Her genes were strong enough to produce a professional baseball player son and two exception daughters. One was a well known ballerina and the other was a top profiler for the FBI. Mack found her family inspirational and liked to tease her, "Like your offspring, Ruby, you've got game, always on your toes, and, when you need to, play with a 'criminal mind.'" Her favorite game was Omaha 8 and Under, but she enjoyed Texas Hold 'em, 7 Card Stud, and her Bridge league on Tuesdays. Anytime she was given an opportunity to show a man up, she was 'rip ready' to go. This tournament would be almost 6 to 1 against the ladies. Just the odds that made Ruby want to say, "Deal me in!" She was an experienced player and could contend in any tournament.

Sign-ups were going well. It seemed Mack would have no problem filling the tables. T.R. Ricky was the next mark on the Barnes' agenda. T.R. owned and ran a local trophy company. Ricky had lived in the valley for over 30 years. Barnes described him as having one of those 'motel shower' personalities. He could be ice cold or steamy hot. First timers would be wise to test the waters before stepping in front of him. Ricky could just as easily burn you as give you a cold shoulder. For some of his customers, T.R. was a refreshing experience. For others, they didn't feel quite clean as they turned to go. Ricky was a good guy wrapped in a sarcastic façade. He liked to get the upper hand before a customer tried the same tactic.

T.R. has been married four times," Mack told Sherri. "Each time the wife got younger; the alimony got higher, and the dog got smaller."

Ricky bought his way into high stakes Vegas cash games and he could hold his own in the short term.

"The best way to describe his ability," Mack explained, "would be 'local talent.' For poker novices, that translates to 'plays like a pro against the amateurs and struggles like an amateur against the pros.' Ricky was up for the tourney because he liked the idea of testing his skills; he had the money; and his newest wife, Coco, would be travelling with *Pompa*, her Pomeranian, during the weekend of the game. Mack felt sympathetic to T.R.'s misadventures with the opposite sex which had tarnished his view of women in general and had tainted his ability to share fatherly advice. Mack once heard him discussing the subject with his boy. "Women," Ricky warned his son, "are like a box of chocolates. If they're not fresh and unopened, they've been handled, tasted or damaged. There's a reason they call the whole bunch 'samplers'. The ones that look untouched and still available are that way for a reason. Guys know to stay away from those types. The empty wrappers are the ones you really wanted. **Sorry,** somebody else beat you to 'em. Move on!"

"He's no Forest Gump," Mack shared with his wife, "his new bride should certainly soften his cynicism or harden his sweet tooth."

Probably no one exuded confidence and attitude more than

Bob Sarkasian. Most people would take one look at Bob and guess he had been a boxer....and they would be wrong! He exhibited a well punched 'cauliflower face' but he had never stepped into the ring. He was a fighter, true, but he would rather knock out an opponent with his arrogance, mind, and well crafted verbal domination.

Sarkasian was Valedictorian at Boston College. His wife, Maddy, as Bob described her, "also graduated Valedictorian but from a little girls' college near by....the name's not important." Actually, that smaller school was Radcliff when it is was the female college within Harvard.

Mack loved to explain Sarkasian, "Bob could write a *Who's Who* by just focusing on his family. Both of his sons became doctors. The eldest became a neurosurgeon who lived in Chicago and, according to his father, 'was very well off'. The younger brother was a plastic surgeon in La Jolla and, Sarkasian emoted, 'was filthy rich'. His only daughter ran a string of dog grooming vans that serviced mobile home parks in the Temecula area. Mention Selena's name and Bob had the same line for everyone, "She could have been successful, but she 'went to the dogs'." He would then, condescendingly add, "God bless her, though, she's got a good heart."

The same could probably not be said for the patriarch of the Sarkasian family. Bob was a lawyer but gambled away a huge portion of income at high stakes poker games from Vegas to Atlantic City and across the pond in Europe. Most true gamblers would agree with Mack, "High Rolling is a drug and just as addictive as Crack and, eventually, much more expensive." While extremely wealthy, Bob was what the casinos refer to as a 'whale'. Whales are treated like royalty until they run out of money and then they're beached. Sarkasian had fun while it lasted. He ended up working off some of his debt doing barely legal, unorganized favors for organized crime elements around the country. "Sark, the Shark" then made a killing as a successful real estate agent in the 90's in an attempt to regain some legitimacy and cash flow. Bob described this period in his life as "going from broke to broken to broker."

Mack told friends, "Bob, as the western song goes, would admit 'he had friends in low places' when he needed them." It seemed to Barnes, that Bob spent half his day at the gym on the treadmill. Barnes once told him, "You'd be thirty pounds lighter if you just lost half your ego, Bob!"

Sherri used to say, "There were times Bob could light up a room just by walking OUT." When Mack invited Sarkasian to the dance, he didn't realize he and 'The Shark' would be doing the Limbo and asking themselves, "How low can we go?" Bob would become a major player in a huge conspiracy. The fact that he knew how to operate both inside and outside the law would be crucial in the months that followed. Sarkasian always considered himself above the law but there was nothing beneath his scope of operations.

As Sherri noted, "The Shark is an innovative and brilliant friend who happens to thrive when he finds himself in the line of fire. His sinister skills elevate to match the task when there's a profit to be made and attention to be had."

Next on the docket was Steve Purcell. Mack knew Purcell would be a catalyst to any game of chance and risk. Steve used to play with some of the top bands in the 60's. He lived in the fast lane, or at least one of the HOV lanes. He had partied hard and taken advantage of groupie girls every chance the tour provided him. He grew up fast and grew old faster. Times were tough now. The old friends got sober, died, or put on suits and made money in ways Steve, or even they, themselves, could never have imagined: They earned it! Purcell was living with his mother, Aleen, 96. She had once performed on stage, as a little girl, with her father, 'The Amazing Man of Mystery'. Harry Houdini had been a house guest for dinner. Purcell and Aleen lived in the local mobile home park. Although Steve sincerely loved and reluctantly cared for her, he occasionally fell off the wagon and resented his present day life. When Purcell was drinking, he could be creatively obnoxious. He had angles, swindles, schemes, and scandals.

As Mack would later explain him, "Purcell wasn't afraid to rob from Peter to pay Steve or borrow from Paul to finance Steve." Most times, however, Purcell's own original soul guided him in aiding others. He truly helped a few of his elderly neighbors. In turn, he helped himself to a few of their things, as a sort of, as Sherri described it, "pay-as-Steve-goes operation". He found a way to pay the entry fee somehow. Some of his funds were on loan from old friends and some of his grub stake was a result of part time work a "spanger'. (compressed word for 'spare changer'). These modern day beggars typically grab hapless customers at the gas pumps who dip into their pockets just to make spangers go away. Some days, Steve could make about $90 to $200. Purcell actually owed more than he could ever pay back to more people than he could even remember. His poker experience was honed on huge tour busses after gigs on the road. His real goal was to go somewhere where nobody could ever find him, with plenty of money and a new start. Steve wasn't afraid to die, or roll the dice, or even play it straight if need be. He was a scoundrel, of sorts, who couldn't be intimidated and actually liked it when some jerk underestimated a guy, like himself, with nothing to lose. Purcell's recklessness and diabolical side would take him far beyond the tournament. As far as the tournament, his ill gotten entry fee was not Mack's moral responsibility. It was time to move on in the recruitment process.

Mack knew Jake Wayland would die for a chance to play his way into the WSOP. Jake was a large, bearded presence. He had a radio friendly voice and was a self-appointed advocate of single malt Scotch. He had two kids with partial scholarships at USC but couldn't rub two nickels together for a movie or a dinner out. Barnes was stunned when Jake showed up at his door with $600 in a plain paper bag. Wayland's fellow workers at A & M Machinery had chipped in to stake their friend's entry to the tourney as a 30th anniversary present. His improbable benefactors/workmates had the look and fashion style of Duck Dynasty and they all expected Jake to make them money as a group. At least, they'd all have a great story to share on Fridays, after work, at the local watering hole during happy hour. Jake's wife, Carly, would rather have had a weekend in San Francisco but she knew her husband worked hard enough and deserved a night out. She knew he could appear to be as financially unencumbered as the rest of the competitors. Wayland wasn't a bad poker player but he always thought Mack was bluffing. Barnes used that belief to draw Jake into the proverbial 'lake for a swim.' Jake was an actual sweetheart who took his mother-in-law into his home when she lost control of her right arm at a casino many years ago. Mom blew her entire savings at the slot machines. Jake and Carly had been care-giving ever since. Truth be told, Jake wouldn't have a legitimate chance of winning but, Mack confided in his wife, "Two sips of Scotch into the action, he'd picture himself and his machinist co-workers waving Confederate flags in celebration. In that vision, they'd be driving down the streets of his hometown of Memphis, hanging out the window of a car painted like the General Lee from the Dukes of Hazard." Carly just made her husband promise to get enough money to 'take me to a hotel in San Diego with a recognizable name and one that provides matching bath robes, candy on your pillow, and a breakfast buffet'. In some sense, people like to root for underdogs like Carly and Jake. Who knew? Stranger things have happened.

Sherri got a call from one of the most demure and classy poker ladies she had met at Pechanga. Nurse Joy and her doctor husband, Herb Santos, were two of the most likeable and truly gentle people on the planet. Herb had been fighting pancreatic cancer for years and was about to lose the battle. He was quite the subtle poker player. The 'Filipino Force', as Mack called him, never seemed to make a foolish move in tournaments. Herb didn't just read people. He wrote reviews in his mind and kept their tendencies and history abridged in his personal mental library. The couple had spent most of the last two months in hospitals recovering from chemo and radiation. Joy wanted Dr. Herb to have one last hurrah. He wasn't going to last too much longer. This would be the memory she wanted to have of Herb doing what he loved to do most. Sherri and Mack agreed. If Santos won, Joy could take his place and represent the group. The tournament suddenly included a frail man who would strengthen its stature. Herb Santos held the sober respect of all the other players. Mack had just added class to the field.

As Barnes looked to complete his 'dirty dozen' gamblers, he learned that a local football legend was putting on his own tournament in a couple of months. Coach Stan Buck was a thin man with a massive shadow. 'Coach' had led the local high school to championship after championship. Other teams had more talent but less heart. He was an inspirational figure who had held the entire community together in triumph and through tragedy. Buck was also a referee so he prided himself on knowing all the rules inside and out and how to play the spread between the two. He played cards the same way he coached. Mack once said, "It really doesn't matter what you have as an opponent. Coach Buck will use your strengths against you and punish you with what you assume are his weaknesses." One phone call was all it took to convince the pigskin guru to join the game. Stan didn't expect to lose. He never expected to lose. He was the odds on favorite, in Mack's eyes.

"Certainly," Barnes admitted, "opposing coaches dreaded locking eyes with Buck across a field of grass in the stadium on Friday night. If you had to lock eyes across the green felt at the poker table, it would be even more intimate and intimidating." Barnes now had his twelve gamblers. The other eight would turn out to be much more than seat fillers, however. As Mack would later describe them, "they'd be a mix of 'where'd they come from?', 'what just happened?', 'who'd have thought?' and 'how the hell?'"

CHAPTER THREE

Wyllie Twins

"Too bad I just couldn't have stopped with those dozen feature players," Mack thought from his French Valley lock up, "I'd have never spent one day in jail. I never imagined the next two entrants would be both my admitted doing and undoing?"

Those two young men grew up right down the street yet had to call in their entry from the Middle East. Mack should have been able to recognize it as a harbinger of things to come. After all, isn't that what poker experience is all about? A true poker player can smell danger when the action takes a turn for the weird. Nobody checks and then raises a call without every player at the table, not just the original raiser, replaying the hand in their heads. A 'check/raise' is like a young boy waiving a lantern on a train track in a driving rain storm with an old bridge just up ahead. It's like a flock of speedy little dinosaurs running toward you in Jurassic Park. It's not good. It's all bad. You've got something coming your way and you don't have to know what it is to know you don't want any part of it. You better duck and cover. Live to see another day!

Simply put, at a table, in a tournament, one of the best ways of winning is not losing. Mack should have heeded his own advice, "Most of the time," Mack told Sherri, "When the ship seems to be sailing without you, it's better to wave from the dock than swim toward the propellers." As Mack replayed that comment in his mind, "This time, it just happened to be *twin* propellers!" When the phone rang around 3 AM at the Barnes home, Mack instinctively hit the alarm button. Getting no response, he hit it harder and harder until he realized it was the phone and that he would probably have to buy a new clock. It was Dottie Wyllie calling from Dubai. She didn't think to allow for the time difference. Her sons were celebrating new positions with impressive law firms and had whisked her away as a thank you present for "just being mom".

"Mack, I hope I didn't wake you guys," she said, "what time is it there?"

Mack was awake enough at that moment to try to save her embarrassment, "It's early in the morning and a wonderful day down here. Where are you calling from?"

"Dubai, Mack. It's like Vegas on growth hormones. But that's not what I'm calling about. Are you still having that poker tournament next Friday?"

"I am," Mack replied. Do you know some sheik in the desert, Dot? We can always use an infusion of foreign oil wealth."

"No Mack, the boys heard about it and you know how much they admire you as a mentor. Can you use three more?" Dottie sounded excited….and awake.

"Sure," Mack replied, "but why three?"

"Their uncle, Calvin Moffett wants to play too, Dottie added. You know Calvin, Mack. He's got a good job as a jailor with the county. It can't hurt to have a former professional football player with a gun for security. You're going to have cash around, aren't you? What do you say? The boys love poker but have never played in a live tournament before and they'd love to be part of it. I'd like to buy their way in as a career celebration present to both."

"Fine with me," Mack consented, "I'll take good care of David and Dennis. We don't have any twins at this point. Do they really know that much about poker or have they just watched it on TV?"

"Oh, they've played online. They belong to something called the WPT. I think it stands for World Poker Tour. It's new, I think." Dottie answered. "I think they've got that gambling bug but they're also really careful with their money."

"The kids have enough money to play," Mack thought. "We need some young bloods to mimic the Main Event at the Rio. Good Chemistry," Mack concluded softly to himself. "Good Chemistry and good practice for the real thing." Actually, the twins were brilliant. Both had passed the Bar and each had a Ph.D. along with a J.D. for their efforts in school. David graduated from Cornell at the age of 19 and his brother, Dennis had advanced degrees from ASU, UCLA and Stanford by the time he was 22. The two gangly youths were sponges for knowledge and magnets for money. Every time they had ever applied for a position, they got the same response, "When can you start?" Each was climbing the legal ladder or, more appropriately, "Running up a moving escalator," Mack had observed.

In spite of their success, Mack had been a surrogate father and advisor for both. Their dad, Herschel, had been a scientist. He worked with rockets. Mack had, obviously, connected the two. 'Hersh' was always inventing, modifying or radically redesigning some sort of mechanical magic. Unfortunately, with the genius came the demons. The polite, kind and generous Herschel Wyllie suddenly lost it one day. He ran through a security checkpoint with a gun in his hand. He was screaming as he made his way through a rival space agency and was surrounded by police. For some 'God only knows' reason, he lowered his head, shut his eyes, and pointed his weapon at the security officers. Immediately, that threatening gesture brought a hail of bullets from all directions. His own gun never fired. He fell to the ground, mortally wounded. His wife, Dottie was devastated. Nobody ever saw it coming.

Mack and Sherri stepped in and the two families had been extremely close ever since. Dottie had worked as Mack's aide at the high school and was a riding partner for Sherri in local recreational horse shows. Even though the boys were light years ahead of Mack intellectually, he kept them off balance with his quick wit. Barnes had kept them grounded after their father's death with his sage, albeit, off beat sense of humor. Their bonding and the ability to work as team would be challenged unlike anything they could ever have imagined. Their uncle Calvin wouldn't be the only taste of law enforcement to deal with in the next few months, either.

CHAPTER FOUR

Best of the Rest

Mack's good Hawaiian buddy, Randy Halemano accepted an e-mail invitation. He had to move his yearly trip back home to the mainland up a week to join in the festivities. Randy was an island spiritualist, tempered by an infectious laugh and a downright funny personality. Once, while visiting Oahu, Mack had asked Randy why his computer ran so slow. Halemano explained, "In da islands, we respect spam, Mack." Hawaiian humor can be playful on tour and painful when you least expect it. Mack had known Randy from his early 'recreation and parks' days back in college. The two, admittedly, "reverted to infantile behavior at the drop of a pineapple drowning in a Mai Tai," as Barnes liked describe it.

Randy was living large on the Big Island. Halemano had pensions from the military, education, civil service and social security. His wife Nancy was still working and hauling down big bucks in the rejuvenated Hawaiian real estate market. She came from a melting pot family. She was Irish and Puerto Rican with red hair and freckles. "I guess we're all mutts in some way," Mack used to tell his students, "I'm German, French and Irish. Guess that means I can attack myself; surrender; and go to a pub."

Randy and Nancy couldn't just sit back and make it on two good-paying jobs and three retirement accounts alone. Halemano wanted to come back to Temecula and build an upscale, tropically themed, manufactured home park. He was inspired by the Magazine, **Dwell**, and envisioned a modern, all-view complex for seniors which would be constructed up against the foothills. He tried, with little success, to talk Mack into investing in it. A win in Vegas, Randy hoped, just might be enough to set those wheels in motion and win Barnes over. This motley band was starting to take shape and only Halemano had a premonition. He told Randy, "The Mainland calls and you answer. The Island will find a way of calling you back. Sometimes the gods are jealous or angry and make you bring friends." The very volcanoes that formed the Hawaiian archipelago and their legends would make Randy prophetic.

"Just another reason," Mack reflected, "that Halemano's feel for nature was usually 'spot on'. It was remarkable how many times the gods seemed to talk to Hawaiians. Maybe California talks to us and we aren't good listeners."

The surprise of the group was Bryce Tanner who called Mack and asked if he had an open seat. Bryce was not a gambler or a wealthy man. He wasn't even someone looking for a challenge. Turns out, Bryce was in the process of selling his house and moving to Austin, Texas. He wanted to go out with gusto and he thought the contest would provide him a great story when he got to the Lone

Star state. Bryce worked at Disneyland in his youth and had bought stock options with Disney when he had the chance. Turns out he made more money selling his Disney memorabilia when he needed a cash flow. Goodbye original Mickey Mouse watch and hello poker tourney. Who wears watches anymore, anyway? Mack knew that Bryce was dead money but he needed live bodies. Tanner would certainly add a jovial personality to the table and keep everybody entertained as long as he lasted. Besides, Bryce liked being part of the team and would share in any profits. Tanner was a dreamer of immense proportion and expected the tourney's winner to advance in the Vegas Main Event. Bryce was now officially a "playah" and his money was as good as anyone else's. Mack never imagined that a "Jack Tanner" or a "Tanner Twice" would become new nicknames for a pair of Jacks and a permanent part of local poker jargon in the not too distant future.

Mack and Sherri's neighbor at Big Bear was Dick Galliano. Galliano was probably not as great as he thought he was, but who could be? Like so many Italians, he pictured himself as Rocky, the stallion. It was a fair comparison in Dick's vision of himself. He'd always lived his life running wild and in search of new pastures. As far as people could tell, Galliano had never been gelded. Anyone who, during his youth, had made a living at things like worm selling, muskrat skinning, and wearing a Mr. Peanut suit, qualified as a vagabond in Mack's book. Dick was even a cabin boy on search vessel that retrieved missile nose cones off Cape Canaveral. That was back in his merchant marine days. The fact that he made and lost millions in real estate and marketing businesses; worked as a highway patrol officer; and been CEO at several top notch businesses just added to his sense of adventure. Mack always reminded him that "somebody who goes by the name of 'Dick' feels compelled to live up to the billing." Galliano and his wife, Shannon, lived between Big Bear in the summer and Palm Desert in the winter. Dick could never say 'no' to an invite that involved testosterone and competition. As a poker player, he was aggressive and a bit of a performer. Unfortunately, his karaoke prowess didn't carry over to the table where his skills were more than a little off key. Given the right situation, however, he was cunning, calculative, intuitive and down right opportunistic. Galliano always chided others, "Poker is not life; Life is poker. You play the cards you're dealt and sometimes, when you don't get what you want, you play the cards you DON"T have."

Mack chimed in, "You play the other guy, the environment, the momentum or the moment. Poker players are shape shifters who morph themselves to fit the eye of the beholder. Good pokers players can be one person on one hand and another person on the next. Great poker players become non persons. They fold into themselves and everybody at the table sees a different person at the same time." Dick Galliano had been that kind of door to door 'salesman'. As a youth, he once sold a three year subscription for a magazine that catered to black audiences. His customer was a wealthy white woman. She liked Dick and bought it for her son who loved airplanes. To be honest, Galliano was just going by the publication's name: JET Magazine. Mack noted to himself, "Dick's skills and intuition would be valuable assets at the table. Fame and fortune can create marketing opportunities. People can find themselves buying what other poker players have to sell."

CHAPTER FIVE

Open Seats

With only two days to go before the home tournament, Mack still needed two more players. He decided to try all the people he originally considered but dismissed because they might have been a bit too rational. Joe Staley, a school psychologist was a pragmatist. He coalesced to the point of giving Barnes a conditional 'Yes'. Joe said he would do it if Mack was unable to find someone and his boat sold for the price he was asking on Craig's List. Three other friends responded, each with differing variations of a common sense 'NO'! Typically they would say, "I'd have better odds picking red or black on a roulette table and far better chance of making money at craps or playing blackjack." And they were right. This was not a **smart** poker tourney. In Mack's mind, the home game was supposed to be more like a magic carpet ride. He even painted it that way, "You don't ask how to steer the rug or how tight the weave is, you just get on and let it take you away. You don't fasten your seat belt. You stand up and admire the surrounding wonderment.

The majesty of being transported to another land does not involve the fear of dropping off in mid flight. Imagination demands that you soar above the clouds wearing a turban, some puffy pants and curly shoes. The final touches include folded arms and head raised in pride."

"Good God, people," Mack internally added, "how can humans make it through their most ordinary schedules without, when offered the opportunity, taking a timeout to try extraordinary things?" Mack had pulled the twins aside in high school and reminded them, "Sometimes there are no *keys* to unlock happiness. Sometimes the secret is finding the right combination." Mack was known to utter such philosophies after any drink that had a shot of Meyer's rum. As mentioned earlier, Barnes was a 'hopeful' romantic. For the younger generation, including the twins, he was sincere, if not always relevant. "It is what it is," Mack would lament, "and, for a baby boomer, it will never be what it was."

In an admittedly low percentage shot at a final player, Barnes and his wife, dropped in on the local school superintendent. Tom Knight was blessed and cursed with a perfectly compartmentalized brain. Every poker grunt would give his or her arm (not their hand) for his recall abilities. If he had decided to become a poker pro, he could have had tells on every player who ever sat down at a table. His mind would give him an insurmountable advantage in reads over even the best in the game. Unfortunately, when a third Queen he was waiting for, hit on the flop, Tom couldn't keep his chin from hitting the table or prevent his pupils from dilating like the Looney Tunes logo. His opponents could almost hear that cartoon sound track coming out his ears. As far as making money at the table: "That's all Folks!" Knight politely declined even though his wife, Katy, tried to convince him otherwise.

"Tom, Mack needs one more person," she said, "You know it would be a blast. It's like fantasy football. You can just sit back and have fun. I think you should play in the game." Tom would have loved to play poker but he had to be careful how it would appear if the game, for example, was busted by the cops.

"I have an image to protect," Knight reminded her, "People don't want their school superintendent to be gambling. It's just not professional."

"Besides," he politely scolded his spouse, "fantasy football isn't gambling. It's a game of insights, research, opportunity and calculated risk. It's not gambling. It may have just as much frustration and exhilaration, but it's not just a game. Fantasy football is real. Women just don't get the distinction."

Truth be told, there is one other difference between being a fan and being an 'owner'. Mack had a team in Tom's fantasy world and agreed, "Actual, real life football *fans* pour out their hearts for their teams on Fridays and Saturdays. Fantasy football *owners* tear out their souls on Sundays." Barnes and Knight had shared years of injury and anguish in the fantasy game. Only those who have 'benched' a four touchdown receiver would ever know what it's like to know someone else had done worse. "The annual fantasy football draft," Mack claims, "is done around a table but everyone knows it's actually held at the altar of ESPN or Yahoo Sports. One of Mack's friends had it all figured out. "Old school charts and New

Age apps meet on an imaginary battlefield. One of Mack's language challenged students saw a flyer on his desk and asked, "Are you a gambler, Mr. Barnes, or is this one of those 'male bondage' things?"

"Sometimes, Mack reasoned, "it's just better to ignore a question than try to explain the difference."

"Sorry," Tom softened his objection as he turned to Sherri, "but Katy and I just can't take the chance on being misperceived in the Temecula community or school district."

"We understand," Sherri responded, "we're just getting a little desperate and thought it was worth a try."

As they headed to the door, the phone rang and Tom went to answer it, sharing his goodbyes and pleasantries as he walked away.

Katy leaned in and whispered to Sherri, "Don't say a word to my husband, but what time do you want me there?"

Katy was a sound player when she wasn't drinking her favorite Champaign at the table. Even then, she had an effervescent nose for the game. The chances her husband would even find out about her playing were slim. She forgot this was, to some extent, a game of chance. What were the chances everyone in town would know the whole story in the not too distant future? It was just a matter of long odds in short time.

Mack and Sherri were 'bubbling' with excitement that the tables were finally full.

CHAPTER SIX

Dealers

Why hire real dealers for a home poker tournament? Can one question have so many answers? Poker dealers are the envoys of the poker gods. When they fan the deck to make sure every card is accounted for, players are confident that the dealer knows his or her stuff. When they mix and swirl the deck with both hands, they do more than make sure cards are randomly dealt. They are mixing the pot, stirring the cauldron, and brewing a potion. The dealer, some poker players believe, adds three ounces of good luck and two ounces of bad luck; a predestined flop and the 'buried cards' someone really needed. The dealer 'buries' a card (puts it face down and 'dead') each time he adds to the common cards. This tradition goes back to riverboat dealers who dealt from the bottom or prearranged the order of cards in their hand. The dealer unveils the holy 'turn' (fourth common card) that stimulates the action and the consummate 'river' card (final common card) that blesses some and curses others. The dealers are the high priests and priestesses of the poker world. The table is their sacred shrine honoring the golden geese and surrounded by fatted calves.

To others, the dealers are faceless, emotionless, mechanical and inconsequential to the final outcome. For those players, the dealer is an hourly employee of the casino who just wants to finish his day without hassles. Disciples of this quasi religious point of view agree that these automatons find tables that make the time go by quickly and, hopefully, deal out a jackpot where everybody tips their fortuitous android hundreds of dollars for something.... couldn't be for *luck*, you know. By the same logic, these players probably leave a tip for the slot machines when they win. After all, the only difference between dealing cards and the slots, it would appear under this theory, is that one of them is 'reel' and the other one is 'real'....and wears a vest. Mack wanted professional dealers at the table because they provided a stable, unbiased, and an acceptable control element to the tournament. The only alternative would be to rotate the deal among the players and, as Mack always says, "Even the word, Trust is 80 % rust." Seasoned dealers have seen it all, heard it all, and ruled on it all. People trust them to make the right call and to do so without emotion or investment. Barnes wanted an impartial decision maker at each table. Mack instructed his poker ambassadors to "be Solomon when they had to think outside the rules; Clint Eastwood when they had to put people in their place; and a nun with a ruler when they had to take control of a player, a situation, or the entire table with just one look or one line." Besides, the dealers were usually the only truly mature people in the room.

"If you have never played Texas Hold 'em," Sherri told a friend, "I can assure you, in the estimation of many, each dealer is actually Santa Claus and every hand dealt is like Christmas morning. Although the players' façades bely their emotional anticipation and excitement, I can guarantee you, they can hardly wait to open their two-card 'presents' the dealer delivers each hand."

"You can almost hear their internal voices as they look down at the pair of face down cards in front of them," Sherri added. "What'd I get? What I'd get? I wonder what everybody else got. Hope it's not as good as mine. Hope mine's the best." Each player's inner child shivers with anticipation." Mack's wife made a good point. Some players have to look at each card individually as it arrives and then decide if they go together. Others want to wait until they can open their entire gift at once so they don't get their hopes up with an Ace or a face card, only to be crushed by a lowly little 5 of a different suit. Still others wait until it's their turn to act. Following Sherri's analogy, they want to see 'what the other kids got' before deciding if theirs is worth playing. Can you tell I came from a big family? Actually, if any 'Mack' comes through at times, it's because I'm related to a couple of people in this story. "In any case," Sherri continued her analogy, "a couple of terrible 'hole' cards are like a pair of socks from your aunt Judy. A decent duo like an Ace/10 suited is like two tickets to a ball game. A great pair, like 9's, is like that shiny new mountain bike you can hardly wait to take out on the trail. You look at your bike and you want people to call. One by one they fold their presents: A new shirt, a box of candy, a wallet, and, from the greasy biker chick who threw her cards away like a

Frisbee, what must have been a Chia Pet. Then, as you are about to jump on your bike and raise the stakes, the guy two down on your right raises 'All In'! The player next to you makes an immediate 'snap call.' Suddenly your two wheeled transport has lost its luster. You can't afford to go against that many 'over' cards. It's time to put your bike in the garage for another day. Your early excitement has been transformed into simple statistical probability. You throw your 'once wonderful present' into the muck."

"Damn it!" you say to yourself. "One of them must have gotten an I Pad and the other guy must have opened an X Box to call." Then, what would have been your third 9 shows up on the flop. You reminisce about that two-wheeler you locked away in the garage. You know how much you would have enjoyed playing with it now that it became a 'tri' cycle. Wait 'til next Christmas morning," you tell yourself but you lean back and try to imagine riding it 'to the river.'" Some sound of remorse is muttered under at least one player's breathe on every hand. Someone at the table has turned to his neighbor and lamented his decision to fold. "This dealer sucks!" You say to yourself, "Maybe I just was a bad boy this year and didn't deserve it."

Five minutes later, the 'jolly old' Dealer has another present for everyone and it's Christmas Morning once again. Ho, Ho, Ho!" by Sherri's standards.

Mack picked up two of his favorite dealers from Pechanga. Washington Evans was a savvy, sage and seasoned dealer who had learned his trade as a recovered poker pro. Evans had started his career winning big, including a quarter million dollar payout.

Like most players who win big early, Washington bottomed out in places like Commerce and the Bicycle Club before finding a career working for the casino. Evans looked and acted a lot like Morgan Freeman when he played a chauffeur in the movie 'Driving Miss Daisy'. He's paid his dues and learned his 'don'ts' in the world of poker and he can chuckle to himself at a humorous comment or, if need be, spread his arms across the dealer's position with the stone face of a drill sergeant. Those lucky enough to be sitting at a table when Mack's other dealer arrived, heard an affable, "Hi everybody, my name is Jimmy!" Jimmy Gilmartin also found himself tempering poker playing with poker dealing. From riverboats to casinos; from lodges to home games; Jimmy was jolly and jovial. The white bearded, rosy cheeked Gilmartin, especially in his white shirt and red vest, looked like a cross between Kenny Rogers and, well, Santa Claus.

CHAPTER SEVEN

The Pay Outs

Mack made copies of the payouts for each player. He had given one to each as they signed on. This was official and it was on money green paper. "From the Champ to the Chump," as Mack put it, "everyone has a percentage."

The Pay Out sheet was a Barnes original:

The Payouts for the Tournament

Last Table FINALISTS

1st Place	15% of the winnings, a $10,000 entry in World Series of Poker Main Event, $1200 for room, board, and vacation along with the right to represent or pick any other player to go to Vegas as the representative of the group
2nd Place	14% of the winnings and 1st alternate in case the actual winner could not compete 'for any reason'

3rd Place   12.5% of the winnings and 2nd alternate
4th Place   10% of the winnings
5th Place   8.5% of the winnings

Last Table Runner Ups

6th Place   7% of the winnings
7th Place   6% of the winnings
8th Place   5% of the winnings
9th Place   4% of the winnings
10th Place   3% of the winnings

First Table Players Eliminated

Places 11-15   2% of the winnings each
Places 16-20   1% of the winnings each

If the tournament champion made it "*to the money*" in Vegas, each player would receive $200 to $3000. If the tournament champion made it to the *final table*, each player would receive $7500 to $112,500. If the tournament champion should **WIN the Main Event**, each player would receive $100,000 to $1.5 million.

CHAPTER EIGHT

The Home Tournament

On Friday, the 13th, Mack was up with the sun and had a better glow. He was proud of the way everything had come together.

"This will be a unique experience, Sherri," he told his wife as her feet hit the ground next to the bed. "When things culminate in a successful activity, I feel like it was all worth the effort." Not to completely equate the two, but this tournament, Mack would later recalculate, "was a culminating activity in much the same way the Last Supper was the culmination of Easter Week. The best and worst were yet to come." Father Jinks once told Barnes that, at Easter services, he had asked all the children to join him around the pulpit for an inspiring homily. At his beckoning, nervous parents reluctantly let their little ones travel up the aisles and sit around the priest on the altar. Dressed in his colorful and brilliant vestments marking the end of Lent, Father strolled around the crowd of innocents.

"What do you think the first thing Jesus said to his disciples when he appeared after rising from the dead?" he asked the youths. No one wanted to say the wrong thing. No one wanted to say anything. Finally, one little girl timidly raised her hand.

"Don't be afraid to guess," Jinks told her. "Imagine that you had died, were buried, and then appeared perfectly fine to your friends on that first Easter. What would *you* say?"

She looked up at the priest. He lowered the microphone to her face and, after taking a quick look at her parents for approval, she replied, "Tadah!" The audience loved it. Not quite the answer he was looking for but it fit perfectly into the message and the magic of the moment. Mack would find there were many more 'tadah' moments in this group's future as well.

The poker tables had been delivered the night before. Sherri had confirmed with the dealers and made the customary middle class trip to Costco for snacks, drinks and paper goods. The living room was a mini casino. Mack had counted out the chips and had placed rules and disclosure packets on the chairs of each of the 20 seats. At about 4 P.M. the dealers arrived. Sherri had the buffet ready as the Barnes management team answered questions and went over typical scenarios that might occur at the tables. In the end, the dealers would settle all disputes and Mack would back them up. At 5 P.M. the players started arriving.

Domingo Fernandez, the Barnes' handyman was just finishing up the final touches on the new canister lights over one table. Over the years, Domingo had done just about every type of work around the Barnes' house. For $20 an hour plus parts, he could do anything from building a gym on the porch, to the present patio cover out back. More than that, he was thought of as family and friend. A better worker and a more wonderful person could not be found anywhere. The phone rang. It was Joe Staley. The boat deal on Craig's list fell through. Joe had made his entry contingent on the consummation of that sale. Staley offered to pay half if Mack knew anyone else who wanted to take his place. Domingo was standing there with the bill for his services and purchases in his hand.

"Just a minute, Joe," Mack interjected, "I think I have an idea."

Barnes put down the phone and turned to his handyman, "Domingo, someone just put you in the poker tournament."

Domingo looked bewildered and caught off guard. "I don't know anything about poker Mr. Mack, and my wife has food on the table waiting for me with mi familia."

"Do you know someone who could play for you?" Mack asked.

"I have a friend, Angel Vasquez," said Domingo, "He loves poker."

"Can you get hold of him quickly?" Mack inquired.

"Si, he was supposed to come for dinner tonight at our casa," answered Domingo, speaking a mild form of 'Spanglish', "but I know he would rather play poker. Is that okay? I can call him."

"Any friend of yours is a friend of ours, Domingo. Besides, we need at least one 'angel' in this group. Get on the phone and give him directions," said Mack, "even if he's a little late, that's fine." Mack would match Joe Staley on the other half of the entry fee. The group was back to two full tables of 10.

In a home game, the players' first sign of commitment is the

BYOB. That's more than bring your own buy-in. Big Jake had his single malt Scotch. Bob had a bold Cabernet. Katy came in with a bottle of Cabernet Blanc. She didn't want to come home with Champaign breath. She planned on staying a while. Most had one of the many various beers: imported, home brewed, crafted and non-alcoholic. For some reason 'IPA's' were in vogue for the present, and light beers marked the dieters and the recovering Colorado River party crews. Randy Halemano had his traditional Long Board and a few utilized tequila, gin, vodka and bourbon on the rocks, in a mix, or straight up. At least three drinkers in the group were soda pop aficionados. In the background, Ruby poured herself a cup of coffee and jolted it with a little Irish whiskey. Calvin Moffett had the only Malt Liquor but you would expect that from a retired Oakland Raider. Dr. Herb had cinnamon tea. T.R. and Dick walked in with the same six-pack of Mike's hard lemonade. Sherri had a little shot of Fireball and Mack had to stay alert so, tonight, it was just Meyer's Rum and diet Dr. Pepper, 'A Dr. Rum'… and just one!

As Mack surveyed the group, he asked himself, "How do I know so many *old* people?" When he suddenly realized that he and Sherri were in the same age group, he amended his assessment of the crowd, "What an outstanding assembly of experience," he touted. "Vitality and brilliance counteract youth and inexperience every time."

Just then, the Wyllie boys walked in….with their mom, Dottie. They looked so young and innocent. Suddenly the red balloon of hyped energy that had permeated the gathering to that point was punctured by the giggly smiles of the youthful twins. They seemed so young. They seemed so 'new'. Maybe the realization of what the next generation had brought to the table suddenly made the players realize what others their age must be willing to face in the Main Event.

"Surely, the veterans' years of poker and life situations would give these two young men no chance tonight," many muttered to themselves. The reality of one of these veterans surviving a weeklong tournament against youth, health, focus, and energy was a daunting challenge to imagine.

Sherri introduced the boys to the group. "This is David and this is Dennis Wyllie. Their mom is a friend of mine who worked with Mack. We've known them since they were in middle school and this is their first poker tournament."

"Actually, this is our first **live** tournament, Mrs. B. We've both played online since college but we never played against anybody face to face."

"Welcome," Ahmed said from the back of the room, "most of us have dabbled online, but I think you'll enjoy this even more."

It was time to grab drinks, fix plates of snacks, count chips and take on the competition. Mack, stalling for time so that the final player could get there, upped the ante by announcing a 'prop' (proposed wager) of his own. "I have $100 for anyone who can answer this question without the assistance of Google or the like," Mack challenged the group.

"When I first started teaching, I had two boys in my class together. They looked exactly alike. I learned that they had the same mother and father and were born on the same day," Mack announced. "They were born in the same year just minutes apart. They were born at the same hospital and were delivered by the same doctor. Both were the same age and had the same DNA but were not twins." Mack went on, "How is that possible?"

The group looked at each other and asked questions that were not well thought out, "Was it a leap year?" one asked. "Were they fraternal?" another queried without thinking. "Were they conjoined?" another embarrassed himself by asking. Just then the relative calmness of the moment was shattered by the unmistakable sound of Domingo's friend, Angel and his Harley Davidson pulling into the driveway.

"Oh, I think our last entrant has arrived," Mack told the group.

Angel walked in draped in leather and revealing any number of gang related tattoos as he uncloaked.

"Tonight," Mack explained, "I'd like to introduce Angel Vasquez, a friend of my handyman, who will be playing for him in his stead. They have agreed to split any winnings."

Angel took his seat and Barnes continued, "I understand you love poker, Angel. Where do you play?"

"I haven't played in a casino since I was released," explained Angel, "but we used to play for cigarettes in prison." With that revelation, most of the oxygen was drained from the room. The sober silence that had accompanied Angel's entrance was even more noticeably pronounced. Players turned to their respective tables. Each struggled to regain focus on the game and devote less interest to the festivities and histrionics.

"Are we gonna play poker or what?" T.R. called out. The crowd seemed to agree. They even forgot about Mack's prop and the $100 'non-twins'.

Mack smiled at the crowd, gave Domingo an inquiring glance out of the side of his eye, and responded with a slight bow of approval, "Thank you, Mr. Vasquez," Mack acknowledged, "glad to have you here with us." Mack nimbly shifted his role to tournament organizer. He stood up, took center stage and made the hallowed announcement every poker player recognizes. In much the same way racing fans respond to "Gentlemen start your engines" or baseball fans make it through the national anthem for "Play Ball!" everyone was energized by Mack's, "Shuffle up and Deal. Dealers put the cards in the air!" Game on!

The always loud and affable Bryce Tanner proclaimed, "I'm going to take it slow; get to know everybody; study their tendencies; and make sure I stick around awhile." Before the first flop of the night, you guessed it, Bryce declared, "I'm all in!" If that wasn't enough, within a heartbeat and an accompanying breath, Angel responded, "I call!" The entire cast of characters, had just settled in at both tables but rose to their collective feet and leaned forward to witness the play. It was a classic 'race' as they call it, with near 50-50 hands. Bryce had a pair of Jacks and Angel had a King and an Ace, suited in spades. When the first three common cards (or flop) hit the table, two of them were Kings. Bryce was gone in less than a minute and the Harley huggin', prison playin', last-to-arrive Angel, 'doubled up' and was the game's first chip leader. Twenty minutes later, Katy, who was filling in the 'Blancs', over bet her straight and was taken out by a flush. "I guess diamonds aren't this girl's best friends," she said. "In this case, they're just lovely parting gifts."

Before the action could travel around the table again, Calvin Moffett, the boys' uncle tried to bluff Ruby on a board of Kings and Jacks, she looked past his gold necklace and wasn't blinded by his 'bling'. She saw him for what he was as a poker player. Boudreau had seen the same move at Caesar's Palace many times in her career. Ruby recognized the male ego and how it represents itself from the waist up. She called Moffett and scolded him, "Might work in the locker room, sonny, but this is the real world and I'm not wearing a towel. If I'm right, and I know I am, looks like you're not wearing one either." The table was down one ex-Jock and Ruby was on a roll.

Before the end of the first hour, Randy Halemano found Dennis Wyllie's big raise too much and folded a better hand. He went out several hands later with a huge "Aloha" to the crowd. Randy, like most other eliminated players went out on the patio to watch the Dodger game on the big screen.

As the second hour ended, David Wyllie took out Ahmed Kahlid and Big Jake on the same hand. David had 'flopped' (those first three common cards) 'the nuts' (an unbeatable hand) and carefully, checked, called and raised like a surgeon with a scalpel in a 'take all' operation. Ahmed had just sent in one of those home DNA tests to find his ancestral heritage. It had come back with Italian markers. It was, to say the least, not what he expected. "Must have been during the Roman Empire," Ahmed told himself, "or maybe one of my predecessors had a great Mediterranean Cruise." Either way, the hen house had a visitor from outside Kahlid's neighborhood. Most people wouldn't have let it bother them but this Middle Easterner was obviously distracted by the news and couldn't keep his concentration on poker. Ahmed had tried to split a pot with an ace high and walked away muttering something about forensics. Big Jake always thought somebody was bluffing and sometimes, they were. In this case, they weren't. Within the next hour the player numbers had shrunk from 20 to 14. The two tables were down to 7 players each. Fewer players at the table meant the relative value of each starting hand had increased. 'Bluffing' became more viable and 'calling with the best hand' was a more fashionable money making strategy.

Dick lost to Sherri who sucked out with an Ace on the river (the last card). Dr. Herb, markedly weak from bouts with Chemo and radiation, had to leave the table. His wife, Joy, took over for him. Even though the doctor's 'Queen of Hearts' played well, she was more concerned about her husband's health and gambled loosely. It was too loosely. The tables were down to twelve.

As the blinds and antes increased, smaller chip stacks took chances and were gone, eaten by chip rich intimidators with little to lose and much to win.

In the fourth hour T.R. called with a better hand and lost to Mack who found his 'three of a kind' on the turn.
Father Jinks was never blessed with good cards all evening and decided to push it all in with a pair of 8's. When two people called, his fate was sealed to another 8 which never came. The clock

struck 10 and, appropriately, the final 10 went to one table. Jimmy now became the floor man and would have the final say in any confrontation. Washington Evans continued to deal but his fun loving banter became more relevant and professional. He knew the stakes had risen for this little band of card sharks and he faded into the shadows of the action. He had become invisible to most at the table. Players counted, canvassed and calculated odds and positions. Things were beginning to become all too somber and serious for a neighborhood contest.

After a 20 minute break, Angel, Bob and Mack went out in that order. The odds changed again. Jonny went out in 7th place, shoving all his chips in the middle with his favorite hand, Queen/10 suited. As he rolled away from the table and out the front door to his van, several players' jaws dropped as others complimented him on his play. Those late arrivals hadn't even noticed he had been playing in a wheelchair.

As the play approached midnight, the biggest surprise to everyone but themselves was that the twins were still alive and had healthy chip stacks. Sherri found out how healthy when she failed to hit her straight or flush, unsuccessfully bluffed her 'nothing' hand, and had to say goodbye in 6th place.

Ruby continued to demonstrate her lifetime learned abilities and Coach Buck was every bit up to the task. Steve Purcell gave it a great effort but departed in 5th place when his pocket Aces were cracked by a Wyllie straight.

Sometime after the bewitching hour a huge hand went down among David Wyllie, Coach Buck and Ruby. The flop was 7-8-9 rainbow (all different suits). Ruby and the coach had hit trips or three of a kind: Nines for Buck, Eights for Ruby and David's Jack/Ten of Hearts had given him a straight. He still had to dodge a full house if the board paired…but it didn't. Everyone had bet their remaining stacks, pot committed.

Unbelievably, the two brothers were head to head for the championship. Not much drama followed since Dennis' stack was dwarfed by his brother's. In about twenty minutes, before the clock struck two, David was crowned champion. Dennis was runner-up. The representative of the old would be the new. The old farts would rely on the two young 'whippersnappers'. Since only the old would know what that expression even meant, the twins could only surmise that it wasn't a compliment. The group saluted the Wyllie boys with a toast by Jake Wayland, "Don't let the big boys outplay you, outflank you, or outhouse you!" he said. Everyone let out a cheer and Ruby added, "Outhouse is appropriate. Most of them are full of crap." Ruby never missed a chance to 'tell it like it is'.

It was off to Vegas for the boys. Mack, retired, would chaperone and everybody would win tons of money. Of course no one really believed *that* would happen. For the time being, it seemed a simple road to Vegas. "You guys drive carefully," The spiritual Hawaiian, Randy Halemano, cautioned, "The highways can be dangerous. The off ramps are many; the traffic can be both real and metaphorical; and car crashes can be both horrific and life changing."

"May the gods be with you," Katy shouted out.

"And with our money," the good Father responded, ecumenically.

CHAPTER NINE

WSOP Registration

When one chooses to think of themselves as 'incarcerated', it seems to suggest that they are more hospitalized than imprisoned. They can convince themselves that they are there for chemo or radiation. It certainly doesn't have the harsh overtones of 'lock up'. Either way, the confinement does give one plenty of time to reflect on the misadventures that led to their interment. For Mack, the solitude gave him periodic reflections of everything that led up to his isolation behind bars. He flashed back to the road to the Rio Hotel and Casino.

The trip to Nevada was to be the culmination of his financial folly. In retrospect, the finances would be exaggerated and the folly would, at times, border on cataclysmic. Like so many things in life, it all seemed to be going as smoothly as expected and according to plan. Barnes picked the boys up at Dottie's house and assured her, "You have nothing to worry about. David, Dennis and I will have a great time in Vegas and you can text them every 50 miles along the way. When we get there," Mack implored her, "Let *them* text *you*. They'll know when they can talk and for how long. We expect that most of the thousands of participants will be registering in person like us. They want to get the feeling of the crowd." The big names pre-register and already have the feeling of the crowd. In fact, the registration is all about those excited first-timers who are looking to rub elbows with a hero, a movie star, or a legend. Almost every newbie arrives with a cell phone camera, a 'selfie stick', or a pen for autographs. The young guns all turned 21 in the last decade and some of them in the last month. Many come with backpacks, baseball caps and shades. Inspirational stories abound. Ahead in line, might be a blind man whose son is allowed to whisper the cards in his father's ear or an armless 'phenom' who holds, raises and folds his cards with his feet. This year there was even a mother in a T-shirt replete with her late Marine Corps son's picture. She promised him to buy his way into the WSOP when he came home. When he didn't, she decided to play in his honor.

Every year there are stories about players who are battling terminal diseases or horrible experiences. In most cases, families and friends are bankrolling them in a tournament or two. Last hurrahs are tear-jerkers and make most people count their blessings while fingering their chips. Mix tragedy, inspiration, admiration, dedication and desperation and you get the most unlikely collage of players in one place, at one time. It's the most mixed up menagerie of cross cultural and cross generational beings in the galaxy. Only Comic Con has more costumes, clowns and devoted fans. Who are these people and how do they see themselves?

Obviously, you have the pros. They come to play smart, win a lot and lose a little. Some are the 'up and comers' who arrive hoping to make a name for themselves. Most are just solid players who want to 'make it deep' into the tourney and, of course, 'make it *to* the money'. The rest of the field consisted of dreamers like Don Quixote; believers like Kevin Costner in 'Field of Dreams'; and wish-come-true'ers like Jiminy Cricket. Dennis was in awe, "Most of them seem to be just everyday people hopelessly caught up in following their own yellow brick road. To them, this must be that place they've dreamed of somewhere over the rainbow. It all seems so wonderful and pathetic at the same time, Mack."

To that last point Barnes offered, "Does it really matter that this city, Vegas, is gold and the other one was just Emerald?" The Wizard of Oz comparison is a fair one if you realize that you can't be a tin man, a scarecrow or a cowardly lion on this trip. *This* tournament requires brains, courage, **and** heart. If you don't have those three things, kick your damn heels together and get the hell back to Kansas....or Temecula....or Brussels....or Shanghai. Poker really is wonderful and pathetic at the same time." Yes, they do come from every country and every walk of life: old and young, rich and poor. They represent every color, creed, size and shape. They play side by side and literally 'elbow to elbow'. Poker doesn't care who you are or where you come from. The Main Event just wants to know what you got and how you're going to use it. The WSOP is a great equalizer. The outsider thinks it's all about cards or odds or gambling. The insider knows it's all about people, situations, confrontations, luck, talent, skill, and strategy. On any given day, in any given hand, any given player can win. Going back to the favorites, the established pros *are* here. Some local legends are always advertising with their appearance. Some of the players have incredible nicknames: Kid Poker, The Unabomber, The Grinder, The Duchess, The Mouth and The Bloody Hand of Fate. Okay, the last one Mack invented to try to intimidate the boys. It doesn't really exist….for now. You get the idea. Make a name for yourself and then change it or let someone else change it for you. Nobody starts out a winner. They all pay their dues. The vets will tell you, "If you look around the table and can't identify the sucker in the first ten minutes, it must be YOU!"

Mack and the twins had made it a noisy trip to Nevada. They had discussed school, jobs, life, and just about anything but poker. "The difference between being excited and being nervous," Mack told them, "is that *you* need to be the one who makes people nervous and *they* need to be the ones who make you excited." After registering at the front desk at the Rio and dropping their gear off in their suite, the Temecula trio found their way to the WSOP sign up.

The Main Event was just the last and grandest in a series of tournaments that had been going on for weeks. A series of tournaments had awarded bracelets and payouts for different variations of poker: low ball, Omaha, high/low and more. One tourney was just for the seniors and another was for the ladies title. The entry fees ranged from $600 to $10,000. Several contests were down to the last few tables. The boys checked the big board to see who was hot this year and who was still in the action. The inside of the Rio was remarkably orderly. By the time David made his way to the front of the line, it was more like buying a movie ticket and not nearly as exciting as when he became a contestant of *Jeopardy: Teen Week*. He did well and won that one. Hopefully, he thought, this tournament would be just as easy for him. As the boys and Mack were heading across the floor and up to their room, a small group of young men approached and confronted them.

"Wow!" one in the group said, "It is!" Another one followed up, "You're Wyllie Won and Wyllie Too, aren't you? I recognize you from face book. Can we get an autograph and a picture with the both of you? Are you guys in the Main Event? That's awesome. I'm gonna tweet everybody I know back home. They, well, we all think you guys are incredible."

Mack's jaw was hanging slightly open as he was being backed away by the slowly growing crowd. Barnes would later describe it to Sherri, "It was like Harry Potter had been recognized as he boarded his first Hogwartz Express." Everyone was taking pictures and getting the boys to sign their programs and registration forms. After ten minutes, Dennis said, "We gotta go now, but we'll see you all at the tables."

"What the hell was that all about?" Mack asked, flabbergasted at the whole entourage thing, "Why did those guys want your autographs and pictures? Are we going to have to dodge characters from the *Big Bang Theory* all week?"

"That's just stupid stuff from online poker, Mack. I told you we play there," Dennis replied.

"You told me you played there. You didn't tell me you two

were celebrities," Mack shot back.

"We're certainly not celebrities, Mack," David quipped, "We've just been moderately successful and we have a following. We did okay the last two years, particularly in "sit and go's" and people have interviewed us. We have a ton of followers on twitter. We've made a couple of cable radio appearances and we started a poker blog. Again, we are not celebrities. We're what you might call poker personalities. Some of our fans howl when they see us and call themselves Coyotes because our last names are Wyllie. Get it?"

"I know I'm going to hate myself for asking this, but how 'moderately successful' have you 'two non celebrities' been?" Mack asked.

"In the last year or so," Dennis carefully commented, "we were able to win just over $220,000 but that was together…not individually. Your live tournament was the first time we'd ever looked at our opponents in person."

"Holy Crap!" Mack barked. "Do you two realize what the other players are going to say when they find this out? I told them it was your first tournament and this will look like we set them up and played them like marks in some hustle. You guys are professionals, for Pete's sake, and I'm looking more and more like your pimp."

"Mack, can I be the one to point out the obvious?" Dennis asked. "Do you know how to get a professional poker player off your porch?"

Mack waited for the punch line.

"You pay him for the pizza and tip him so he can pay his rent! All young poker players think they're professionals and some of them even drop out of college to get rich," David added, "we didn't lead anyone on and we didn't hide anything. We're just two intelligent kids who seem to have a knack for playing cards. Is that a crime? It's all about fun. Relax."

"All I know is that there will be shit to dodge when the fan's turned on and I can tell you, for a fact, I'll be the one it hits, not you two. I'll be the one who can only stand there in front of the spinning blades and sample the flavors. When I tell them about you two, people like Coach Buck, Ruby, Bob, Kahlid, and Jake will have a field day. Even my wife, who loves you guys, will be a tough sell. Holy Crap! I can't even imagine what Angel will say. I think I hear his Harley pulling up in my driveway as we speak."

"Wyllie Coyotes? Wyllie Won? Wyllie Too? A quarter of a million dollars?" Mack screamed in his head,
"I hope this is the last surprise I have to deal with, explain or cover up. **Holy Crap!**"

CHAPTER TEN

Day One: Chips, Chairs, Champs, Chumps

_____

David picked up his bag of starting chips and made his way through a labyrinth of tables to find his assigned seat. Some people call the first day at the Main Event a zoo. To the two kids from the Temecula Valley, it was Jurassic Park, Disneyland and Wall Street rolled into one. It was obvious that, for some players, it was more like Halloween. It seemed like every table had one of those tricksters who thought the whole day was his or her treat. Sitting two seats away from Wyllie was an attention seeking Blue Man without his 'group'. At one point, the boys saw a pirate with his parrot doll perched on his shoulder. A Jedi with a laser sword stood nearby. Later, a genie walked up rubbing a lamp.

When a fully costumed Statue of Liberty walked by, David took the chance to poke fun. "Still carrying a torch?" David called to the pale green Liberty. "That's tired, and poor!" the statuesque figure replied. Obviously he wasn't the first in the crowd to use that line. By Day 2 *most* of the obviously narcissistic poker pretenders would have used their Warhol minutes of fame and been sent home. In the middle of the muddle, everyone, even the clowns and freak shows had posted a legitimate $10,000, either as individuals or through investors. Most were there to play some serious poker. A few years back, some unlucky rookie had lost everything in the first five minutes when his full house lost to the bigger 'boat' of Sammy Farha. Sammy was already famous as a professional runner-up to the first 'nobody' to win at the final table. The name of the guy who turned the World Series upside down and ignited the poker frenzy was Chris Moneymaker. You can't make these things up. That was his name and he won the whole kit and caboodle as an amateur over the pros. From that point on, it was game on for the whole poker world and anyone who ever played the game.

The camera crews were everywhere. ESPN would film and, eventually, show the hole cards of everyone at the tables on delayed telecasts after editing. During the months of September and October, a week of play would be shrunk to less than 10 hours for 'viewing and commentating'. It was shown weekly while the final table players went on hiatus for a couple of months to train. Each finalist would use the time to prepare for battle against each other for millions. The ability to involve the people watching on television by knowing what hands players were playing, folding, and using to mount bluffs was largely responsible for the game's universal popularity. It allowed everybody at home to follow the drama, appreciate the plays, and play/predict the 'next move' in classic confrontations. Very little is missed by the film crews as they comb the floor looking for stories. Tables would even hold the action for a crew to arrive.

Ray Romano once changed seats and sat down at an early table to find one of the most incredible hands of all time developing. The crew that followed Ray stumbled onto the final play. With an Ace and two other suited face cards on the board, the betting was heavy. Such a board, because of its bluffs and made hand possibilities is called an "Action Flop" and the betting is usually fast and furious. The last card was also an Ace. Both players put all their money in the middle. One of the two was so excited he shoved his stack of chips like a bulldozer moving sand. Both raised their hands and yelled triumphantly before they saw the other's cards. The edited film cut to Romano who said something like, "Are you kidding me? Are you kidding?" One of the players had drawn his **Fourth Ace** and was already jumping up and down. For the other player, that same ace had given him an absolutely unbeatable **Royal Flush**! That 'Ace on the river' was a once-in-a-lifetime combination. Ray Romano had made his mind up that he was at the wrong table. The cameras and the editing had captured the drama. The dealer arranged the hole cards on either side of the common cards. People left their assigned seats from all over the casino floor to take pictures of the hand to prove they were there when it happened.

"It's more than that menagerie," Dennis thought to himself as he inhaled the circus-like atmosphere in which his brother was playing. It's a cavalcade of chance, enhanced by an organized orgy of card crazy pleasure seekers. If it seems surreal to me, it must bug the hell out of the real poker players. They must hate all the flamboyance and tomfoolery that marks the first couple of days. I bet my bother is in hog heaven though. He absolutely thrives on the attention. Better him than me."

Following an extraordinary display of pomp and circumstance, the shuffling commenced and the cards were in the air. The first goal was to survive the first day. The second goal was to 'get to the money'. Everyone had a third goal but they wouldn't jinx their chances by even mentioning the words: FINAL TABLE. The young Wyllie started slowly and had just half his original money after the first hour. Mack's phone rang. It was Randy Halemano who had received a cell phone picture in Hawaii of David at the table.

"What is that rock in front of the kid, Mack?" Halemano demanded to know, "I hope it's not what I think it is."

"I'll call you back at the break," Mack said, "I think he said it was a lucky rock he picked up in your neck of the woods. In fact, he did mention it was volcanic rock from the Volcanoes National Park. I thought you'd like that, Randy."

Halemano went ballistic, "That's the reason he's losing. Madam Pele, the volcano goddess curses people who simply remove her rocks from the islands. Everybody knows that! Who knows what she does to those who flaunt their criminal contraband? You've got to get that rock or those rocks and promise goddess Pele that you'll return them as soon as you can. Bad things will happen and they'll only get worse. I'm not kidding here. Get that rock off the table or we'll all lose in ways you can't even imagine." Randy, of course, was hyper and superstitious. Because Barnes had seen some of these legends in action as a student tour guide, he decided not to tempt fate and promised to have David change card markers. He promised Randy (and Pele) he'd personally return the rocks to their Hawaiian volcanoes. Barnes picked up a Wile E. Coyote marker from the MGM gift shop over the break. Problem solved. Mack thought it might be a good thing if the Wyllie family joined the Barnes family on a cruise when all this was over. They could use the rock return as an excuse for closure once David was eliminated. Hawaii was his favorite place to cruise. Problem solved? It depends on whether or not you believe in those Hawaiian legends and curses. As Mack later told Sherri, "Sorry, honey, but I just promised a man we'd cruise Hawaii."

Sherri took it bravely, "If we have to, we have to. I have to get a new swimsuit and some glasses." Madam Pele, it seems can also promote tourism and fashion sales.

After most of the distractions had subsided, one late arrival would prove Wyllie wrong about costumed amateurs. Phil Hartwig, one of the bad boys of poker, entered the room. Phil was famous for making dramatic entrances, donning outrageous costumes, and flanking himself with gorgeous girls, also in costume. This was Las Vegas, of course, and it was all just 'part of the act' for most. In light of the legendary Hartwig histrionics of the past, this one was, by comparison, quite subdued. As always, Hartwig had arrived late to draw focus on his entrance. Phil came in dressed as a doctor with 'Dr. Phil' embroidered on his chest pocket. He was accompanied by a half-dozen beautiful nurses. Play stopped for the 'Poker Pout'. By all personal accounts, Phil is a great guy in real life. As a pro he's prolific. 'The Pout' had won more than his share of bracelets. People either loved him or hated him. Like most famous people, Phil knew either would do, as long as they noticed him. When David saw how Phil was dressed, he made a poor decision that somehow turned out to be brilliant. During the break, he borrowed a white medical lab coat from Dr. Herb who had made the trip to Vegas with his wife. David hastily used a magic marker to write "Phil Hartwig's Doctor" on the back (The PHD was in capital letters and heavy. He had spent too much time with Mack). When he walked through the arena, the reactions were mixed, at best. Some jeered. Some shook their heads from side to side. No one seemed to be amused. Most people in the crowd, including the alerted Hartwig, thought it was disrespectful and immature. For Phil to think someone else was disrespectful and immature is like Lady Gaga complaining someone else was 'showboating' or 'over the top'. Joy Santos knew this whole poker adventure was going to be her husband's last hurrah. They had joined the young Wyllie as part of his gallery of fans. Joy saw that David was bombing in his attempt to 'one up' Hartwig. Santos and his wife both leaned toward each other the way married couples on the same wave length do that sort of thing on a regular basis.

"The boy realizes that the prank didn't work, Joy," the weakened Santos said.

"I know," his wife replied, "I was just going to suggest that I go out to the car and …." She didn't have to finish the sentence.

Dr. Herb completed her thought, "It's in the trunk and get the new one. It'll show up better."

"Got it," Joy said, and rubbed her husband on the shoulder, "I'm so glad I married you."

With that, she ran out of the building and reappeared within minutes holding a doctor's bag. Joy went to the rail and whispered something in the ear of the table security person. Beautiful women don't have to whisper much. They just lean into a man's body and press their lips against his cheek and ear. The guard motioned her to the table and gave an okay sign to the floor man.

Joy reached into the bag and said, "Take this David. Herb thought you could use this for effect."

With that, she placed one of her husband's stethoscopes around the Coyote's neck as though it was a lei of Hawaiian flowers. The other players seemed more interested in Joy who, though Filipino, could have easily passed for an island girl. Only a grass skirt around her waist and a couple of well placed half coconuts could have heightened their attention or improved the ceremony. Wyllie still wasn't sure the 'doctor gag' was the right idea or not, but the whole Joy thing seemed to be the right prescription. David looked into the gallery and gave Herb a thumb's up. The attractive Santos sat back down with a smile and the rest of the table seemed rejuvenated by the 'Joy' of it all. David decided to stay in character. Good thing he did. About an hour later, the Coyote was in a hand with two other players. He checked, hoping for a straight and guarding against a flush. When the last card hit the felt, so did one of his middle aged opponents. The man gasped, clutched at his chest, and fell, face first onto the table. Poker players are not always the most sensitive people in the middle of a hand.

"I guess he's all in," one said, hoping to make light of the situation.

"Is that a flop or a fold?" another quipped.

The man remained motionless. This was no laughing matter.

"He's not breathing. Call 911. Get the paramedics." the dealer yelled as the other players helped the slumped figure to the ground.

"I think he's dying. I can't feel a heartbeat," one panicked woman cried, "Does anybody know CPR?"

At that very instant, David remembered his training as an eagle scout and noted what he was wearing around his neck. He rushed to the victim, plugging his ears with the listening ends of the stethoscope. Tearing the man's shirt open, he held the metal disc to the chest of the victim.

"I have a heart beat!" Wyllie announced. "Everyone step back and give us some air." Those around the scene retreated and gave a collective sigh of relief. A few, for some reason, applauded. Two things then happened, almost simultaneously. Real paramedics arrived and went into action. Just prior, however, one of those many camera crews had snapped a picture of David on one knee listening via medical apparatus to the chest of man lying motionless. He was still wearing the white lab coat complete with the "PHD" text on the back. The man sat up and was taken away on a gurney with a 'thumbs up' for the crowd. He recovered, signed a release, and returned to the table before he could 'blind out' and be eliminated. He was just fine as long as he still had chips on the table. The same could not be said for Phil Hartwig. The next morning's papers had front page pictures of David. One mentioned 'saving a life'. One caption under the picture mistakenly identified Wyllie as "Phil Hartwig's doctor". A fellow poker player brought the papers to Phil who was, by the friend's account, incensed. He had been shown up by this "little twit," as the Poker Pout described him. Phil was then handed one more picture, in another paper, taken from a different angle that showed the whole "**Phil Hartwig's Doctor**" on the back of the coat.

"Who *is* that kid?" Phil asked his poker pal, Daniel, "Who the hell does he think he is?" Phil asked before being put in his place by his fellow bracelet bro.

"He looks a lot like you when you came on the poker scene," Daniel reminded his friend. "He takes chances, knows entertainment value, and has the instincts and timing of future hall of famer like you."

Phil rubbed the back of his neck and then turned and agreed with his poker pal, "You know, buddy, you might just be on to something. The kid's got moxie and he *does* remind me of myself before I went from cute to good looking. I'd still like to know who this kid is." He added to his friend, "He may have this year's 'mojo', my friend." Better yet, a ton of people, inside and outside the poker world were asking the same question, most through social media. Like it or dislike it, they noticed David. Phil, at least for the moment, got second billing and had class enough to appreciate it.

Flashing forward to Mack in the jail cell, Barnes made a mental note, "That should have been a sign that this was not going to be a simple story." The fact that the film clip made its way through the news trailers and late night monologues was flattering but only a hint of how far inexplicable coincidences could eventually take you.

"Wouldah, Couldah, Shouldah," Mack drifted, "why wasn't there a fourth choice? I really thought Day One went well. David doubled his chips after we retired the volcanic rock, and, at the time, I was actually looking forward to Day Two and just plain poker." David loved the adrenaline flow and had other ideas. David had a plan."

CHAPTER ELEVEN

The Magician's Story

On day two, the carnival was starting to die down. Many of the costumes were gone, most in bags carried by busted poker players. David had decided to take the role of a different, famous poker player every day as long as he remained in the hunt. The remaining costumed characters were dwindling. As he snapped off picture after picture on his phone, others were taking pictures of him. He bumped into Charlie Chaplin while gawking at one unbelievable Marilyn Monroe. He texted pictures of Mr. Clean, the Michelin Man, and even a hairy fat guy in a Tinker Bell outfit. Who knows what kind of bet *he lost*? Most were soon out of the tournament and just hanging on as spectators. Soon, even they would be history. In any event, so to speak, David had too much respect for the game to dress that ridiculously. Wyllie came as Antonio Esfandiari. Antonio was an incredibly talented high-stakes player who just happened to be an accomplished purveyor of 'sleight of hand', as well. As such, the boys automatically gravitated to "The Magician" since the two shared, with Esfandiari, a love and an interest in the art of prestidigitation.

"Today, Mack," David explained, "I've taken Antonio as my role model. I hope that he, more than the Poker Pout, will be flattered and see the move as a sign of respect for magic and the magician. I want to do it with only the best of good taste. Antonio has tremendous insights into both poker and illusion skills and plays and performs incredibly! He also might be the best TV poker analyst in the business."

Mack had an instant reply, "Why anyone would sit down at a poker table with a man who can 'make any card appear or disappear at any time to anyone in any place' is something I can't even begin to comprehend. If a professional magician sat down at a poker table I was playing at, he'd make me disappear before the first ante. If there is honor among thieves, magicians, and poker player, I don't want to explore the crossovers or combinations."

David was dressed like Antonio with horn-rimmed glasses and he liked the 'facial hair' version so much he added a goatee and a moustache. Props were so important to the roles he hoped to play that he carried a large, leather bag that the recently arrived Sherri had tooled with the word: ACME like the bag Wile E. Coyote carries when he needs a gimmick or a gizmo invention to catch his cartoon nemesis, the Roadrunner.

"Maybe this will bring you luck," Sherri told David.

Wyllie wore a short tuxedo jacket and carried a black top hat that Esfandiari would never wear at a poker table. It enhanced the performance in David's eyes. Some people took pictures of David and most realized who he was emulating and went along with his disguise choice.

As he sat down to his assigned table and seat, one of the other players, a rotund man wearing red suspenders, asked, "You have any tricks up your sleeve today, kid?"

David simply bowed and removed his top hat in a sweeping gesture of gracious recognition, "I will, myself, be devoid of some of my obvious talents," Wyllie announced, "and I shall not hide behind the pretenses of abracadabra. Sir, I say to you and your cohorts: many cards will appear and disappear today and any player who tilts the odds with parlor tricks shall be dealt with accordingly."

Obviously, for someone who had acting experience on stage and screen, his words were rehearsed in anticipation of the opportunity to recite them. In poker terms, 'he knew what was coming and he was ready for it.' David already had five more roles to play if he lasted that long in the tournament and this one got him 8 seconds on one of the roving cameras. That's a winning time for cowboys when they, like Wyllie, sit down and try to ride their way through different types of bull. Of course, he knew he could be thrown off at any time. Without the right moves, he would be knocked off now and then. It was important to know how to 'dust yourself off and get back in the saddle'. Most poker players are eliminated when they are still playing a prior 'bad beat' in their mind. It's called a 'meltdown'. The player loses control of the concept of playing one hand at a time. The best poker players recover quickly and the worst players are gone. For the first four hours and through the dinner break, David managed to increase his starting fund twenty-fold. He and Mack met 'on the rail' (between the audience and the tables) several times to consult during breaks in the action. No actual coaching is allowed when hands are being played.

Mack paraphrased an old adage when he told David, "There's plenty of hind sight to reflect upon if a player has the foresight to ask advice on being a damn sight better in the future." None of the players, in the hand or out, can make observations about the cards except those who are playing head to head. Such impropriety can be met with admonishment by the dealer or the floor man. A penalty can be assessed. The offender can be forced to leave for an allotted time while the action goes around the table before he or she can return to play. Chip-wise, the offending player can lose one or more rounds of antes/blinds in the process.

Just before the dinner break, David was involved in a hand where the pot in the middle of the table had grown significantly. That big man in the jeans and red suspenders had challenged Wyllie by pushing his remaining chips 'all in'. David had plenty of 'outs'. He could win with a 6 or a Jack for a straight. He needed one more diamond for an unbeatable Ace high flush, or he could even take it all with an 8 for three of a kind. He could also loose or be drawing dead since there was a pair of 10's and a 7 and 9 on the board. It was tempting. He had plenty of cards that could have won it for him. He sat until all of the other players, not involved in the action, had departed for dinner. A couple stood and stayed to witness the outcome. David finally decided to surrender and folded his hand, face down into the muck. He turned and asked the dealer, "Can we see the 'rabbit card', sir." The 'rabbit' they 'chase' is the next card that WOULD have 'landed on the river' had David not folded.

"You know I can't show the rabbit card," the dealer said with disdain, "that kind of crap is okay in home games but it's taboo in a tournament. I would if I could but I can't, so I won't." To be fair, any dealer could lose their job if they revealed it. David gave the dealer a pathetically pleading look. He took off his hat, shook it to show that it was empty, and then turned it over and pulled out a small white rabbit by the nape. He placed his own face along side the bunny and said, "PLEASE, PLEASE, PLEASE, Mr. Dealer? One time?" The dealer ignored the originality of the appeal and simply fanned the cards around the felt in all directions. He glared at David and his little white, wiggling friend. The answer stood. Occasionally, a dealer will 'accidently' expose the card in a fumbling effort to entice a tip. That, too, could be grounds for discipline. All hands and dealer moves are filmed from cameras above the floor and poker savvy ex-dealers monitor all the screens constantly. David placed the rabbit back in the hat on the table and walked off to dinner. The fat man, who actually held the best hand, slowly walked over, made sure David had departed, and took a peek into the top hat.

"Where's the rabbit?" he said to an empty table, "where the hell's the fucking rabbit?"

No one was left at the table so he stuck his hand inside and started to feel around.

He hadn't noticed David coming back for his prop.

"Careful!" Wyllie shouted, "He Bites!"

Good thing the guy was wearing those stupid suspenders or

David could have easily scared his pants off.

CHAPTER TWELVE

The Fable of the Giant on an Outer Table

David Wyllie would build his first huge following from the television audience the next day while playing on an 'outer table' as ESPN commentators Norm Chad and Len McEchearn refer to it. Wyllie was dressed like another of his idols, Phil Laak, the 'Unabomber', who wore a simple grey 'hoodie' sweatshirt and sun glasses like the infamous criminal. When things got tense, Phil would put on dark glasses and tighten the draw strings on his sweatshirt like a turtle. It was Phil's way of revealing as little as possible for his opponent to evaluate. David had just moved to a new table in seat 8 well into day three and was sizing up the chip stacks and the competition. It was obvious from the get go that there was a giant at this particular gathering. At the other end of the table in seat 3 was a monster of a man: almost 7 feet tall with a deep and powerful voice that resonated like a sonic boom. For Wyllie, Darth Vader came to mind. In David's first hand he drew an Ace and a Jack of different colors. He'd play, he thought, until Goliath went 'all in' and the next three players cowered in submission. The action was on Wyllie. He thought for a minute and asked himself, "Do I really want to risk my tournament life on a marginal hand against someone I haven't had the chance to study?" He had a feeling he was being bluffed and pushed around but he decided to wait for a better hand and measure the reads and tells in the meantime. Sometimes, heroics are more about discretion and information than valor. As he threw down his cards to fold, the behemoth roared, "I intimidated you, didn't I?" It felt like David had stumbled upon a medieval village dominated by an ogre. All the peasants at the table turned their heads to witness the domination of another peon.

"Let me think," David said calmly, as he removed his hood and took off his glasses. He then immediately replied, "No…not really."

The villagers turned back to the oversized bully who first made eye contact with his victim and strengthened his observation, "No, I *know* when I intimidate someone and YOU were *definitely* intimidated! The rest of the crowd followed the words back across the table like fans tracking the flight of a tennis ball at Wimbledon's center court: A made-for-TV moment and the cameras were close at hand, a fact not lost on the young Wyllie. David knew his table image was under assault. "Actually, I'm quite comfortable in situations like this," he quipped gingerly, and then added, "I used to work for a proctologist!" David had used his backhand to continue the rally down the line to the other side. A feeling of tension excited the spectators and the crowd anticipated a solid return to the low shot from the challenger. The cameras were focused as well. Surely the next words out of seat 3 would end the contest once and for all. The dominator's nostrils flared as everyone, at home and at the table, zeroed in on his reaction. Outraged, the massive figure pushed back his chair, put both his fists on the green felt of the table and let rip with an aggressive, baseline forehand pall mal.

"Worked for a proctologist? Are you calling me an *Asshole*?" the angered titan bellowed. It was a question but it seemed like so much more. The words reverberated beyond this smaller crowd and stopped play nearby. Much of the room turned to witness the accelerating scene. Before the dealer could admonish either on their lack of table manners and decorum or call for the floor manager, David simply deadened his volley just over the net with the calm look of an innocent and the subdued instinct of a master.

"Oh my god," he replied, "I certainly didn't mean *that*, and I apologize if you took it that way. I just meant that I'm used to operating in tight places."

Game, set, and match!

The entire table dropped their eyes. The sound of muffled laughter crippled the hulk. He was left both speechless and devastated. David had made his point.

One of the announcers later described the action on his own scoreboard, "Well Len, he proclaimed, "That makes it David 1; Goliath zero."

As the story spread throughout the room, retold from player to player and exaggerated from table to table, the legend of "Wyllie

Coyote" grew by leaps and bounds. '*The Giant Killer*' was one tag many hung on David. More importantly, no one in this tournament was ever going to test his metal again with intimidation alone. He now had what every poker player longs for and aims to build on. He had a reputation.

At the break, the young Wyllie was resting on the rail and talking to his brother, when he noticed Dennis backing away and looking skyward. A huge hand grabbed his shoulder from behind. "Hey kid!" he heard as he felt a warm and heavy breath back side. It was that unmistakable foghorn of a voice David had earlier silenced. The Coyote turned and looked up at a face that seemed to be three feet above his own. The giant's hair above his face seemed to be rubbing up against the ceiling. Wyllie's abbreviated life of twenty-four years flashed before his eyes.

"I like you," the creature snorted, "Nobody around here has had the guts to stand up to me." David tried to retain what he *had just* demonstrated as superiority. He was losing hold of it quickly.

With sincere relief, he replied. "I really appreciate you saying that....really!" His first enemy had become a newest friend.

"Thank God!" David said to himself as his heartbeat slowed to just above normal, "Thank GOD!"

CHAPTER THIRTEEN

The Raise'n Asian

The next day, David was on top of the world. People had viewed his confrontation on you tube and were posting it, passing it, tweeting and just flat 'on-lining' it to death. Forget being face book friends, people of all ages wanted to be 'Wyllie Coyotes'. Suddenly the price of Road Runner memorabilia rose in value and volume on e Bay. David, Dennis and Mack could see dollar signs for the young man if he could just keep momentum moving forward. People were starting to see him as a contender. David was, in fact, on the leader board for the first time in 17th place. His confidence was so pumped that he decided to dress in a costume imitating Jackie Chiang. Chiang was considered to be one of the best players in the world for decades.

Chiang played himself in a few poker movies and was a classy dresser who loved exotic race cars and fast women. Wyllie came in wearing Chiang's trademark red leather jacket with large, reflective sunglasses. He pulled a tangerine out of that new ACME leather bag of tricks Sherri had crafted for him. Jackie Chiang had originally used the tangerine to scratch and sniff in an effort to cover up the smell of cigarette smoke at the table. Nobody smokes in casino poker rooms anymore but the tangerine was still an identifiable and effective Chiang prop. The announcers, the media and a growing cast of followers watching live or streaming on line took note of David's costume and near unanimously approved. The first hour was typical David. He played like the man they call "The Raisin' Asian". He smelled the tangerine and held it to his face before making his moves. His goal was to play inscrutably like Jackie himself. He meant no disrespect. In fact, Wyllie hoped word would spread to Chiang who was still alive in the tournament. David even imagined Jackie coming by. Hopefully, the Asian might appreciate the homage Wyllie felt he was paying to the poker icon. After eliminating yet another rival and increasingly moving up another notch or two on the posted leaders, David looked up and saw the Poker Hall of Famer heading in his direction. The Coyote smiled until he saw what Chiang held in his hand. It wasn't a piece of fruit. It was the one thing David ever wanted to see. It was his worst nightmare. At that point he could only shake his head and shrink into his own seat. In Jackie's hands were chips. Suddenly he was playing twins with a man who'd had millions in career earnings.

"Howya doing, kid?" the affable new arrival asked with a smile.

"Up to now, I was doing great, Mr. Chiang. I think I'll just get out of this outfit, though." David replied.

"Naw, naw, you go right ahead," said the man who had made

over a dozen final tables, "Do what you do. We'll just see who wears the red leather better. I heard about you, kid, this should be fun." It was obvious at least one of the two was truly inscrutable. Add to that, affable, unshakeable, and probably unbeatable. It was like Payton Manning dropping in on your first game as quarterback or sitting in on drums with the Rolling Stones. No, it was more like having the Pope hear your first confession. You might as well be talking to God, himself. Suddenly the young Wyllie was speechless, contrite, and felt he wanted only a quick blessing and to be sent off to do the penance for his sins. Instead, he refocused. He remembered Mack telling him, "There is no such thing as a problem, just a challenge that presents us an opportunity to grow."

The champ had just said, "this should be fun." David recalled Mack telling the brothers as their JV basketball coach before a big game, "It will take defense to win," Mack had shared with his players, "defense is spelled W-O-R-K. You can always count on defense. If you *work* your heart, your legs, and your mind, it will always be there. Offense, on the other hand," Barnes went on, "is spelled F-U-N. Sometimes it's just spelled F-U because you don't always get *out* what you put 'N'. David certainly felt like playing defense and he avoided playing against Chiang in every hand. Certainly, if one of the biggest winners on the TV show, *Poker After Dark*, went on the offense somebody else was about to be 'F-U'd". Wyllie was not about to go 'head's up' with the other man in the other red leather jacket if he could help it.

Sometimes, however, you just can't help it. David looked down at an Ace of Hearts and a King of Clubs in the big blind. He raised the pot by $20,000. Jackie Chiang made the call. Suddenly it was *mano a mano* to the flop. The dealer laid out an Ace, a King, and a 10. All three cards were Spades. David had flopped top two pair. Chiang checked and David checked. The turn was a deuce of clubs. Both checked again. The river was a seemingly harmless 4 of diamonds. Chiang bet $200,000 or half his stack. All David had to do, he felt, was call and he'd walk out a winner. At worst, he was being sucked into a bottomless hole and the Asian would roll right over a hapless Coyote like a bad cartoon. David felt in his heart that Jackie didn't have the straight and certainly didn't have the flush. In fact he regretted checking the flop.

"What to do?" Wyllie asked himself. "Go with my gut or put the ball back in his court?" He did the latter.

"I'm 'All In!'" David said without inflection. Since he had three times the Asian's money, he was actually putting Chiang 'All In' for his tournament life.

When he didn't snap call, David felt he had been right about his opponent. He would have called instantly if he had the flush and he was probably wondering if David did. "What else makes sense?" Wyllie pondered, "Jackie Chiang certainly must see that it's going to take a straight or a flush to win. Maybe he has a small flush," David speculated.

The Coyote put down the tangerine and Chiang picked his up. David pushed his card marker of the cartoon character, *Wile E. Coyote* out in front of him, as if to play with his opponent's mind while he made his decision. As he did so, he scolded himself, "Don't fart around with the master. Don't give him anything to pick up on."

Were David's two pair enough? He was beginning to think so. Chiang picked up his tangerine and started to peel it. The youngster had seen this before on television. "When Jackie peels the tangerine in front of you," people say, "he's metaphorically stripping off the layers of your soul until he can read your spirit." The Asian tore out a section of revealed fruit and bit into it. David chewed on some imaginary gum to hide any facial tells.

"Maybe I've just seen too many zombie movies recently," the rookie thought to himself, "but that felt like someone just put a pin in a voodoo doll."

Opponents tend to make long speeches before they fold a hand. It's a way of saying, "I know I've got you beat but I'm going let you have this one." Translated that means "I ain't got the guts to follow through on this one."

Just then, Chiang took a deep breath, stretched his arms and reached into his inner jacket pocket. David felt he was hearing 'fold!' When he started to hear one of those long, aforementioned dissertations, he relaxed a bit.

"Kid," The Asian said with an all-knowing smile, "On my way over to your table, a fan stopped me and told me I might need this." He pulled out a colorful plastic cartoon card marker of his own. It was the *Roadrunner*! Chiang slammed it on the table.

"Beep Beep!" he announced to David and his Coyote, "I call!"

"He must have had the straight," David said to himself as he replayed the hand in his head. Wyllie turned over his two pair and was prepared to see that 'obvious flush' or Queen and a Jack for that straight. What he did see, however, would rock his entire concept of playing poker. Jackie, the 'Raisin' Asian' Chiang turned over two 4's for three of a kind. He had floated the flop and turn to hit it on the river. David couldn't account for the fact there was a straight and a flush on the board. For the very first time in his life, he felt overmatched.

"That," The Coyote said to himself, "was the greatest call I've ever seen. Straights, flushes and face cards all over the table and Chan called with trip 4's. That was amazing." David found himself standing and applauding. Later, the victorious Chiang told the Coyote, "You're pretty damn good, kid. What they say about you is true. I thought I picked up on something you were doing. I got lucky, that's all." Whatever it was: talent or tell, it turned out to be a defining hallmark for Wyllie Coyote.

"From now on," the young David told himself, "I play as myself." He went to the ESPN Zone and bought a Phoenix Coyote jersey and would wear it proudly at the table for the rest of his tournament life.

He made a commitment, "I am David Wyllie, 'The Coyote' before, during and after the Final Table. I don't have to be anything or pretend to be anyone else. Who I am is good enough from this point forward."

In one sense, he was right on. In another, however, he would be dead wrong.

CHAPTER FOURTEEN

Playing in the Zone

Maybe losing to Jackie Chiang made the surrealism of the whole Main Event seem mundane, if not just plain ordinary. Maybe finding someone who seemed to be one step ahead of a Wyllie made the next step a challenge. Whatever it seemed to be, the 'Roadrunner' besting the Coyote seemed to ignite the competitive juices in David. From that hand on, he seemed invincible. Chiang went out the next day when he couldn't bluff a kid from India. David suddenly realized survival was an active process.

One of the oldest adages in poker goes something like this: "When you lose, lose the minimum and when you win, win the maximum!" David was in that 'zone'. Every card player will tell you there are times in that zone when everything seems to be on cruise control. You know the second hole card before it's dealt. You know what you need and you know it will be there when the dealer reveals the flop. When you need a heart for the flush, it arrives. You need a 9 or a King to complete the straight and you see it hit the table before the reveal. You bet the perfect amount consistently. Other players call you when you have an unbeatable hand and you sense how much to bet to get them off their better hand. The world not only revolves around you at that moment; you ARE the world!

David found himself in that zone. For the next few days his stack of chips became a mound, a mountain and finally a fortress. He found himself constantly apologizing during a hand because he was still sorting, stacking and arranging chips of all denominations. On a huge winning streak, chips are like Lego pieces. The Coyote was in that time and place. David Wyllie was the owner of Lego Land. When it comes to stacking any amount of chips, poker players range from standard to creative to maniacal. The only rule at the table states that all chips must stay *on* the table and that the most valuable chips have to be in front for all to see. Usually players arrange their stacks by color and amount. Rebels and those just plain sloppy will play with 'dirty' stacks that have different colors in no particular order. In a tournament, when they close one table and send the remaining players to another, no one is allowed to put chips in their pockets. Instead, clear plastic racks or bags are issued for transport. Each rack holds 100 chips: 5 rows of 20. Some players carry multiple containers to another table, impressing their new neighbors with a hint of what's in store for them. Occasionally, someone will have to carry a single chip in their rack across the floor to their new seat. It's worse than ordering from a dollar menu. It's worse than asking for directions to the Dollar Store. In the poker world, there is nothing worse than sitting down at a new table with one chip. The real world has nothing tantamount to that humiliation.

Mack says there may be something close. "I went to my wife's 10 year high school reunion," Barnes admitted shamelessly and illustrated the point. "I had to work all day and she picked up my new tailored suit. I was in a hurry and she had hung it on the door in our hotel room. I showered and dressed hastily so I could join her downstairs in the ballroom. Later during the reunion, I removed my coat and danced the rest of the night. After clean up, a friend, walking behind me in the parking lot, asked, 'So you're a 38-32?' I had danced all night with a huge SEARS cardboard sticker on the back of my pants. Not cool." Yeah, it's like that except, in poker, with your one chip, you know it's happening *as* it happenings. Everyone else in the room gets to watch it 'on parade' and praise God it's not happening to them.

Players love to use chips to show off their experience and talent. Counting out exact amounts in seconds is impressive. Using a technique similar to a cup stacking contest to raise or call can wow the novices. Taking two equal sized chip stacks, 'smooth' players will fold them together and split them apart repeatedly using just one hand. The dexterity is impressive and tells others "I'm thinking but I know what I'm doing." Some players actually pay money to take classes on how to play with their chips. It's cool and just another way to build presence. "What the hell," Mack said when informed there were classes for chip tricks, "Nobody's immune, Sherri got me to line dance and I still haven't forgiven her for that!"

"So many of those chip trick strategies are bullshit but veterans of the game would prefer to treat them like fertilizer," Ruby had

advised the brothers, "Both smell the same but one of them has an organic value 'in the garden'. The table is a community garden and only those who 'weed,' 'water,' and 'feed' their plants will find the opportune time to harvest the benefits of their toil."
Conservative players show their bluffs and aggressive players show when they have the nuts." Make no mistake. David had learned almost all the chip tricks of the trade. He and his brother, Dennis had competed and won numerous origami contests. As demonstrated earlier, they were both advanced amateur magicians. David felt fortunate to be playing in the home of his two favorites, Penn and Teller. They were masters of illusion and knew how to distract their audiences and redirect attention as they created their own zone. Chip leaders can be so focused on their stacks that they lose track of time and space. When operating 'in the zone', time stands still or it ceases to exist at all. Other tables were folding all around the young Coyote.

The amount needed for blinds and antes skyrocketed. Suddenly everything was measured in the number of Big Blinds you could muster to survive. David never noticed. Just like the namesakes of the Rio's Penn and Teller Theatre, he seemed to be performing magic in the moment. To paraphrase Billy Joel, Wyllie was in a 'Vegas state of mind'. Suddenly, it seemed, more than half the players were gone and a loud voice came over the room, "we are now hand for hand. We are now, officially, 'on the bubble.'" Translation, "After one more, dumb schmuck is eliminated, all the rest of you lucky stiffs will go home with, at least, twice the money that you started with." All eyes searched for the small stacks. One of them would soon be forced to play. One of them would lose and everybody else could breathe a sweet sigh of relief. Recently, the powers that be decided to take away some of the 'pop' when the bubble burst. The last player eliminated before the pay off would now be given a free entry for the next year's tournament. It was a gesture of condolence and a chance to be just as frustrated again next year. Schmuck bets; schmuck loses; schmuck departs with a little consolation prize.

The next announcement was much more civilized, "Congratulations ladies and gentlemen. You are all now 'in the money' and guaranteed a minimum of $20,000. One by one, each of you will be given a chance to make ever increasing amounts. Good luck to the survivors!"

This was a sweet victory for all the Wyllie Coyotes back home. Each would be seeing a pay day. In fact, it marked the day most of the home players in Temecula packed their bags; reserved their room; and headed for Vegas. From that point, they carved out a corner in audience to hoot, holler, and howl. From here to the Final Table, the big stacks would either bolster their own advantage or throw away their money frivolously. Each knew they could become instant geniuses to the masses. Just as easily they could be remembered for bonehead plays and laughed at. Someone would be a sudden idiot to millions of television fans. The small stacks could die quickly or become incredible 'comeback stories' to that same audience. In any case, David would be neither. He knew how to play and how to win methodically. David Wyllie would not only survive, he would thrive. From the bubble to the 'double bubble', the Coyote would fatten up on the other critters. At some point in every tournament, the remaining players, invariably, look around the room and count heads. The remaining players started thinking, "Shit, I could actually win this thing!"

Getting enough sleep is almost impossible without pills or potions. The adrenaline, the interviews, the long days of action and mounting prize money took their toll on amateurs and professionals alike. Suddenly, David found himself, after almost a week of day-long play, with only two tables remaining. He also found himself near the top of the leader board along with a couple of pros and a few of his 'young gun, on-liners'. The rest of those who managed to make it to this point were inconsequential to David. He already developed 'lines' on most of them and held an advantage on each thanks to his twin. Dennis, it seemed, was proud rather than jealous of his brother. The twins would sit down at the end of each day and modify or discuss strategies for the next day's action. Dennis shared insights and observations from a twin perspective. David, however was starting to selfishly separate himself from his alter ego.

"Dennis," David said reassuringly as he put his hand on his brother's knee, "I know you are only trying to help but I think I have evolved on my own. Kick back and let me take it from here. Are you enjoying the fact that you're related to a famous poker player?"

"You might not know this," Dennis reminded his ego inflated twin, "but I play poker too. Every day, hundreds of people come up to me asking for my….your autograph. Do you know how it feels to deny them and have to explain? Sometimes they ask if they can get a picture of the *two* of us."

"Just tell them you're me, bro," David advised his twin, "bask in my glory. Make someone happy. Play the role. Enjoy the attention while it lasts. You can't be me forever but you'll still be able to milk it for all it's worth."

"I can't believe I'm talking to the same person I grew up with, David. I wonder how you'd feel if it was reversed. You'd probably explode. I'm glad for you but not enough to pretend to be you. You know, I don't want to argue so I'll just wait until all this is over. Good luck with the tourney and I sincerely hope you win. Maybe then we can sit down and shrink your head to match mine. People are starting to distinguish us on that alone."

"Good luck to you too, brother. I still think it's easier to pretend to be me out there. Enjoy opportunities I've earned and make the most of it." When his brother turned and left, David reevaluated the other 9 competitors. Only one person's name on that list caught his eye and that person was one of his superheroes. Destiny, he felt, brought the two of them together. This unlikely combination of opposites would meet in, what would turn out to be, the most talked about and the most internet viewed hand of the entire Main Event. Both players must have both known it would happen, but when?" It was about to happen half way between sooner and later.

CHAPTER FIFTEEN

Double Bubble, Toil and Trouble

As described earlier, the last player to bust out of the tournament without winning any money is the 'bubble boy' or 'bubble girl'. It's time now to talk about a 'double bubble," of sorts. This 'double bubble' may well carry even more splash as it loses its form and fill. It carries with it a stigma much like being eliminated in fifth place and having to watch the "Final Four" play in college basketball. It sucks! It has more emotional rejection, albeit, less financial exclusion than the 'money bubble'. As the remaining players numbered 10, they joined to form one table. The glory of the actual final table in three months time, with all the hype and hoopla, would not be shared by the next person eliminated. People can bask in the glory of having reached the "November Nine" for the rest of their lives. People buy you drinks; have pictures taken with you; and ask for your autograph. You are 'royalty' of sorts, at least at local casinos. Your picture may not adorn the halls of past champions but, goddamn it, people know your play. People want to be you. Poker fans name their children after you if you're lucky or maybe an occasional dog, cat, or goldfish if you're not. The last 10 players at the table ranged, in age, from 23 to 55 years of age. One was from India and had already been burdened with the nickname, Slum Dog Millionaire' in light of his current chip stack and projected winnings. David figured he must have been the kid who knocked out Jackie Chiang. Another was Russian born. He had no nickname but boasted an icy stare and a heavy accent. Mack told the boys the Russians play poker like their late countryman Boris Spassky. Boris had a series of Cold War chess matches against Bobby Fisher around 1970. "Spassky played with a chip on his shoulder," Mack advised David, "and he lost his title to a brilliant young Fisher who frustrated the defending champion at every turn. Boris, the older man, was overmatched by the American. Let's do it again!"

Those last two players were mid stacked and confident to make the November Nine on live TV in a couple of months. Several players were in jeopardy, desperately trying to protect their assets against the chip leaders. They were looking for the right moment to shove all their chips into the pot and move up the leader board. Two main stories shared the interest of the poker elite and the fans at home. Young Wyllie Coyote had gathered the charisma and the star power usually reserved for veterans like Doyle Brunson. Doyle, as past Main Event Bracelet winner and 'grand old favorite' got a standing ovation every year when he was eventually eliminated. Wyllie was the new kid on the block but he had howling fans and market value. His story was unique in that he would only receive 15% of his winnings. He would be forced to share the rest with his home game friends, the original Coyotes. His goal was winning the most cherished bracelet in the poker world and touring the country in the poker limelight with his runner-up twin if Dennis, he hoped, got over his jealousy by then.

In most years, he would have been the leading story but this time he had competition, *female* competition. For one reason or another, sheer lack of numbers has minimized the skills of women at the Main Event. Mack's wife, Sherri told him, "I don't like tournaments for women. Women are harder to read than men."

Mack agreed with his wife, "That fact, alone, is not lost on most men. Men have trouble reading women whether they're poker players, wives or blind dates." Legally, men cannot be excluded from women's events, although, most men can't imagine what those guys' motives would be. If a man wins a women's tournament, and they have on occasion, what does it prove? At Harrah's Rincon Casino, when a woman knocked a man out of a ladies tournament, she got a standing ovation from her poker sisters. The eliminated man made his way through jeering women who shouted Seinfeld-like insults, "No chips for you" and "don't like women with bigger hands?" The management provided the coup de grass by awarding the lady who sent him packing, a certificate for a free hot dog.

The Coyote was in a virtual dead heat with the lady who sat down next to him at the table. It was the person the twins admired most in poker. It was Annie Duke. Duke was the first female to be in a legitimate position to win it all. She had almost as many chips as David and he realized that he could easily face her, eventually, in a duel for all the marbles. Under that scenario, not only could she become the first female to win the Main Event; but David could end up notorious for preventing her from achieving her goal. Either way, Wyllie would be disappointed for personal reasons. Either way, he would be playing against a legend.

Annie Duke had won a cool half million as champion of the National Heads-Up Tournament. The top pros had been invited to battle one-on-one in a single elimination tourney for a nationally televised classic. It was winner-take-all. Duke emerged as champion. David would be at a distinct disadvantage in such a format. David had his growing pack of Wyllie Coyotes but 'The Duchess of Poker' had an even bigger following. Many of the professionals were her friends and most women were in her corner. She was classy, sassy, sexy, intelligent, experienced, respected, and, probably more than anything, she was Annie Duke. That's right! She was the same Anne Duke that had been 'robbed,' in the boys' opinion, when Donald Trump picked Joan Rivers as 'The Apprentice' in season seven. The smart money had been on Annie. She led all women in career poker winnings. She finished 10th in the 2007 Main Event while 8 months pregnant! (At this point, the obvious interjection would point out that no man will ever match *that* accomplishment!) She won a Tournament of Champions for $2 million over other top pro qualifiers. The Duchess was admired as one of the great ambassadors of the sport, having raised millions in charity work. Beneficiaries of her efforts included African relief, refugee projects throughout the world, the USO, fallen heroes, cancer research, and a slew of other charities. She had also added her name and celebrity to countless other charity poker tournaments.

Originally Duke had championed online poker interests but she ran into some unscrupulous business partners and shifted her focus. Annie testified in front of a congressional subcommittee and advocated for the regulation of gaming on the internet. Annie maintained that such sites could be monitored and policed legally in the future. David didn't even feel he had a significant intellectual advantage against Duke. Annie was an Ivy League grad from Columbia, the mother of four children, and coached the likes of Ben Affleck and Matt Damon on the strategies of poker for film and competition. Affleck hired her as a mentor on his way to winning the California State Poker Championship. Damon relied on her input in the poker movie classic, '*Rounders*'.

The whole table was just settling in and sizing up their roles. Those with over 5% of the chips were careful. Players with smaller stacks were exchanging glances. Mack described it this way, "The looks they give each other are always pathetically competitive in the way fat kids eye each other when hoping not to be the last one picked by teams in a P.E. class. You know the routine, 'That leaves Roland. You got him!' The last team to pick says, 'we don't want Roland, you take him!'" The few remaining picked-over poker players tell themselves, "Avoid embarrassment. Look confident! Look competitive, or at least healthy. Look like someone who can, at the very minimum, stay out of the way of the real players." When you consider what *all* of these players had endured to get here, looking for the weakest link is like comparing lightning. Each one of them was brilliant, unpredictable, shocking and potentially deadly. They'd have had to be. Even the least of these players survived almost 7000 others all week. In spite of their incredible talents, skills, and resilience, some stacks were dwarfed by huge chip edifices built by rich and powerful poker barons. Even your shadow seems to shrivel up around you. A player can be both an Adonis of a man in the real life and a chip poor street urchin in relation to the others. The small stacks become the 'Roland' of that gym class. Their chances were similarly slim and their days were numbered.

David and Annie had too many chips to worry about being this 'double bubble'. If it came down to the two of them, Wyllie would be, once again, the underdog. People were already presuming that these two would probably finish up in November, *mano a femenino*, for the title.

One thing for certain, they would avoid each other in big pots and let everyone else eliminate each other. They could possibly take turns pouncing on those who could least defend themselves against either of the two powerhouses. Annie would, most likely, finish higher than Barbara Enright, the only woman to even make a final table (she finished 5th in 1994). David would, most assuredly, avoid Duke even if he thought he had a better hand. Annie would do likewise. It was poker policy. Big stacks stay clear of big stacks and smaller stacks stay clear of bigger stacks. Big stacks chase off small stacks. Mack had dubbed it 'DarWINian' in nature. The strategy was accepted as standard operating procedure in tournaments, especially when 'on the bubble' or, in this case, on the 'Double Bubble'. This was not your predictable, standard operating procedure (SOP). This was the **W**SOP. In one sudden confrontation that might only come up every three to four thousand hands, all the strategies would change. All the tournament drama would be condensed into a few moves and minutes. All the rules would go out the window. The players, fans, and the entire poker world would witness history once, twice and for all time. Not only would one player be crippled or eliminated as the double bubble boy or girl, but the action would be dead for months. There would be little doubt as to who the champion of this main event would be. Even more remarkable was the fact that, after this epic battle of titans, the real drama would be, by comparison, barely set in motion. How then did it happen? Would one of these two lose their minds? Would David overplay his testosterone? Similarly, would Annie challenge his manhood or ability? There is always one other option. Cards are like the Sirens of mythology. They can beckon with irresistible temptation. They can take hope and dash it upon the rocks. Cards can do that to people. For one of the chip leaders, this 'double bubble' was about to become one of the worst shipwrecks of all time.

Like most specials on the Weather Channel, the deadly encounter started innocently enough with positive possibilities. David looked down at his hand: Two Queens, Diamonds and Hearts! This time he would just call and hope some innocent would shove his chips all in. He'd pounce on the fool! The Russian and the Asian called. Annie, who woke up to a pair of black 6's, wouldn't have played but she was in the big blind with money already on the table, she tapped the felt. Four would play and she would eventually fold, she assumed. Annie caught a glimpse of the Coyote out of the corner of her eye as she folded her legs in the lotus position on the seat of her chair. The Duchess wanted to see if she could pick up another 6, otherwise she was gone. Duke might even fold trip 6's to be safe, depending on what three cards hit the felt on the flop. David had the same thought about another Queen but that would be too perfect and he might just eliminate one of the foreign challengers. I might remind everyone, at this point, what 'action flops' are. When the three common cards hit the table for the next betting round, there just might appear multiple opportunities that would be good for more than one player and great for bluffing. This, then, was the 'mother of all action flops'! David not only got his third Queen but also a pair. He had hit a full house and 'that would have been that' in most cases. Did I mention that this was NOT 'most cases'? David tried not to look at his hole cards or the cards on the table. That would be a sign of strength. "I've got this one," David sighed to himself, without a movement, "Will one of these other guys call me? I can't believe I got my Queen *and* the pair." Incredibly, the "pair" that sat on either side of the Coyote's Queen of Clubs, as it turned out, were red 6's. Annie had flopped quad sixes, four of a kind. The announcers went wild when it was aired on ESPN, "Oh MY!!!" shouted Len McCearchen, "The world is about to change forever," added Norman Chad, "Is there any way the young Coyote avoids a total skinning?" You'd never know these two had monster hands by the looks on their faces. Wyllie appeared disinterested and Duke adjusted her turtleneck and looked directly at the dealer and kept her breath soft and her heartbeat hidden. David bet a million.

Annie, knowing he had a pair of A's, Kings, or possible Queens, slowly formed three stacks the same size and re-raised to three million. The other two remaining players 'folded faster than a hotel maid' as Mack would say. David knew there was only one hand that could beat him and he pushed all his chips into the middle. "I'm All In!" the Coyote announced calmly, hoping the Duchess would call. Annie knew he couldn't have a Queen/six and he wouldn't go after her with a Pair of Aces. "He must have Queens," she quickly calculated. Any of the players at the table could have mucked the other Queen. David could be drawing dead. She was a prohibitive favorite. The words were calm, clear and resolute, "I call." Half of the chips in play were collected in the center of the table. The total was almost $100,000,000 in the pot. The other players realized they were all coming back in November. More importantly, though, they all seemed to realize they would be playing for 2nd place. The winner of this hand would be the odds on favorite to win it all in a few months. Both David and Annie already knew what cards each other were about to turn over. There's a place in a poker player's head that says, "I know what they have but I hope I'm wrong." They were both correct. David was down to 1 out, as he asked, "Did anybody fold a Queen?" No one responded. Either answer would cut into the excitement of the moment. The turn card came up with brilliant colors, wearing a suit and embossed with a huge K on the corners and spades beneath. A collective sigh and swelling yell came from 'Annie's Army'. David, an avid trivia buff, tried to avoid unrealistic hope. He ironically remembered that the kings were named after real rulers. "It's David, the King of Spades" Wyllie reflected. He knew each of the cards was designed to honor of a famous king in history: Alexander the Great, Charlemagne, Caesar and King David, the King of Spades. He recognized another odd similarity. King David held the sword of Goliath in one hand. He remembered the giant he, himself, had defeated earlier and fancied the idea both had been linked by fate. The young Coyote concluded softly, "The next one will be his wife, the Queen of Spades!" It seemed the dealer was waiting forever to bury one card and reveal the river. Wyllie found the words he thought he'd never say, come streaming out of his mouth, "I've never used a 'ONE TIME' in my life. I hate it. I hate people who yell it. I hate people who think it works.

"ONE TIME! ONE TIME! ONE TIME!" he screamed and the dealer turned over the final card. It was wearing a suit. Was that a J on the corners? No, it was a Q! It was the last Queen in the deck. The Queen of Spades sat next to her King. The Queen had eliminated the Duchess.

"GOD SAVE THE QUEEN!" David yelled. The Coyote didn't even need to reach into his bag of tricks. His pack howled from the bleachers. Annie Duke, the class act she remained, made her way over to congratulate David. "That's poker," she muttered, and all her friends and fellow pro players rushed to console her with hugs and tears. David was mobbed by his Coyotes, interviewed by ESPN, and did a victory dance that reminded people that white men can't do that either. He stopped and had an epiphany. David looked off into the distance and saw a woman being comforted by her friends. He ran past his own fans and made his way back over to Annie. The game was over for a couple of months. The rest of the players were mobbed by their own supporters. Wyllie bent over, hugged Annie and asked, "Would you consider being my coach for the next couple of months? You are so much better than me. There's no question I sucked out on the river, big time. I want to win the bracelet and I'd make it worth your while."

"You want ME to make you my 'Apprentice'?" Duke said, finding a way, even at that moment to find a smile.

David looked at her, smiled back and replied, "Of course I do. I think we just found a way to "Trump" each other." A beautiful friendship was born and David had made a move that would virtually guarantee his victory.

Mack got a call on his cell phone. It was Randy Halemano. "Isn't it great, Randy," Mack asked. I guess you want to congratulate David."

"Of course it's great but what you don't know is that the goddess Pele has a way of shooting you to the top just to pull you down. Did you make plans to bring those rocks over here where they belong? For all we know the fun is over and the drama is about to begin. Don't mess with the gods. The real drama could be beginning as we speak."

"One thing about Halemano," Mack reminded himself, "he's a true believer and usually eerily accurate when it comes to the future. I think I need to get tickets to Hawaii. Madam Pele might appreciate the fact we immediately made reservations."

CHAPTER SIXTEEN

Angel in the Wings

It didn't take long for the expected payouts to plague Coyote Nation. Dividing the spoils, while everyone profited well from their investments, was going to be disproportionate by design and unfair by interpretation. Nowhere were the confusion, complications, and unclear expectations more evident than in the case of Domingo Fernandez, Angel Vasquez and the actual sponsors of their seat, Mack and Joe Staley. Once shares reached 6 figures, Domingo's vague promise to 'share any winnings' with Angel became less a gentleman's agreement and more of an episode of American Greed.

Barnes found himself echoing his advice from economics class, "Funny how a little money can be a problem; a lot of money can be a dilemma; and a shitload of money can escalate to a war." Neither Domingo, the handyman turned late entry, nor Angel, his 'hired gun' ever imagined that they would have to disseminate and appropriate funds in excess of three years earnings for the two laborers combined.

Domingo told his friend that, as the official entry, he was himself entitled to "the lion's share" of the prize. Even that estimation could be contested. Most people assume the 'lion's share' means 'majority'. Some people even take it to mean 'most'. A few think it means 'everything.' Very few have had the privilege of spending time in an actual lion's den. If they had, it was either through a misguided safari or 'name your own price' ticketing through Priceline.com. The lion or 'king of the jungle' gets all the spoils he wants. That which is left is divided amongst lioness, cubs and scavengers in descending order. The bugs come last. Domingo was thinking a 75/25 split was more than fair. Angel agreed. The only thing they disagreed on was who got the 75%? Each soon to be ex-friend had a solid rationale. Domingo reasoned that he "gave up the seat he was 'given' to someone who knew and enjoyed the game. Without Domingo, Angel wouldn't have been there." Angel, on the other hand, argued that, "without my experience, skill and execution, Domingo would have gone home empty handed." Mack hated when ex cons used the terms like execution. After all, Vasquez had given up a couple of hours of his life while Domingo had only transferred a gift to someone who knew what they were doing. Angel reasoned that he had earned more than Fernandez could ever have won.

Mack always said, "Worth is more important than value because it means more to the buyer." In addition, the two undocumented immigrants had little legal standing in a court of law. Angel was worth every penny he never contributed. Domingo had value in the fact he owned the gifting. Even Mack couldn't find a precedent for this one. Complimenting the share question was the fact that the cash put up for the seat was paid by neither. Joe Staley put up $300 and paid Mack before the World Series started. Mack paid the other $300 to complete the 'stake'. The two investors figured they would, at least, get back the money they shelled out. It seemed the civilized thing to do. The whole matter was a corporate dilemma. You have two entrepreneurs splitting their risk without a verbal or written contract as gifted investors. Fernandez became a silent venture capitalist who banked his fortune on a working partner who acted as a middle management developer and accountant. College Econ 101!

Mack decided this could only get uglier if the prize money went 5 or 10 times higher. He suggested they all work out an agreement ASAP. Domingo's old friend, Frank, of Frank's Home Center, was his father figure and loyal supporter. He had advised Domingo, "You received the entry as a 'tip' and then employed Angel as an 'independent contractor'." Frank was educated at the University of Bill Handle and his weekly radio show, "Handle on the Law". Mack's feel for contract law reinforced the fact that everyone who grew up on "LA Law" or "The Practice" knew there was no *quid pro quo* arrangement and that, for a contract to exist, there had to be a 'meeting of the minds'. Mack backed his opinion of the dispute with daily Judge Judy episodes like the rest of the retired generation. He suggested 60/40 for his handyman and $1000 each for himself and Joe out of Domingo's pocket.

Angel came unglued. "I got to play. I get paid," Vasquez argued,

"You two can go to hell. I have no legal way of fighting you because I'm not a legal yet." As he reached the driveway he was lathered in sweat and getting louder, "Sometimes," he yelled as he revved his hog's engine, "people end up dead and then the survivor gets it all! You give me my 75% I earned or I'll be back for my inheritance. You know what I'm saying?"

The two men still standing in front of the garage knew what he was saying but hoped he didn't mean what they heard. Mack turned to his handyman and asked, "How well do you know this guy? I have the feeling one or both of us just got threatened. Is he dangerous? What's he capable of?"

"I wouldn't worry if I was you Mr. Mack," Domingo answered, "he has too much to lose. Angel will calm down. He's getting his citizenship soon. His new wife, Consuela, has a good job as a nurse at the hospital. She works in the heart attack room. My old friend's got a bad case of machismo right now, that's all. In our culture, real men don't look to their wives to support them. With enough money from the poker game, he could give up his job as a cook and finance his own body shop. You know what I mean?"

"I know what you mean," Mack explained, "and, by the way, it's not called the 'heart attack room. It's the cardio pulmonary unit. While I'm at it, what was he in prison for?"

Domingo reassured his friend and boss, "He just has a bad temper some times. He only went off once and he served his 10 years. To this day, Senior Barnes, nobody who knows him believes it was 'voluntary' manslaughter, it was an accident. The other guy just fell wrong. Get some rest. We'll work this whole thing out.

Trust me, my wife and I are having dinner with them next week at the restaurant near the hospital. We'll work things out." Domingo smiled and waved as he got into his pickup truck. Mack wasn't convinced but, if Fernandez wasn't worried, Barnes would move on to other concerns. "Maybe they could barter a better deal next time," he pondered, "nobody wants to end up in the 'heart attack room' over this." Unfortunately, as to meeting as a group, there would be no 'next time'.

CHAPTER SEVENTEEN

Delta Force

David was almost 6'2". When he went to open the door on the eve of the Hawaii trip, he was eye to eye with an incredible fem fatale under the porch light.

"David Wyllie?" the stunning figure asked.

"That's me," the young man answered, "What can I do for you?"

"I need to talk to you in the worst way," she replied and David seemed to sink into her deep emerald eyes.

"Come on in," Wyllie responded invitingly as he silently added to himself, "talk to me in the worst way you know how." Some social intercourse is often social for one and more intercourse for the man. Delta recognized the Coyote as prey and she knew how to hunt for what she wanted. In this case she used innuendoes as her weapon of choice.

He opened the door wide and she got even taller in those 4" heals as she took the step up through the doorway from the porch.

The girl, strike that, woman looked even more beautiful in full light. As he closed the door behind her, he noticed that she just kept on looking good as she passed him and continued across the room.

"To what do I owe the pleasure?" he continued.

He was still captivated by athletically toned female in his apartment. Some women wear business suits beautifully. This green-eyed, redheaded, Amazon just let the powder blue jacket and thigh length skirt tightly contain every curve, every movement, every undulation and modulation of what seemed to the perfect body.

"I'm sorry, what was the original question?" Wyllie asked, interrupting a perfectly good conversation he was having mentally with himself.

"I just asked if you were David Wyllie," his guest continued. "I know you are. I recognize you. My name is Delta and I'm hoping you and I can get to be the best of friends.

"When somebody like Delta tells someone like me something like that," David deduced internally, "It can't be just socially motivated."

In high school, he and his brother were self proclaimed nerds in the very best sense of the term. They had joined and were active in clubs like robotics and the Model U.N. delegation. College and work took up most of their free time since. They played chess for excitement. Those were the only 'moves' he really had. Online poker was a distraction but certainly not like a pick up bar. Social media dating was more of a gamble than poker. His entire social life passed before his eyes. It didn't take that long.

"Boy, that was quick," he said to himself as he redirected his attention to Delta.

"Okay, why don't you sit down?' David said, still confused but now intrigued, "I'm interested. Well, I'm motivated. Actually, I'm glad to have you."

"Why didn't I just ask her if she would enjoy being 'had'?" David asked himself disgustedly.

He was mumbling and bumbling over his words. He was even stumbling his way around the apartment he had lived in for three years. Suddenly, the floor plan, the furniture, and even the carpet, were all new to him.

"I'm here for business but I usually find pleasure to be the oil that lubricates the relationship," Delta shared.

David thought to himself: "Would you say 'lubricates' again? Why did I envision her unbuttoning her blouse when she said 'pleasure'? Hold the presses! Did she include 'relationship' in the same sentence with those other two words?" The world continued to stand still for a minute or two. Delta was a mistress of sexually charged suggestions and she could always tell when she could throw out pure innuendo and let others field it as sexually impure as they chose to. It was the mental/physical part of her game. David was playing right along.

"David, my name, for this assignment, will be Delta. "The boys in the office thought it was the perfect cover name for a poker girl. They, like you and others, always seem impressed with me when I stroll into the office. You had the same reaction when you invited me in," she shared as she shifted to business, "I represent a small financial group that is interested in investing in your upcoming economic redistribution. You know what I'm talking about: the Final Table."

David, who was not easily confused, appeared bewildered by that last statement, "What are you talking about?"

"David, I'm talking about the poker game and the $10 million dollars you plan on winning in November. My partners want to buy your effort for $4 million right now and guarantee an immediate pay day for you and your friends. Of course, that also includes more money to be made in advertising, endorsing, and representing our interests in online gaming." Delta added, "We're interested in bringing back all that action from off shore or where ever. You *do* like 'action' don't you?"

In his mind, David just kept flashing back to "lubricating the relationship". In high school he had some 'friends of the opposite sex' but never dated. In college he considered himself a bit of a player since he started dating girls with good personalities. He later moved on to some cute ones and had finally hit his ultimate plateau at 'attractive'. That was more than he had ever expected. He just kept analyzing the situation and concluded, "Delta left 'attractive' in her rear-view mirror years ago. Her eyes radiate enticement in much the way some video games project laser kills. Her hips are more avatar than human and her legs go all the way to the ground!"

"Wow!" David screamed without sound, "I'm way out of my league but, like my fantasy basketball team, I'm ready for draft day."

"I can honestly say 'tell me more'," he offered, trying to channel his classic movie hero, Cary Grant. "How does this work? I don't know why my homeys would want to listen to me," Wyllie said.

"Did I actually refer to the home game players as 'homeys'?" he asked himself. Instant replay confirmed the call.

"Honey," she replied, "You are *hot* property and you've seemed to capture just about everybody's interest in the sport. My people tell me you 'cross all the lines'. They all love you. That's what 'image' is all about. Nobody wants to say 'no' to y'all. In the end you could work for us and so could some of your fan base in the crowd and on TV. They look adorable wearing those little cartoon outfits. I love when they dance around and howl." At this point the fact Delta had used the term 'cross all the lines' was not lost on David's fully activated and thoroughly stimulated imagination.

"We could find a way to get them more money too! Some of them are so cute! I don't know how you did it but our experts say they seem to check all the boxes, demographically. You've got blacks, Arabs, Mexicans and people in wheelchairs. You even have a gay twin and a priest. You are a regular melting pot billboard! We want you to be our poster boy. You just think about it and gather up all your little wolves or whatever they are. When you get back from Hawaii, think about and just remember me. I want you to think about it *real hard*!"

Delta leaned into her new, straggly project. "I think you're a leader, David," she prolonged the flatter, "I love leaders. They excite me. I bet you could get all your friends to come around. She pressed her, as they say in those cheap paperback romance novels, heaving breasts into David's chest, "I bet I know how to get someone like you to come around. You might even decide to come a couple of times." She ran her nails down his back and kissed him on the neck, bit his earlobe tenderly and then ran her hands down to his hips.

David's eyebrows were raised in exhilaration. He made a quick, below the belt self-analysis and thought to himself, "I bet the 2nd time will be even better."

CHAPTER EIGHTEEN

Hawaiian Cruise and Curse

After one day back home and the uncomfortable visit from Angel, Mack thought it would be a good idea to get the hell out of the hoopla and help clear David's mind. Barnes didn't even know about Delta. Mack had initiated a 'do not disturb' sign by scheduling the Hawaiian trip for the Wyllie and Barnes families as far away from Vegas and poker as possible. All of the coyote team in the valley had guaranteed themselves a hefty profit with only 'more money to win' at the Final Table. Wilson Creek Winery and the Temecula City Council were planning a 'DAVID WYLLIE DAY' in a couple of weeks upon their return. Mack knew David needed the kind of 'hang loose' feeling of island life before his hometown could honor him.

"Besides," Mack had told David, "Temecula has a sister city in Hawaii. City councils always have sister cities in places like Hawaii, Europe, Japan, or the Caribbean. No self respecting City Councilman or Mayor would ever be caught dead visiting Haiti,

Tunisia or Paraguay."

"I've only been to Hawaii once, on a cruise," David told Mack, "two years ago, and that's where I lost my virginity. She was a cruise line dancer… …that's 'cruise line', not 'line dancer.'"

"We'll sail between the islands," Barnes told the boys, "I made a promise to Halemano and Pele, the fire goddess, that those four lava rocks you showed me would be brought back to the Big Island. It's a small price to pay for winning and a great excuse to relax. Now, let's all get packed for the *Pride of Aloha*. We sail Saturday and I have three balcony rooms near each other: one for you boys, one for Sherri and me, and one for Dottie." Mack was right. Hawaii was the complete opposite of Vegas. The state of Hawaii didn't even allow the ship to open up its casino. As Mack analyzed it, "Even if someone recognized the Coyote, they'd be more interested in the next day's tour in port, David the piano man at the bar, or visiting the 'anytime buffet' on their way to or from any of several themed stages. This was a cruise. People were here to buy overpriced paintings and wear plaid shorts with hibiscus shirts and straw hats. Who would have time for a couple of poker players?"

"Hawaii," Sherri sighed as the ship left port in Honolulu, "land of rainbows, volcanoes, and surfers."

"Next month we'll start training with Annie Duke and some of her poker buddies," Mack reminded his wife, "I really think the kid will go all the way. He's got over half the money and, barring some unforeseen problem, he should be a lock for top prize, the bracelet.

"Mack, this could be a second honeymoon," Sherri interrupted, "do you remember the first one? We had $175 for the week and we lived on love." Barnes, surprised by his wife's memory, seemed a little embarrassed as he looked around the deck to make sure no on heard her.

"You're right. Outside of dropping off a few rocks at Volcanoes National Park, we can escape the drama for a week and pretend nobody knows the boys," Mack whispered to his love. "It'll just be you and me, a Mai Tai or two, and a balcony next to the bed. It's time to enjoy the things life has to offer."

"Surprise!" a familiar Hawaiian voice piped in, "I flew over on a military jump seat and I'm sailing with you. Last night, in a dream, Madame Pele talked to me and asked me to meet you. Pele told me you didn't want any drama, unforeseen problems or any of the Coyotes to argue and break Ohana. She said there was some drama between Coyotes."

Ohana is the family spirit and Mack had no idea how Halemano could have known about his fears or about the confrontation between Domingo and Angel. It seemed as if Randy was really channeling the spirits. Barnes tried to dismiss it but it was definitely in the back of his mind and would remain there for now. After a brief stop in Oahu and the tourist trappings of Waikiki, the ship sailed on to Maui. Sherri and Dottie shopped their way through Lahaina. Dennis took a bus to Kahana to visit an old friend and they all learned how to weave hats on the Promenade Deck. Sherri reminded the whole group, "When you finally decide to drop the pretentious crap and become a real tourist, you're on 'island time'. The only reason to look at your watch is to find out if it's still working." Kauai was rainy and Kona was dry but both were relaxing in their own way. The only 'calls' were for room service. The only 'raises' were with glasses in a toast to 'Aloha'. Even the mention of 'all in' made Mack blush. The whole group was sun screen drenched and salt water seasoned when they arrived in Hilo. Mack rented a Mustang convertible for the trip to the volcanoes and lava tubes. Sherri got to drive with Dottie riding shot gun. Mack and the boys took up the back seat in the open air. The ring tone 'White Sandy Beach' blasted and Mack scrambled to get his cell phone out of his back pack. It was Bob. He had a serious sound to his voice, "People, we just lost one of the pack's best. Dr. Herb passed. We all knew it would happen but, at least, he got a chance to follow the action to this point. One of his last messages was….let me find the text," Bob said, "and I quote, 'Go Wyllie and my fellow Coyotes. Thanks for making my last hand part of a big pot." You won't be back for the funeral, Mack," Bob explained, "A few of us will represent. It'll be traditional Catholic Filipino. We'll sit on Joy's side of the church. The family will be on the St. Joseph side away from the '2nd wife.' Don't worry. We'll eat at one of those table side grills with Herb's family afterwards. Dr. Santos was a good guy, a great player, and super friend. He will be missed." Mack got off the phone and clarified the message for the group. He had to yell against the wind, "Don't think that was part of Pele's curse, but I know I'll get a call from Randy. We'd better get these rocks dropped off pronto." Kilauea is, in California terms, an awesome spot. As they pulled into the park, the sulfur fumes were just too much for the open air convertible. The group pulled up to the ranger station, put on the top, and shut the windows.

"I'll go inside and check the protocol for returning the lava rocks," Mack said, "You guys can drive out to the lava tubes." Mack sought out a ranger who assured him that the rocks did not have to be returned. He explained that the belief in the curse was held only by hard core Hawaiians and completely ignored by the majority of the island people.

"I made a promise to a friend and to the goddess Pele," Mack admitted, "and I won't hear the end of it if I don't get this done."

"I understand, sir," the ranger acknowledged, "As luck would have it, all this weekend the docents are putting out the old display of items returned by those who fell for the curse. We used to have it as a permanent part of the ranger station but too many people focused on its novelty. We're a national park with serious science to share. It didn't really fit in with everything factual. It was more for its entertainment value. Once every year or so, we pull everything related to the curse out of storage. You just happened to time it right. If you don't have time to stay, just Google' Pele's curse' and read how many people blame the rocks for everything from lost jobs to failed marriages to hair loss." Mack headed out back and looked through the cases of returned shoes, rocks, dust, soiled shirts and pleading cases for better luck in the future. He saw one remarkably long letter from a woman in Florida who sent back her tennis shoes with lava rock in the soles along with a hand written message.

"Take this back to the Goddess Pele for me," the letter pleaded. "In the last four years since I took it off the island I have been cursed like the legend foretold. I met two 'Mr. Wrongs', starting with abuse and ending in divorce. I lost a lottery ticket worth $3000 before I could cash it. Someone broke into our house and robbed us twice. My sons, who always obeyed me as children became unruly teenagers. I lost three jobs and now suffer from anxiety, depression and thoughts of suicide. My mom fell and broke her back in her 80's and my dog was hit by a car. I can't take this any longer. Give me back my life, oh volcanic deity." Most of the letters, over a hundred of them, were almost as bad.

"Let's see," Mack analyzed. "She couldn't judge men; was careless with her important papers; lived in a bad neighborhood; lacked parental and employment skills; probably took drugs; and didn't keep the pet gate closed. It sounds like she really pissed off the heavens."

Some of the letters and returns were recent. "….and the beat goes on," Barnes added softly and sarcastically, "maybe she was wrong about her mother's back. That first lady probably stepped on a crack before mailing her letter."

When the Mustang pulled up to the ranger station, the whole group was frantic. "We just got a call from Ruby. She fell and broke her ankle. She'll be in the hospital for three weeks. It must have been the rocks. Bad things always happen in three's," Sherri warned.

The phone was still ringing off the, now passé, 'hook'. It was Randy Halemano.

"Mack, I just did an anagram after I heard about Dr. Herb and now Ruby. Do you realize that if you take the letters in 'DAMNED HAWAIIAN CRUISE' and rearrange them, it spells: HAWAIIAN

CURSE, MAN DIED?"

"For the love of God," Mack insisted, "there is not going to be a third bad event. I'm only doing this for you, Randy. I can't take this for one more minute. We are returning the rocks as we speak. Leave us alone! Good-bye" Mack said with exhaustion and frustration. "Get a life. If you really have the time to play anagrams, you ARE the third curse. I'm actually thinking of bringing the rocks right back there and hiding them in your garden."

"Don't do that. That's not even funny, Mack," Halemano said, "I was just trying to save you some …"

Mack had listened too long. He pressed the disconnect button on his phone and said, "Enough about curses. Let's get out of here. We need to think rationally. We just need a little sanity. Sometimes the fates are more than anyone can explain logically. Sometimes they are more like their namesakes in mythology. They cut the thread of life short and no one knows why. This was one of those times."

Mack's phone buzzed again.

"Randy, leave us alone and put a sock in it," Barnes pleaded. "Let it be and don't call me again!"

"Mack, this isn't Randy," the voice on the other end replied, "It's me, Bryce Tanner. "You know how you recommended Domingo to help me get my house ready to sell?" There was a silence on both sides before Bryce interjected, "Are you ready for this? Domingo's dead! The coroner's here right now."

"Domingo's dead? How? He was one of the healthiest people I knew," Mack said in total disbelief, "What do you know about it,

Bryce?"

Turner was ready, "I was downstairs and Domingo was hanging a light fixture over the bed. I heard a huge thud and thought he might have lost his balance or dropped the lamp. When I went up there he was on the ground and unconscious. My neighbor and I called 911 and started CPR. It was too late. Right now they say it was probably a heart attack or maybe he just fell wrong. The EMT guys took him to the cardiac unit. I can't believe a guy like that would have a heart attack. You gotta wonder if it was something else. We're all in shock!"

"Maybe it was because Bryce had added, 'maybe he just fell wrong' that flashed Barnes back to Angel and the last veiled threats on the driveway. Coupled with Vasquez' fiancée and her cardio pulmonary nursing experience, it seemed to be more believable than a young guy in great health just dropping dead. Suddenly he had a new respect for Pele and Ohana.

"Gotta go, Bryce, I'll call you later. Sherri's going to lose it when I tell her. Gotta go!"

Mack put down the phone without explaining the call to the group. "Where are the rocks?' Mack asked, "Where are the goddamn rocks? Let's get rid of those fucking things and get the hell out of here, now!"

"Relax," Dennis said, "I already returned the four rocks. I put one in a lava tube, one outside the Jagger Museum, one in the steam vats and I tossed the last one off the Kilauea outlook. That should do it!"

"Why the steam vats? Why a lava tube? Never mind. Let's go."

Mack said still in a state of shock, "Never mind, it's done."

Mack seemed visibly shaken with the news. Could there, unbelievably be something to the curse or was foul play involved? He just looked at his wife, the boys, Dottie and said, "Domingo Fernandez, our handyman and great friend is dead." The five rushed to form a teary-eyed hug.

"Okay, we've lost an outstanding young man. We returned the rocks" Mack said as he reflected on his dismissive attitude toward that pathetic letter. The one he mocked at the ranger station, "From this day forward, we pray for the Fernandez family and we ask Madam Pele to forgive us all now and at our own final table. Let us heal Ohana in every way we can."

"Did they get the rocks back on time and with sincerity or was there one more, even more serious price to pay?" Barnes wondered. When Domingo died, they all knew anything that came out of the tournament would be tarnished. The fun part was waning and there were, if you could believe Halemano, even more complicated problems ahead.

The last two nights before the flight home, the group spent relaxing at Turtle Bay Resort, on the north shore of Oahu. David and Dennis stayed in the room and discussed poker strategies. A full-time butler and an X Box were provided as part of their concierge package.

"You know, David," his younger brother noted, "I think this would be less interesting more ignored if the gay brother had gotten this far."

"I think it had more to do with style, strategy, talent and the fact that my own personality was starting to emerge as an independent force," his twin countered. "You had your chance and you came up short, little brother. I think I just took a leap forward inspired by the competition."

"I think we need to talk when we get home, David," Dennis suggested, "You want the real David at that table. Who you are may be more important than who you think you've become. I just want the world to see who we have always been. You're getting a little too sure of yourself. Who pumped you up?" The name Delta came to David's mind but not to his lips. "No need to tell Dennis," his brother reasoned. "He wouldn't get it."

The last night was interrupted by a firm knock on the door. Peterson, their penthouse suite 'gentleman' opened the door and announced, "Master David, there is a young woman and a man to see you, sir." Both Wyllies walked to the door.

"Which of you is David?" the woman asked.

"I'm David," the elder twin replied, "How can I help you?" She looked vaguely familiar and he thought she might be there for an autographed picture.

"You don't remember me, do you?" She continued, "I used to dance on the cruise ship. We spent the night together. I think you might be my baby son's father."

A quiet panic filled David's next words, "Are you sure? I suppose you want to make sure, if you're not.
This is completely shocking to me, what can we do to make sure? Is this your father? How do you do sir?"

The young woman turned to her male companion. He stepped

forward and handed David papers, "This is a paternity suit, Mr. Wyllie. I am representing my client legally and we will require a DNA sample before seeing you in court. I might add that my client is willing to avoid any mention of this and not pursue the issue temporarily for the appropriate monetary compensation."

Mack had arrived near the beginning of the conversation and asked, "Is this a shake down?"

Quite the opposite, sir," the suit replied, "We are prepared to delay any mention of this and agree to keep the whole thing under wraps until after the poker playoffs. We would require David to take the test and enter into a financial reimbursement arrangement should he be determined the father. I might add that we wish him well in Las Vegas. We think that for her silence and cooperation on the matter, for the time being alone, my client should be compensated to the tune of $10,000." If we disclose the paternity issue, we lose the retainer. If it is determined that he is the father, it will be included as part of any settlement."

"So this *is* a shakedown," Barnes clarified, "Is this possible, David?"

"It was my first time. I was dumb and we were just irresponsible. Yes, it is possible but it was just one time."

After working out the details of the nondisclosure, money changed hands, conditionally, to avoid distractions until after November.

"What time is the plane in the morning?" Dennis broke in, "I think we all need to get out of Hawaii and never come back. Temecula will be a better distraction."

Everyone nodded in agreement. Mack wanted to put superstitious Randy, possibly pregnant women and the unpredictable gods in his rear view mirror, the sooner, the better.

CHAPTER NINETEEN

Delta Force Two: The Rake

After the Turtle Bay stunner and the things that erupted around the volcano, David was looking forward to some quiet time before his hometown day of recognition. He almost decided to ignore the doorbell when it rang.

"This better be good," he thought to himself, "No autographs, interviews, the guys, or new found friends." It wasn't one of the guys. It was his newest found friend who seemed a little eager at the door. Frustrated with pushing the button, Delta knocked on David's door just as he opened it. She threw it back and strode past the young Wyllie. This time, she was more direct about using David to her advantage.

"Did everyone agree to sell? I have the check for the entire $4 million. You can disperse it as soon as I have every signature on the contract or you sign it for the group," Delta explained. She seemed less the temptress and more the business woman this time.

"Hypothetically," David offered, "what if some of the players would rather take their chances on my skill and wait until November?"

"The deal was for the whole group. If we have to go individually, we can't offer as much and we might have to deal with the more reluctant people in our own ways. Sometimes that requires a little more of a hardball approach. Sometimes people have to be persuaded in creative ways."

"That sounds like threats and intimidation. I'm wondering if you might represent the mob!"

"The Mob," Delta shot back, "is an outdated term for a completely different group. That group goes from urging to persuading to convincing. Please! The people I represent are more of a consortium," the leggy redhead explained, "They think of themselves as a co-op. They are just smart investors who try to simplify situations by reducing them to achievable equations. They assume minimal risks to realize maximize benefits and increased opportunities for profits. They are simply trying to take small hits for big gains. I swear, didn't you ever watch Shark Tank? This is not even a big venture for us. We are diversified. I can count on you and your brother? Can't I? I'd even enjoy meeting him someday under different conditions."

"I know you are just going to use me to get what you want and I can't say I wouldn't enjoy the 'negotiations' with you but my Coyotes are my believers and I can't disappoint them. We will not be bought!"

"You might be surprised how many of your opponents at that final table have already signed 'letters of intent'. Those are our 'hedge bets' and you'd also be amazed at how little convincing they took. We have access to more than money. We can pay you in discounted luxuries, pharmaceuticals, and even 'previously owned' property at more than half off. I, myself, can barter with my own 'professional services' that, though expensive, are more than worth it to the virgin buyer."

"Not interested," proclaimed Wyllie, "Well, I'm interested but I have my own moral compass."

"And which way was your moral compass pointed the first time we met, darling?" the all-woman negotiator suggested, "From where I was standing, it was due north."

David wanted an equally provocative sexually charged comeback. He fancied something right out of a Bogart movie from his Classic Films Club. He ran through the dialogue in his head, "From where I stand, you're just a good looking dame with an ugly soul. You're the kind of girl who would rather spread her legs than open her mind or heart. You're sick, kid, and I can't heal you!"

That thought never made it to the real world. What came out was more like, "Oh yeah? Well I'm going to meet a girl some day and she'll be even neater than you!"

"Geezus," David berated himself in his mind, "I have a law degree and won a state speech and debate championship but when there's a beautiful girl involved, I suddenly turn into some sort of Jonah Hill in Super Bad or Raj from the Big Bang Theory.

Delta adjusted her sweater which, was already adjusted just

fine in David's estimation. As she rose to leave, she looked over her shoulder like some sort of Jessica Rabbit.

"If you change your mind, or anyone else's" she offered, "I wrote my number on a post-it note and stuck it to your headboard. Watch yourself, David. You never know when you might have a red dot on your forehead. As always, I'm just speaking figuratively and I know that's how you see me."

"Damn!" the Coyote steamed silently, "Why does she get all the good lines? Sometimes attitude and experience trample on a great mind and a good upbringing."

"Mr. Wyllie," Delta concluded, "Don't always look for a moral to the story. The best stories, I've found, are immoral or amoral. Again, I'd love to seal a deal with a kiss but I can also pursue binding arbitrations and enter into mutually satisfying resolutions. I think you know it's better to screw than to get screwed. I may see you one more time or I may never see you again. Everything is either in your hands or in mine. I've worked my way from the bottom to a dominating position and I'm comfortable with either. Hope you make good choices. When you think about me, and you will, call me for anything and I'll get on top of it. If not, there are always consequences to delayed gratification." She was, if nothing else, an expert at mixing that business with pleasure, sexually charged metaphors, and hormonally driven conversations. David knew she could talk the talk and he watched her walk the walk. As she swung open the front screen, the young Wyllie knew she was careful enough to leave the door open to the future. He considered Delta's experienced promises and contemplated her equally suggestive threats. In poker, the house takes a few dollars in every hand. It's called 'the rake." David realized that He had gone from being cultivated to being 'raked' by Delta. What a Whore. "Shit," he told himself, "I could have even used 'rake' and 'hoer' against her. I would have killed for either of those lines a few minutes ago as parting shots."

Meanwhile, Randy Halemano was having another dream about national attention and the twins breaking Ohana through an act of selfless betrayal. He saw a picture of the twins being torn in half by the gods. "They must be having problems in their own relationship," Halemano thought. "I'll call Mack next week."

CHAPTER TWENTY

The Homecoming

If there's one thing Temecula knows how to do, it's throw a party. The Balloon and Wine Festival attracts tens of thousands who gather at Lake Skinner each spring. The people come to float in hot hair balloons or taste the nectar of the gods on the ground and get high. Thousands watch in awe as the ascending fleets of baskets are raised aloft by thunderous furnaces under colorful silken canopies. The Annual Rod Run in Old Town draws car enthusiasts to the classic car-lined streets. The local restaurants, beer gardens and dance spots teem with enthusiasm at night and into the wee hours of morn. The hot rod crowd has been known to approach or exceed overflow in more than one sense of the word. Ice rinks at Christmas, hundreds of concerts throughout the year, over forty wineries packed on any weekend and gaming at the many nearby casinos are but a few examples of "valley fervor". All this is just an hour or so away from everything and makes Temecula the perfect 'staycation' for travelers from Orange County, San Diego and Los

Angeles. The town is an entertainment 'wander' land that draws from the San Bernardino Mountains to the Mojave Deserts to the Mexican border to the Pacific Ocean. Mack and Sherri saw two Gary Sinise 'Wounded Warrior' concerts on the lawn of City Hall in years past. Major acts perform at Pechanga weekly and no other town has as many poker fans in the Inland Empire or, perhaps, in the world. When the City Council proclaimed a day in September, "David Wyllie Day", the mayor seconded it by adding, "we should have a parade down Main Street." Another councilman joined in, "and the parade marshals should be Wile E. Coyote and the Roadrunner." Someone in the audience called out, "with Looney Tunes playing in the background."

A few years earlier, Jerry Yang had won the Main Event, claiming Temecula as home. Although, Jerry did a terrific job, he did play usually play at Pechanga He was really a Lake Elsinore gambler. Besides, Yang came into the final table 'short stacked' and not given much of a chance to advance. Pechanga followed the action at the final table live on dozens of big screens in their poker room. The fans went crazy when he blasted his way through the pros with huge bluffs and bets. David, on the other hand, was a prohibitive favorite to win it all and, if there's one thing Temecula would loves, it's a winner. It's a champion. It's a WSOP Main Event Bracelet!

The day, the parade, poker mania, and the Wyllie Coyotes howling their way through town was overwhelming and featured David and his little band of investors. Everybody in town knew the story by now. Once David defeated Annie Duke, The Press

Enterprise had started a daily insert called 'Know Your Coyote' which featured each of the home game players with pictures, interviews, how and why they bought into the tournament and what they planned to do with their share of the money.

At Pechanga Casino, the Coyotes basked in the radiance of their 15 minutes of fame. Some incorporated it more than others. One of them, we won't say 'who', turned the adventure into a series of Sunday Mass sermons called, 'Getting to Heaven, What are the Odds?' His marriage counseling sessions were titled 'The Better the Pair, the Better the Action'. The article the Enterprise did on Father Jinks' homilies was headlined "Now he's speaking to a 'full house.'"

Jake Wayland was interviewed with his co-workers dressed as ZZ Top, holding guitars and wearing sunglasses. In a month or two, this would all die down and disappear but, for now, everyone in the group was a rock star in some sense.

Katy, who entered without telling her superintendent husband, was conspicuous by her uncharacteristic silence. Most guessed the money was good but the attention and her clandestine entry were not as popular at home. Remember, she entered without telling her husband because, "Who'd ever find out, anyway?"

By the day of the parade, others had jumped on the bandwagon. In various plays on words, businesses followed "suit". Guidant, a world leader in cardio pulmonary equipment had a sign out front that read "our *Hearts* are with you'.

Chaparral High, the former school of Mack, Sherri, Dottie and the boys, scheduled a special assembly. The students and faculty were proud of the two boys and everybody loved an excuse to get out of class.

"I don't remember the cheerleaders hugging us back then," David told his brother on the stage, "it would have been even more appreciated when I was 17."

"Back then we weren't athletes," Dennis reminded his counterpart, "Now we have money. If we would have come back with the 'before and after' look of a couple of nerdy teen geeks who blossomed late and became exotic male dancers, we'd have been hugged. This is nice, though. I guess we should just sit back and enjoy the attention while it lasts."

"You should thank me, Dennis," the older Wyllie replied, "I told them that the two of us should be together for this day. It was something I *earned* and something you *yearned to have*. Sit back and bask in my limelight. Not many of us have the opportunity," David bragged.

Dennis just shook his head in total disbelief at his brother's attitude, "I'm glad it's you, David," Dennis thought, "I honestly wouldn't want to be in your shoes. If I were, I'd wear them with more style and humility. The 'new you' is too much and the 'real me' is just fine, for now. If you change your mind or want to act a little more like me, I'll, of course, be there for you." Dennis decided to concentrate on the celebration.

"Remember Dollars for Scholars? We were the studs that night but I like this better," Dennis admitted. "God, I'm glad we're not still in high school, though. Did we ever look that young?" David asked.

"The real question, brother," Dennis pointed out, "is just how old we actually look to them now?"

"We've always looked younger," David reminded him, "if we hadn't been so tall, we'd have looked like middle school kids at our own graduation. Unfortunately, we fit in with this crowd."

The boys had gone from the parade to the high school and, eventually, made their way out to the vineyards. Wilson Creek Winery was sponsoring a luncheon ushered in with the help of a quickly formed city council caravan. Wilson Creek Almond Champaign is nationally, if not internationally, renowned for its unique flavor. Today the winery would honor both brothers: 'Coyote Winner and Road Runner-up' as they billed it. Charlie Wilson brought down the house when he passed around a specially labeled, limited time edition of the popular bubbly. On the bottle was a picture of David and Dennis wearing Phoenix Coyote jerseys and, above their heads were the words, "Almond Brothers Champaign". Each of the Coyotes who attended got a 12 bottle case to take home with them. If David won, they would certainly be collector's items. The Wilson family had prepared a five course luncheon with a different wine to match the cuisine. With the exception of the head table of Coyotes, everyone paid $100 for the privilege of meeting the guests of honor. Singers sang, speakers spoke, and the whole group was roasted by civic leaders. In the end, a fun time was had by all.

"You certainly made an impression with this town!" Mack told David as they were finishing their *la tois petite filets*, the main course. It was also their fifth glass of wine since sitting down in banquet room, "Enjoy all the fuss and commotion but don't let it go to your heads," Sherri suggested. "Same with the wines but don't overdo it." They both overdid it.

The Wyllie brothers had taken on the attributes of the vino. Blush red from all the attention; hard pressed to thank everyone; and a little too 'corked' to drive home. Unfortunately, aging was also soon to be in question.

By the end of the afternoon festivities, Mack and Sherri had to drive separate cars home with a different brother passed out in the back seat of each vehicle.

CHAPTER TWENTY-ONE

Heads Up: The Showdown!

Mack and Sherri drove the boys back to their house where the two were staying for the month. David was seeking insulation from Delta without referencing her visits. The twins fell into their beds after drinking the afternoon and evening away. Neither one woke up until late morning the next day. They continued to defy sobriety. The drink of choice was beer during the day and shots at night with friends. For David, it had already become a constant distraction. For Dennis, it had developed into a growing concern for his twin. Mack sensed that the two boys were growing apart. The grand luncheon celebration at Wilson Creek might have been the impetus that sent them over the top. The merry band of 'Wyllie Coyotes' found themselves the Posse Pro Tem of the entire Temecula Valley. The newspaper interviews, autographs, at least one proposal of marriage, and even talk of a possible book deal continued mount. Their Instagrams and Facebook pages had blown up and their Twitter followers numbered in the countless thousands. Nowadays, it appeared, fame could last a month for some people if they had sat back and took it slow. Because of all the attention and the fact that the brothers had over imbibed at the winery, things seemed strained between the twins. They were novices at adjusting to their hangovers. For the first time in either's memory they were picking at each other and arguing. Complicating the situation was the fact that they were drinking to feel sober, David more than his brother, saw in his twin the first trappings of celebrity. He was glad that David had found a way of becoming an individual. It had always been something David wanted far more than his younger brother. "Did he really know how to handle life on his own?" Dennis wondered. He always wanted to be famous and he even touted recently in one interview, "David Wyllie," he declared, "the name will outlive me and will stand on its own merit! When people mention my name, long after I'm gone, they will know I accomplished more than even I had ever imagined!" To Dennis, it was time to step up and set his brother straight.

Dennis got nose to nose with his inebriated counterpart, "I really don't want to get in your face," Dennis insisted, "but I will when I have to!" He went on, "It seems like you've already crowned yourself champion but all I hear is the voice of false pride. I smell expensive alcohol on your breath but it's mixed with the stench of uncharacteristic self-promotion. You're as full of yourself as you are of the Cabernet, Bud Light, or Jaeger shots. Either way, one, or all of them will bury you! From one twin to another: get serious!"

David flew into a rage. "You're just jealous! You've always been satisfied to be *just a twin*." Do you have any idea how many times people still ask me, "Which one are you?" Dennis dealt back, "ALL twins go through those things but I have never been offended by those remarks." There was an awkward pause. "I think you need to go to bed, brother," Dennis said. "Maybe, you need to get some rest away from all this. It would help you clear your mind." At that point, Mack, who had been staying clear of the escalation between the two, stepped forward, "I think that's a good idea, David. Here are the keys to the trailer in Big Bear. Drink a pot of coffee and take a little time away from it all. Don't take a phone. It's quiet up there. The people there don't give a flying crap about who you are. Most of them only know fishing, boating, driving around in golf carts, and Saturday evenings pot lucks that build to a crescendo with $1 bingo cards. You can sit on the porch, read a book and take a hike. I guarantee you'll come back in a few days as the David we all know and respect. In any case, take the keys, and, since you'll have your truck, bring back three folding tables for next weekend. Sherri's putting together a little private party with more food and less vino, suds, and pure poison."

Both boys let Mack leave before David reinitiated the confrontation. "I'm not finished partying right now, brother, David argued. "My straight friends are down at Friday's in the bar and I plan on surprising them and the rest of the crowd." For some, unexplained reason, Dennis' sexuality only came into play when David was either drunk, angry or, as was usual recently, both.

"Life can be short, Dennis," Wyllie Won said to his openly gay brother, Wyllie Too, "You only live once and I intend on making every minute count. If you're honest, you have to admit that you want to be in my world far more than I want to be part of yours. *You take the keys to the trailer, and try to be careful with my truck. You're the one who needs to chill! I'll take your 'faggy' little red Z4. I don't need to leave. YOU* can get away from *ME!*" At that, he grabbed Dennis' keys from the entry table with the wallet along side and stormed out of the house. Dennis pleaded with him to reconsider but to no avail. The little BMW disappeared in the distance. "OH Heavens!" Dennis said to himself, thank God he only has a few miles to the Promenade Mall." If roles were reversed, David would have said, "No Shit! I'm leaving too." Get one of them angry and you could always tell them apart. Sometimes, friends, who weren't sure who they were meeting, would say something aimed to anger. The choice of expletives was a dead give away. One brother relied of forms of feces to emote and the other turned flaming religious. Dennis looked around and didn't want to be there when his brother returned. He decided *someone* had to get away from this madhouse situation and both needed some time to themselves. He picked up the keys to the truck and the remaining wallet near the front door. He packed an overnight bag for Big Bear Lake just a few hours away. No cell phone for him either, he had to do some soul searching and find a way to help his brother achieve his dream without letting the recent fame sabotage everything. All he could think of was letting his brother realize how much everyone had grown to love him for who he was.

    It's a nice relaxing drive to the rustic little trailer campground called the 'Lighthouse Resort'. Even though he had been drinking a little as well, he felt, with a Latte' Grande to console himself emotionally, he could find a non decaf that could and would renew him spiritually. His mind was clear enough to sort through strategies that could bring the twins back to the singularity they shared and still maintain David's success.

When Dennis turned the key in the truck, that simple ignition sparked as wild an adventure as he could ever have imagined. Along the way, Dennis noticed the fuel gauge. "Oh, blessed Jesus" he softly cussed, "David left me with a new truck and an old problem." The tank was nearly empty as he got off the road in Yucaipa, the halfway mark before ascending the hill on Old Highway 38. Dennis pulled into the gas station, his last chance to fuel up before Big Bear, almost an hour away. He got out of the car and slid his credit card at the pump.

"Rejected, try again," the hard-to-read monitor instructed.

"No problem,' he told himself, "I must have punched the wrong zip code because I was still distracted by the thoughts of fighting."

He tried again. The tiny screen read "rejected!" again. "Oh Holy Redeemer!" he said, looking more closely at the card, "What's happening here?"

In the thralls of their hasty and passionate split at Mack's house, each brother had picked up the wrong wallet. No matter, he knew his brother's zip code in Mesa, Arizona was 85207.

"It serves him right," Dennis thought, "David *should* have to pay the bill this time."

Then it suddenly occurred to him, "What if David was somehow arrested for a DUI? It would go on Dennis' record instead. He knew his brother, still incensed at him, would play the whole thing off as younger twin.

"He has my license. He has my face. Please David," he pleaded silently as he looked back to the valley, "I'll pay for the gas."

"Would David really act like that in something as serious as a DUI?" he whispered as he drove, "I don't think even David would impersonate me on a matter that serious.

He took the 'back way' as flatlanders referred to it. It was definitely more scenic and less travelled. The flora went from valley brush to mountain top pines and changed in increments. The gradual shifts in terrain seemed to help bleed off any latent hostility toward his twin as the evening darkened into night. Dennis wanted to make sure this was the first and last argument the brothers would have for a lifetime. He made a vow to make sure it never happened again. As vows go, this one would be a hard to evaluate. As he headed up the mountain, it started to rain. At first, it was no more than an annoying mist. The twists and turns were frequent and unforgiving.

"I wish this defogger worked better," Dennis mentally gauged, "I'm glad I can see headlights or I'd be leaning out my window to get a clear view." The rain started to come down harder. Within minutes it was a deluge. For some reason, people tend to lean into a hazy window to get a 'clearer' view. Dennis tried that too. Suddenly a huge truck rounded the corner on a curve and its headlights blinded him. He tried swerving right toward the mountain but the truck overcorrected and headed toward a tree and a couple of boulders guarding an extreme drop off. Dennis did his best to avoid an accident. Not every accident, however, can be avoided. Some people are lucky, some are unlucky. Sometimes, luck has nothing to do with it at all. Car crashes are always hard to explain. Being in the wrong place at the wrong time is a poor explanation to a mourning family member but it happens every minute of every day in some place or another. This time it was a tragedy that could have been avoided 'in one place or another'.

A local driver, who happened on scene, called in the accident. Law enforcement arrived at the site within minutes. The staging area was marked by flashing red and yellow lights and a gathering crowd of passers by. It was too late. Inside the twisted metal was the lifeless body of the young Wyllie. Paramedics arrived and confirmed the worst. There was no breathing and no heart beat.

"Looks like he died instantly," one of the uniformed officers stated, as he started to mark off the accident scene, "must have lost control and flipped off the road. From the look of the grill and hood, he hit something before he flipped it."

One of the onlookers pressed forward to get a better visual, "I think I know that young man," he yelled to one of the medics as they were about to cover the victim, "I've seen him on TV. He's from Temecula, I think. He's in that famous poker tournament in Vegas. I could be wrong but I think he's that 'Big Bad Wolf' or something like that."

One of the investigators pulled out the wallet on the seat of the vehicle, "Is his name Wyllie?"

"That's it!" the observer confirmed and amended his former statement, "He's that Wyllie Coyote. That's who he is."

The clipboard was out and the report was started. The primary officer removed the driver's license from the wallet and wrote down the name and address. He noted the site and then took pictures. There was no CSI team. It was a one car accident and, it appeared the driver had been speeding. There was a noticeable smell of alcohol in the car. "Street sober or dead drunk," the officer told his partner, "He died on impact. The decease's name is Dennis Wyllie of Temecula. He and his little red car are history."

At almost that exact time, Dennis was pulling David's truck into the outskirts of the town of Big Bear.

"That was a close call coming up Hwy 38," he reflected. He turned right on Division and headed toward the trailer. He had no idea his brother had lost his life minutes earlier in Temecula. "Whew! Dennis breathed faintly, "I could have gone off that cliff back there. Thank you, God. There was almost one less Wyllie twin in the world tonight." Dennis had no way of knowing that, back in Temecula, he, not David, had just been declared dead and officers were in the process of notifying next of kin based on his wallet and the info inside. He just kept thinking about how David had his I.D. and how easy it would be for his brother to misuse it if he got stopped by the police.

"It could happen," Dennis told himself, "other twins have done worse." Dennis remembered the story of the Van Ardsdale twins from Indiana University and the NBA. All identical twins have changed places at one time or another: a schedule conflict, a blind date, an awards ceremony, or even classes in school. He and David were guilty but not on as grand a scale as the Van Arsdales. 'Tom and Dick Van Arsdale," he recounted the story to himself, "scored within a dozen total points of each other during their college careers as Hoosiers. In the NBA they were quite similar guards who had made one '*Twin Promise*' to each other the day they were drafted by different NBA teams. If, by some stroke of timing and coincidence, they each made it to the NBA All-Star Game, and if, by some quirk of fate they were on opposite teams, they swore that they would put their plan into action. Preplanning, it's called. During half time of the game, so the story goes, each would make an excuse to leave the locker room. They would meet in a prearranged location; switch their EAST and WEST uniforms; and play the second half as each other. They, supposedly, agreed not to tell anyone until they retired. They wouldn't face any recrimination from the league that way. They also didn't want to jeopardize their own integrity and wanted to act 'in the best interest of the game.'" To this day, only twins Tom and Dick Van Arsdale, themselves, know whether they did it in either of the two opportunities they had to pull it off. "Maybe they where satisfied to just create an urban legend," Dennis speculated. When they had heard that story, both Dennis and twin David had marveled at the guile and creativity it would take to pull off such a feat. They questioned if, under a similar situation, and in the face of national attention and magnitude, they would ever have the balls to attempt to try something that incredulous. Both, knowing the chances were slim they would ever be put in that position, agreed to, at least, find a way of creating a legend of their own. "To do it," Dennis had told his brother, "would be incredible."

"To do it," his brother had argued, "would be a 'twin/win'

proposition."

"Never promise what you can't deliver and always deliver what you promise," Mack often touted. That quote sounded very philosophical until the boys found out where Barnes had picked up that slogan. As a teen, Mack used to write down pizza phone orders and take pies to his customers. His boss, Alfredo Persico, at Al's Master Pizza was the 'philosopher' who coined the phrase.

Dennis was reflecting on the Van Arsdale plot when he arrived at the gate of the Lighthouse. He dropped the chain and headed to the trailer. Wyllie decided to go right to bed and resume the story in his dreams. Even a little intoxicated, Dennis found his spinning brain stopping to refocus. "The craziness that was Temecula this month and the constant adulation afforded my brother was well deserved," he had to admit." Dennis, for this solitary moment, was just a young man in the mountains on a well deserved campout. He made it to the bed and crashed. He didn't even remember his head hitting the pillow. The 'younger' Wyllie slept soundly in the compact bedroom quarters of the forty foot park model. The smoke from the many open air fire pits, along with the emotional exhaustion of the last few days, had done their magic. The coffee had only kept him sober enough to climb the hill.

Just before sunrise, Mack's Honda Ridgeline pulled into the Lighthouse campground. Sherri loved the area and called it 'quaint'. A million dollar 5th Wheel RV park was just down the road. Mack knew 'quaint' was just a nice way of saying 'cheap' but he and his wife were what you would call 'quaint.' He drove past five to ten trailers before stopping behind his own rental space. Devastating news rarely evokes as much pain for the bearer as it does for those who receive it. This was a solemn, heart breaking moment reserved for family but played out by the closest of friends. Barnes dreaded the walk up the porch and coming face to face with, who he assumed to be, David. He wished he had played the part of peacemaker and encouraged the boys to resolve their differences rather than separating. Maybe all this could have been prevented. Maybe the days of pageantry, parades and winery luncheons had been too much for the young men.

"If they'd been together, this might not have happened" he tortured himself, "then again they might both be gone." Mack counter speculated. People seem to play mind games with alterative outcomes until they finally arrive at acceptance of 'it is what it is,' a term Mack and Sherri hated. In this case, it seemed to be the theme for the next hours, days, weeks and months. Right now the whole WSOP adventure seemed so silly, so petty, and so inconsequential.

"So quiet," Mack thought, "so serene in the mountains. The stars and the heavens seem closer and yet feel so far away."

Dennis had heard the sound of a car just outside the porch followed by the unmistakable sounds of footsteps on the boards that led to the front slider.

"Maybe my brother decided to come up and apologize," he thought, "If he did, that was a bad decision. Driving up the mountain can be dangerous and driving up drunk can be deadly," he told himself, "If he did and he made it, just be thankful to God. Don't start another argument. Just be glad the two of you are both together again."

As he threw off the thick comforter and slipped into the only shorts he could quickly locate, he noticed the clock read 4:42 AM. On the porch, Barnes walked as slowly as he could, delaying the inevitable, until he was standing under a yellow bug light by the slider on the deck. He held up a fist to knock and pointed a finger at the doorbell. Mack just couldn't quite bring himself to choose a way to announce himself to David. Dennis arrived at the door. He slowly slid open the curtains and unlocked the sliding glass. He and Mack were eye to eye in silence. "Something was wrong," Dennis decided. People always ask themselves, "Why would so and so be doing such and such?" In the middle of self-questioning, the answer always comes back, "Bad news." It's always followed by another internal question, "*how* bad?"

Mack Barnes was holding his words. He had rehearsed a dozen approaches on the drive up the hill but was suddenly speechless. Dennis broke the silence, "What's the matter, Mack? Is it my mom?"

There was another awkward pause that seemed to bind the two before Mack, tears running down his cheeks now, managed to say the words that changed the game forever, "Dennis is Dead, David. He was killed in an auto accident. We tried to call you but couldn't get through. I was the only one who knew where you probably were. Let me take you to your mom, son. You're twin brother Dennis is gone."

"The argument, the switched wallets, the truck and the car," Dennis thought to himself, "Everyone thinks I'm dead! Mack could never tell us apart. How do I explain this?" He saw Mack with the keys in his hands, he heard David's rant replay the only serious argument the two had really ever had. Maybe it was the switching Van Arsdale twins he dreamt about. His vision was still clouded with sleep as his eyes welled up in tears. He suddenly felt a connection with his brother unlike any before it. It seemed his course of action or reaction was unavoidable. Maybe it was the fear of losing his twin forever that brought the next five words out of his mouth. In an instant, as easily and resolutely as he had ever delivered any line on stage, Dennis looked disbelievingly at his mentor and blurted out, "NO SHIT! Dennis is dead?" He moved to the couch and began to bawl like a baby. It would be the first thing he would ever do in the role of as his departed brother, David. It would certainly not be his last. He was now playing with a new deck, new dealers, and as a new player.

CHAPTER TWENTY-TWO

The Looking Glass Funeral

Dennis's first true test occurred when he came through the front door of the family home and shared a hug with his mother. Dottie leaned back and looked into his eyes. She studied his face with her mouth slightly open. Suddenly, she threw her arms around him and collapsed. Dennis picked her up and carried her into the bedroom and laid her down softly. Moms always know but they don't always know why. When she came around they were alone and she just held her finger to his lips as if to say, "No need to explain….for now. I know you have a reason."

"Why doesn't she say anything?" Dennis wondered, "Why doesn't she ask? Dottie had stolen her son's instinct and claimed it as her own. She, like the new David, would try to understand their roles. "He could be in shock," she deduced, "or maybe he has a plan. Trust in God, trust in your son. All things will be revealed in due time," she had decided.

"All the world's a stage," the Bard wrote for the Old Globe,

London and 'The King' reminded us from Graceland, Tennessee. Appropriately, Elvis did it in a song called 'Are You Lonesome Tonight'. For the time being, each of them was more than lonesome in only ways only a mother and an identical twin could feel. This was merely Act One and both remaining Wyllie family members had decided that, for this one moment in time, they each would play a part and the show would go on for David's sake and Dennis' reasons.

Although fans, friends, and family all called or came by, the 'new David' remained in seclusion. Surprisingly, no one had any questions about the accident. People were so kind and Dennis had plenty of time to fine tune his impersonation. He combed his hair slightly differently and cut it shorter. He exchanged the limited wardrobes they had in common with his brother and Dottie bought him some new clothes. He would have to set aside his gay mannerisms and expressions. He had already been successful in switching roles on a short term basis. This time he would be substituting for his brother in the biggest poker tournament, incredible purse and ultimate prize, the most coveted bracelet. To dilute the somber overtones of the situation, he mused to himself, "I can do the purse and bracelet thing. It's the poker world that will be tough." He had no idea how tough.

Five days after his brother's death, Dennis got up early and prepared to attend his own funeral. He had been careful to isolate himself from friends he and his brother shared. It was a blessing, of sorts, that the two brothers were such self-proclaimed geeks. They had few friends and even those few had been fooled in the past. The boys had common friends in drama, young republicans, speech and debate, and yearbook. It's not the sort of social networking that screamed 'popular'. Both brothers were more comfortable with each other. When they were young, they had that special language only the two of them could understand. When their father died, both had taken over as the men of the family to help their mom. Dennis had to admit that the impersonation of his brother had been a helpful distraction from the loss he was feeling each day. Only a twin would understand the familiarity of the charade. "As long as David and I are one in this performance," Dennis decided, "he really hasn't left. I can, somehow, feel him inside me. At some point, I will have to let him go. The World Series will be the last time we will work together. It will be **our** swan song. The two of us can combine our intellects and talents. We can merge forces and attempt to conquer one more challenge. David would have wanted it that way. I'm sure of it."

Dennis found the mirror in his en suite a poor substitute for his alter ego. The two were actually 'mirror twins' which meant that one was a reverse image of the other. From their hair swirl in the back to the symmetries of their individual faces they were reflectively the same. Most people don't realize how different one side of their face is from the other. A computer camera trick can produce three images. One will simulate the subject with two composed 'doubled over' right sides and two similar left sides with a standard photo in the center. The images provide three distinct people. One will be thinner and one will be fuller. People used to view each other similarly at the mall. Two individuals would press their noses against the opposite corner of two glass show windows or mirrors across from each other. They would look down the side of one window and move their heads, hands and feet to create ridiculous images and illusions of themselves. With the advent of the smart phone, a built-in app can morph any owner's face in a similar manner. Mirror twins come from a single, fertilized ovum that doesn't split for just over a week. If it didn't split for two weeks or more, the twins would be born conjoined. Mirror twins are truly unusual. The only more unusual twins are the ones who share the same sack and amniotic fluid for the entire pregnancy. The biggest risk with that group involves entanglement with each other's umbilical cords. Mack told the boys once, "You can lump all twins into one category: Womb Mates!" Dennis, as he recalled that 'Mackism', knew Barnes was going to have to play an important role in his immediate life. The only question was how and when to tell him the truth.

As he looked into bathroom mirror, he realized *that* time hadn't materialized. Dennis stood in front of the mirror once more but this time David was superimposed. We all do it every day without so much as a simple 'hello'. Not so with twins, particularly 'mirror twins'. As he peered into the looking glass, Wyllie wished he was Lewis Carroll's Alice and could just join his brother. He'd ask him for his approval of the ruse. What would the real David say? Would he be happy that his name could still be etched in the hallowed halls of Poker? Would he be disappointed that Dennis had robbed him of his accomplishment? Would he appreciate the chance to share one last adventure? Would he be angry that he was being buried under a name other than his own?

"Talk to me, David," Dennis pleaded, "I always knew what you'd say before it came out your mouth. Now, I can't see anything but me looking at myself."

"What do you want me to say, brother?" the image in the glass replied. "Seems like you've got it all worked out! You never would have had this chance if I was still around. I'm just wondering how you're gonna pull it off." Dennis heard the reflection in the mirror but he had to pinch himself to make sure he wasn't dreaming or hallucinating. "I have more personality, more 'attitude', and, quite frankly, more talent," the glass figure continued. "We've always been close but I had you edged out in almost every competition. Tell you what. You pull this off and we'll finally be even."

"Are you really talking to me or am I talking to myself?" the warm blooded twin asked.

The reflection spoke again, "I'm here but that doesn't rule out guilt, insanity or even conscience. If people discover the truth, you'll have more than a poker title and bracelet to deal with. Come up short, and you won't even be close to me as a player. I'll be the twin who died on top and you'll be the twin who humiliated himself by trying to be 'just like his brother'. Good luck little bro. Remember, I was in this world four minutes before you and I told them you were 'right behind me.' I'm flying with the angels. *You're* the one who's talking to a mirror!"

David and Dennis had never been able to even find an acceptable plural for 'only child'. He and his twin had no other brothers or sisters but 'only children' didn't seem to fit. 'Only childs' was even worse. Now, he had become an 'only child' but he didn't feel like one. Twins transcend time and space. In this case, they might even have a chance to cheat death. Funny, he didn't think about 'cheating' until that instant. The boys were, if nothing else, incredibly honest in everything they had ever done. The only times they deceived people were when they found a need to change places in school. They had once switched classes for exams. David took two Calculus Finals and Dennis took two English Exams. They were both getting A's anyway, so it was more for the thrill of the game.

"Was *that* what this was?" He asked himself. "Was this just one more time the two could enjoy the game? Was it more about the money? Was it mostly about the 'Wyllie Coyotes' and the people back home? For the first time, he realized what it was all about. He loved David. He didn't know if he could go on without his other half. Dennis suddenly understood what, for him, was the overriding reason. He couldn't accept his brother's death and this was the only way to keep him alive. Now, looking at the time on his phone, if he didn't hurry, he was going to be late to his own funeral.

Dennis spoke as his brother at the 'celebration of life'. He had some very sincere, complimentary things to say about himself. He couldn't help but feel that he had led a good life, up to that point. Other speakers praised his work ethic, his robotic designs, and his 'get out the vote' as a Young Republican. Nobody really had anything to say about his personal life. Nobody felt comfortable talking about his lack of dating or even about his gay life style. He realized that nobody really knew him as an individual. The closest thing anybody came to actually giving him any human emotion was when poor Frankie Durawitz talked about Dennis at the state speech competition. Frankie, a SAD (Speech and Debate) member, awkwardly described Dennis as a 'master debater'. It was extremely hard for Dennis to bite down on his lower lip and keep from laughing. Many in the audience that day quickly learned to do the same thing. The fact that Dennis was not actually dead was the one thing that made him feel alternatively alive and deceased. When the casket was lowered into the ground, even though there were tears in his eyes, he felt the curtain closing. After a well deserved intermission, he was ready for act two. He and his brother were in it to win together. In his mind, it was an 'In It T'win' project! He pictured a headstone that should really read, 'Dead, Buried, and Still Alive'. All three were card terms. Dennis realized, "If it can happen in poker, it can happen in life."

CHAPTER TWENTY-THREE

The Shark Tank

Dennis realized that he would need another living person as an advisor, probably a lawyer with whom he could share client confidentiality. Bob, 'The Shark', Sarkasian came to mind. Not only was Bob involved as one of the Coyotes, but he was not totally unfamiliar with deception in his own right. He gave the Shark a call and the two met at Mo's Egg House for breakfast.

"Try the catfish and eggs, David," urged Sark.

"Is that what you're having, Mr. Sarkasian?" David offered.

Just then one of the waitresses put down two plates of complimentary coffee cakes and asked, "Are you ready to order?"

"I'll have the Chicken Fried Steak and three eggs, the buttermilk biscuits and gravy with hot cakes," Bob announced.

"Do you want home fries, hashed browns or fruit plate with that?" the server offered.

"Definitely the fruit plate, Sally," Bob announced, I'm on a new diet and potatoes are out of the question. Oh, and while you're at it, make that nine grain hot cakes and light syrup."

Sherri had observed, "When Bob diets, he has a tendency to be all-inclusive … or at least, most inclusive."

Dennis wasn't hungry but he wanted to make this meal more of a team effort so he ordered, "I'll have the crepes with lemon and powdered sugar. I'll have the fruit plate and maybe a little chamomile tea."

Bob thought to himself, "never known a guy to order like my late wife. At least he forgot to ask for the orange marmalade."

Dennis called out to the waitress, "and a little orange marmalade, if you have any."

Sarkasian looked toward the heavens and whispered to himself, "Sorry, honey, it just means I'm still thinking about you." Turning his attention to the young Wyllie he asked, "Now, what's this all about David? Want a financial investment plan when we're all rich? Sorry, that was uncalled for. I need to offer my condolences on the loss of your brother, Dennis. He was a fine young man. You both …." he stumbled over the use of 'are' and 'were' and then shifted thoughts, "We are all devastated and keep you and your family in our thoughts and prayers." Bob had just equated food, death and money. Mack would have surely noted, "For a lawyer like the Shark, it's as natural as crawling out of a hole."

"I'm not ready to talk about investing right now. I hope you understand." Dennis redirected his focus. "First, I want to retain you as my lawyer. Here's a check for $1000. I hope that makes us a team."

"Of course we are and I'll buy breakfast for my new client,

David," Bob volunteered, "What can I do you for?"

"Secondly, and most importantly, Bob," the younger Wyllie instructed his new confidant and legal advisor, "you can stop calling me 'David'.

Bob was never at a loss for words but, search as he could, he was devoid of vocabulary. Speechless, I think they call it.

"No?" he finally uttered, with a lean in and a hand on the young man's shoulder, "You can't be saying what I think you're saying."

"You got it." Dennis said sheepishly, "For the first time in my life, I'm alone and I need someone to come along for the ride."

Sarkasian paused to assess the situation and the ramifications. The complications were shooting by him at break-neck speed. He tried levity, "You know, in the underworld of crime, when someone suggests that you 'come along for a ride', you might not be coming back."

The humor was lost on his newest client.

"Will you help me, Mr. Sarkasian?" Dennis asked.

"From this minute forward," Bob assured him, "We are a team. How can I help, *David*?"

"We need to explore all possible pitfalls ahead, Dennis proposed, "This affects too many people. I hadn't thought about being disqualified if I was found out before or after the Final Table. I don't want to risk the money the Coyotes and the real David have already won. There may be challenges from people who know David and me. I need to know what I have to look out for; what I need to do to insulate myself; how to respond to any inquiries; and how to keep a low profile until and after November. I need a lawyer to refer to and I need a friend to lean on. Without that, I don't think I can do it."

Sarkasian knew the two were going to be venturing into unpredictable situations and unfathomable surroundings. He could see Dennis was understandably lost.

"When you're in uncharted waters," Bob pointed out, "you need a 'Shark' or you'll be eaten by another."

Bob knew he wanted to be part of the scheme. It wasn't quite diabolical but it made him feel young again. He looked at his new, young client and tried to make him feel at ease, "In this case, I'll be the brains and the mouth. You'll be the heart and the soul. Don't think and don't talk. Keep the faith and find the love. I'm a lawyer. I don't mess with compromising elements like the heart and soul. I operate best without either. They're not parts of the law fraternity I joined long ago. Give me some time to work out some strategies. In the meantime, if you ever find yourself at the mercy of truth, refer the question to me. I need to put myself in your situation and then assume the minds of those who might attack. The best thing about being counsel is that the same immunity that keeps your secret also shields me from the origination of any conspiracy. It also grants me freedom from impunity and immunity from persecution as long as truth can be pawned off as lies and vice versa."

It was just the first of many lessons Dennis and Bob would share in 'Legalese'.

CHAPTER TWENTY-FOUR

Check/Raise: The Media

It had to happen eventually. Dennis woke to the troubling side of lying: The Channel 7 Morning News. Nobody wants to be the subject of "breaking news", especially after a tragedy. Enlarged pictures of oneself should never appear as the backdrop for the lead reporter. The local 'eyewitness news' broke the accusations right after they left the latest car chase. The anchor woman looked directly into the camera and spoke with the authority that comes with the position.

"At least one of his fellow WSOP Final Table players is suggesting that a local poker player may not be who he says he is. In addition, the whistle blower thinks a twin brother may have risen from the dead, so to speak."

The blonde news personality, Josie Wayne, went on reading the monitor and announced to the viewers. "The accuser is suggesting that one twin brother may have assumed the other brother's life after one was killed in a recent automobile accident. For more on the story, we go to sports reporter Wyatt Phillips outside Pechanga Casino in Temecula. Wyatt?"

"Yes, Josie, an unnamed source has sent an anonymous letter to officials in Las Vegas and mailed copies to us here at Channel 7. In the letter, the source claims to have identified some suspicious differences in an interview at the funeral which made him wonder if a substitution may have occurred."

"Wyatt," the blonde anchor interjected, "wouldn't this suggest a cover-up and wouldn't local authorities have to be involved?"

"News agencies always want to find a scandal and when they can't, they 'suggest' one," Mack noted as he watched from his home.

Phillips, not ready to confirm the story or lose the scoop, shot back, "Josie, right now, we want to point out, these are just accusations and, without proof or any supporting evidence, it will just be interesting how the young man known in poker circles as the 'Wyllie Coyote', will respond. This has been Wyatt Phillips in Temecula. Back to you in the studio, Josie."

The phones started ringing in the Wyllie camp. Dennis was the first to call. Bob would be on speed dial from that moment on.

"We need to rally 'round the wagons, Bob. What's next?" a rightfully concerned Dennis voiced. "Will I have to be treated like one of those aliens that landed in New Mexico? I don't want to be hassled. This is tough enough having to deal with my brother and avoiding everybody else. Help me." Bob agreed to meet and told Dennis to defer all inquiries to 'legal counsel'. Mack was the first to get a referral. Barnes was immediately on the phone, "Bob, if there's any truth to what they say on TV, I need to know. I'm hearing some pretty suggestive speculation and I have to know what I'm talking about. I wouldn't even care except that I already called David. He referred me to 'his lawyer'. Let me fucking repeat that. He referred ME to **his lawyer**. What the hell is going on?"

"Mack, why don't you and Sherri come over here right now to my office? We have some things to discuss and I have to get David in here too," Sarkasian explained.

Mack was quick to answer, "Sherri and I will be right over. This better be good. By 'good' I mean it better be all of what I want to hear and none of what I don't!" Mack had already been through enough. He didn't even let anyone know that the D.A. had contacted him, as expected, when one of the home players had complained that Mack entered two 'pros' in a home game and misled the group by misrepresenting them as first-time players. Mack assumed that it must have come from Coach Buck. As a football referee, it was his job to know all the rules and how and when they apply. He hadn't accepted the story Mack told him when he confronted him face to face at the Temecula 24 Hour Fitness. Another 'anonymous' caller had informed the District Attorney that he was being 'cheated out of his share' of the winnings but called back to say that most of those problems had been "resolved". The resolution coincided with Domingo's mysterious 'heart attack'. Now that everyone was 'winning money', and, although charges had been filed, nobody was knocking at Mack's door with handcuffs. "Maybe it went away," Barnes told himself, "Maybe this would, too. ' Barnes hoped so.

Mack and Sherri walked into the Sarkasian offices and Wyllie was already there, sitting on a leather couch.

"We've talked," Bob explained, "and the boy, here, respects the two of you to the utmost. He has a great idea that will help him speak freely and protect the two of you, as well. He knows both of you need to be part of this team. I want to hire the Barnes family and make you part of my staff."

"What the hell are you talking about?" Mack lashed back.

Sherri was even more direct, "Hired for what?"

"I'll pay you each $5 a month. You'll sign an employee letter of confidentiality, and *then* we can talk," Sarkasian directed them, "then and *only* then can we share what we have to explain. David and I are already bound by an even more restrictive covenant."

"I bet David gave you a lot more than $5 for your services, Bob," Mack said suspiciously, "do I really want to work for you?"

"As your friend and as a lawyer," the Shark mentored, "I strongly advise that you not only sign the contract; you would be foolish not to so. You leave yourself and family wide open to the press, the WSOP, and the public at large."

After Mack and Sherri took time to do what all people do when they sign on the dotted line, they reluctantly became part of the team and Bob's employees.

"I feel the same way I did when I went to a free time share breakfast presentation, Shark" offered Mack, sarcastically "and you have the same look on your face as the man who handed me that 22" television for stealing 4 hours of my life. Get on with it. I can hardly wait to hear what you have to say."

Sarkasian stood between the couple and the young man who

had moved behind the desk in the swivel chair. It looked like a solid buffer for the next reaction.

"Mack and Sherri Barnes, I'd like you to meet *Dennis* Wyllie, previously deceased."

"Holy Crap!" Mack blasted.

"Holy Mother of God!" Sherri added.

For the next two hours Dennis explained how the whole thing happened and how it all played out. Most of Mack's concerns were expected. "What about Dottie? Did you really think you could get away with it? How could you jeopardize the emotions and lives of so many people: Coyotes, families, friends, fans, and the poker tournament itself?" Mack's 'Holy Crap' had been right on and he was about to prepare the 'Blessed Fan' for full impact.

"I have to remind you both that you have a nondisclosure agreement now," Bob explained. "It restricts your freedom but it protects your actions."

"And what am I supposed to say to someone who asks if I know about this hoax?" Mack distressed.

"You have to answer with, what I like to call, a 'true' lie," Shark informed the couple. He went on by saying, "Let me give you an example. Someone asks you the question, 'Do you know if David is who he says he is?' You can tell a 'true' lie. You just word it carefully by saying, "No, I can't say that I do."

"And how is that honest? Sounds more like another plate of your world famous legalese to me," Mack observed.

Bob interpreted, "the answer is NO and the reason you 'can't say' is because you're an employee and you signed a contract that says you can't."

"Legalese, it's goddamn legalese, Shark," Mack reiterated, "lawyers get paid to make shit smell like perfume but to Sherri and me, we might as well be rolling in cologne. Somebody's gonna realize we're wrapped in brown turds, no matter how many 'aromatic' scents were sprayed. Hell, I'll know, even if nobody else does. I don't suppose there's anything else to do but make the best of it until it all comes crashing down on us."

"Funny you should mention that, Mack," Sarkasian pointed out to the group. "In the event we are all found out, we will have to be ready. We'll all be meeting back here in the office on Sunday afternoon. Dennis, I mean, David, and I have some research to do. The whole team will be introduced to and given roles in what we lawyers call 'PLAN B.'"

"Must be B for Bullshit," Mack shot back. There's a reason the restroom is the only place in the house that smells like fruits, flowers, or flavors. It's that sickening sweet fragrance that only acts like a cover up. Whenever I smell it I know what's underneath, whether it's next to a toilet in the bathroom or a standing beside a lawyer in his office. Nobody ever gets away with anything like this. It's just a matter of time."

Dennis responded, "Mack, nobody 'caught' ever "gets away' and nobody who 'gets away with it' ever 'gets caught'. That's why, for instance, no one knows how many 'perfect murders' there are, for instance, because they were 'perfect murders'. Let's just sit down and figure this thing out, without getting emotional. The cards are in the air and we just 'sealed the deal.'"

"For the record," Mack shot back, "I suddenly feel like I sat down with Bret Maverick and we're all part of a hustle. These stakes are very high and I don't like our odds and I don't like our 'outs.'"

CHAPTER TWENTY-FIVE

In the Court of Public Opinion

In the National Football League or even Fantasy Baseball, the minute a 'team' is drafted, it starts to play. Not so with this team. After adding Dottie, the legal team of Barnes, Barnes, Wyllie, Wyllie and Sarkasian hoped they'd never have to play at all. If they were ever called upon, however, the need for a game plan for dealing with naysayers and identity challengers was crucial, if not critical. Mack and his protégé, along with Dottie, Shark and Sherri found themselves trafficking in the bold new 'electronic super highway world of high tech sharing'.

"We're all victims and assailants here, "Mack advised the group, "and we have to thank Al Gore for inventing and then tangling the world-wide web he wove." Mack could go off on a rant when he was incensed.

Suddenly fame was not only fleeting, it was tweeting. It was texting. It was 'googling'. It would be something newer and faster tomorrow and each day thereafter. Mack pointed out, "Information already travels faster than the speed of lies."

As a 'stand in' father figure, Mack had helped the twins pick out their first portable computers when they were 9. As Barnes relays the story, "We went to some sort of cow colored store called Getaway, or something like that and the boys picked out the equipment they wanted to buy with the money their late father had left them for educational supplies."

The boys had sheepishly told Barnes, "We found good models for about $2500 each."

Mack exploded, "$2500….each?"

The young sales person interjected, "We have some computers that sell for almost $10,000."

Barnes couldn't believe his ears. "I can't believe they cost that much," he told the sales boy, sorry, tech support associate, who was barely out of high school himself. That freckled faced kid thought he'd be reassuring but did so in, what Mack perceived to be, a condescending remark or an open ended invitation to disaster.

"I bet that was a lot of money in your day, sir," the boy had said politely.

Mack put his arm around the novice negotiator while the twins shuddered to think what they might witness in Barnes' response.

"Let me tell you, sonny," Mack said sagely, "In *my* day, if someone paid $10,000 for something that was designed to work while it sat on your lap, we'd have expected it to do a whole lot more than just compute."

That little message, if digested by the employee of the store, might have been his own 'gateway' to more sensitive sales. For Mack, it was educating the next generation. For the boys, it was a relief that they could make a quiet 'getaway'. In the years since their first lap top, the world of interpersonal communication had spun out of control. News traveled faster the actual speed of light because it fans out in so many different directions. Mack was about to find out what instant celebrity involved. The new David who saw it coming, still wasn't ready for the onslaught. No one ever really is. The media and the paparazzi had latched onto a story that seemed to have it all: tragic death, gay brother, the home game dream and the latest intrigue: unanswered questions of identity. It could have been an episode of the daytime soap, *Santa Barbara*, on which the twins had appeared as pre-toddlers. They, like most twins in the acting world, played the same, interchangeable baby. The long hours of being held, hugged and cuddled took its toll on overworked children. "Thank God for unions," Mack had noted when he learned about their first jobs.

PEOPLE Magazine included a front page picture. Mack was flanked by the boys. It was taken just days after David's 'miracle hand' over Annie Duke. They were heroes. The caption on the cover read: *The Mentalists and their Mentor*. Barnes would have preferred Mack and the Boys. Most of the tabloids focused on the tragedy and a possible plot to replace one Wyllie with another for the money. "Pulitzer pretenders and scandal mongers," as Sherri put it, "claim to reveal all and are, unfortunately, available at newsstands everywhere." Cover pages were full of photo shopped images that included enhanced and manipulated micro birthmarks. One had moles connected with lines to form question marks. A myriad of camera angles 'proved through facial recognition technology' that the public was being scammed. One of these journalistic giants actually suggested that this was a murder case and that the body should be exhumed. According to this scenario, Mack was a 'modern day Rasputin' who held the boys under a hypnotic spell and had been the mastermind of the "deadly deception". Sherri's favorite was the murder plot where David's image was being questioned by the classic TV detective, Columbo.

"Evidently," the now openly 'David' said after reading the last article, "we are becoming historical figures in the Press. I think I would prefer to be close to Caesar, though, rather than to the Czarina. On second thought, Rome had more of a Mediterranean climate and we know how *they* used people for entertainment."

"At least, in the glory days of Rome," Mack reminded David, "when you entered the coliseum, you only had to worry about being ripped apart by the lions. The worst you got from the crowd were thumbs up or thumbs down."

Bob Sarkasian had arrived for the weekly 'employee seminar' and took that cue to center the group on the tasks at hand, "Everybody has to be on the same page and on guard. This whole thing will die out soon and the predators will move on to fresher game. Our job is two-fold. We have to find a way to, as the old song says, 'accentuate the positive and eliminate the negative'. I have my own plans of action for the latter and you all have to put on happy faces and learn to say 'no comment', 'I'm sorry we've been through a lot recently', and 'there really isn't anything new to add'.

"In legalese," as Mack put it, "these non-responses are acceptable, sympathetic and film clip length for the nightly news."

"What if we get discovered somehow?" Sherri asked, "After all, we need to know before it happens, right?"

"I'm so glad you asked that," Shark shot back. "In cases where you think all is lost; you go to that Plan B. Again, in this case that's legalese for 'oh yeah, here's why we did it! Good news from the poker world. They have contacted me and are interested but don't want to muddle their own event. They just want to be assured everything is kosher. I assured them that there is no Lock Ness monster; Big Foot has been exaggerated in both hair and size; and Area 51 is now housing only *illegal* aliens. In other words, I told them, I'm not going to dignify sensationalism by responding. It will only legitimize their accusations." "That, in the court of public manipulation," added Sherri "is 'Advanced Legalese.'"

Sarkasian was now well within his comfort zone. He was acting like a lawyer, had plenty of chutzpah for the confrontations, and knew how to, if need be, fight for his life with the heavyweights. He went on, "I have prepared for each of you arguments that justify our actions from several approaches. We hope we never have to use them but I want you to read them, absorb them and be ready to defend them adamantly, at a moment's notice, should that be necessary. Hopefully, we will never have to go to this Plan B. If we do, we'll be ready. Just knowing we have a back-up strategy should help us all sleep better at night."

"Bob, what happens to all the other Coyotes and the money

they think is already guaranteed them?" Dennis asked.

Shark tightened his lips and grimaced, "I hope it never comes to that, son, but my best guess is that we'd have to pathetically claim that all money to this point was earned by the 'innocent brother' and should be awarded a 9th place pay out to be divided among the group. Good point, though, I'll add it to Plan B. Now here are the scripts and roles we hope we'll never have to perform. Learn them and make them your own."

CHAPTER TWENTY-SIX

Slow Play on a Break In

Mack woke to the all too familiar sound of an early morning knock on the door. It was Bob again.

"Mack, we've got another situation," the lawyer apprised him. "Somebody broke in the kids' dentist office and stole the X-rays of the boys' teeth….both sets."

"Is that something to be concerned about, Shark," Barnes inquired. "Wouldn't they be the same?

Sarkasian shot back, "They're mirror twins. Neither one has had any dental work other than cleaning but their teeth are reverse images of each other. The good news is that this dentist is old school and didn't keep any computer records. It's obvious somebody was out to get information and they might just have succeeded. Believe me, I had nothing to do with it this time. My guy wasn't scheduled to break in until tomorrow. As far as fingerprints, we are also on shaky ground. Right now, their mom, Dottie, has the only baby prints on her copy of the birth certificate. Luckily, and I hesitate to use that word in public, the hospital where the twins were born had a basement fire in 2008 and the whole place was destroyed. Most of the records were either cremated or badly damaged. I sent another guy up there to investigate and he's supposed to get back to me this week. Until then, we're in the clear on that one. As you know, fingerprints are unique, even with identical twins. It's a chemical, environmental and developmental process. The boys once had their fingerprints taken when they first worked for the judge but they admitted using one hand of each twin on the separate cards as a joke. They never thought it would come into play. In that case, those prints don't differentiate between left and right." Dottie has every right to withhold her copy of the boys' prints but, at some time in the future, the courts or the Nevada State Gaming commission might want to subpoena them. Hell, they might even find another set somewhere in the justice system. The boys worked in some secure systems. I'm surprised anybody in Vegas hasn't requested them already. They probably hope this all goes away."

"So we just have to wait for the other shoe to drop? Is that what you're saying?" asked Mack.

"That's pretty much the way it goes, big guy. It could have been an aggressive member of the paparazzi or maybe a bitter poker player. It could even have been someone out to blackmail us. Remember, if anyone asks, more than ever, the only politically true lie is 'no, not as far as I can tell!'"

"And it's why paper is 8 1/2 by 11 inches," Barnes added. "It's the right size to cover your butt." Mack, who could never resist adding insult to injury poured on some hyperbole, "Now I understand why Legal Size is 14 inches. Lawyers must either have more of a butt to cover or they were just born bigger asses."

"Some records survived the fire at the Alaskan hospital," Sarkasian added. "I don't want you to worry about that one. I got that one covered even though the actual hospital where they were born is now just a parking lot. I spoke to an archivist and they are going through their records as we speak. We hope our guy gets there before the rest of the crowd can even find that little city."

"Something tells me I don't want to know how you know those two things, Bob," Mack admitted, "Just tell me that we're not all going to jail in the future."

"That might not be a laughing matter," Sarkasian noted. "I'm glad we have Plan B. We might be standing in front of your referenced scented fan when the smelly stuff hits it." Bob mustered as much nerve as he could generate, "We might want to review our roles."

They both looked at each other with as little desperation they could project, shook hands and gave each other a much needed and appreciated man hug.

"I'll tell the rest of the inner circle. They'll need to know their scripted responses and how to add 'no comment' to their vocabulary," Bob advised Mack.

"You do that," Barnes acknowledged, "I'll talk to Sherri."

Mack turned to put on the rest of his clothes. As he did, he lost his grip and one of his boots fell to the floor. He turned to Shark, who was halfway out the door.

"Don't worry, Bob, that wasn't the other shoe falling, it was *this* one. Sorry."

CHAPTER TWENTY-SEVEN

I'll Cut; You Deal

"Smell this. Do you think it's fresh?"

Mack reminded Sherri when Bob pushed Plan B, "There is little doubt that everyone has been asked that question more than once in their life." According to the Barnes' belief system, "The need to share good news is understandable. The need to share bad news, guilt, malevolent thoughts, evil deeds, attacks, jealousy, dishonesty, moral corruption, cheating, dishonor and shame is irresistible. Many of the countless souls who find themselves stymied by the suppression of spicy secrets yearn to tell all to a confidante. Usually, there is little available. Ah, but if you happen to be Catholic, the confessional can be the answer." In the past, the penitent parishioner used to operate in complete anonymity by simply pulling back the curtain like one of those date night photo booths. Daters sit but sinners kneel. A little divider would slide open to reveal the silhouette of a priest. The shadow on the shade was all the priest could see. Every Catholic with juicy sins to confess developed the voice changing abilities of a great ventriloquist like Jeff Dunham. Catholics had an advantage. They could move their lips. Gone, almost everywhere, was the anonymity but all confidential admissions were protected by the seal of the sacrament itself. In other words, nobody but the priest (and God who sits in on what Mack described as a 'conference call') would ever know what the sinner did. It seemed unlikely that God didn't already know anyway.

Dennis called and made an appointment with his parish priest and fellow Coyote, Father Patrick Jinks. He intended to clear his conscience, examine his soul and, perhaps, keep from losing his mind over the next month or two. Penance would be assigned and he could get some good advice from someone he trusted.

"Bless me Father, for I have sinned," Dennis told his confessor, priest, and friend.

"I hope you haven't done anything like using your magic skills in a poker game lately." Jinks said and then added. "I'm sorry, that's just a bad joke in light of your loss. How can I help you my son?"

"Father, while it's true I am haunted a little by the death of my brother, my biggest sin is more in the realm of 'false witness'. To be blunt, Father, when my brother was killed, I assumed his identity and plan to play in the Main Event as David." confessed Dennis.

"Wow!" Jinks whispered loudly, "You mean you're actually Dennis? Believe me, I've had a ton of 'wows' in my years as a priest but this....this is a new one, even for me! How long did you think you could get away with it?"

"I thought," Dennis said optimistically, "I might be able to *pull it off*. Right now I'm more concerned on whether I could or should *call it off.* I was hoping to get some impartial advice from someone who couldn't turn me in. You always seem to have some story or parable that fits the bill. Is lying always wrong?"

The priest was quick to respond, "My boy, I'm reminded of the man who asked his son if he tipped over the outhouse the previous night. The son denied that he had anything to do with it. The man reminded his son that George Washington cut down his father's favorite cherry tree. When asked by his father if he had done it, Washington said, "I cannot tell a lie. I did it." His father rewarded his son for telling the truth. The boy listened to his own dad's story and admitted to the tipping. His father put him over his knee and gave him a hearty spanking. When the boy asked why he was punished for telling the truth, his dad explained, "George Washington's Dad wasn't up in that cherry tree when he cut it down." Because I am now a Coyote, you and I are *both*, 'out on a limb' and definitely 'in the outhouse'. Do you want me to tell you to yell 'timber' while you continue to push? I can't do that."

"My brother and I would always figure things out together. We still talk about what to do now." Dennis admitted, "We still can't quite decide on this one."

Jinks thought for a moment and then advised, "I can tell you that ethically, you have to tell the truth, the sooner the better. Morally, you might be able to make an argument that there has been no victim. Spiritually, when you ask forgiveness you must promise to avoid lying in the future and correct all wrongs. Psychologically, and I'm not an expert here, it sounds like you might be wrestling with your conscience which is manifesting itself as your brother."

"As for me, Dennis," Jinks went on, "I am required through the sanctity of the sacrament of Penance to keep your secret. As for the money, the good bishop has been following the story and has suggested that the vast majority of my share should go to his 'relief fund for needy countries.' In that vein, I am not financially vested which makes it easier to give advice."

"So many people are affected," Dennis rationalized, "and David was so close. It's really not about the money. My brother and I never even liked money. This would be our final project together. One twin starts the action and the other one completes it. Maybe I just want to do it in his memory. In fact, I don't think he will rest in peace until I do. I know that sounds at least a little neurotic but he has been very encouraging. I have always known how he felt and I know how he feels now,' Dennis explained further. "Doctors know that a person still feels pain in their foot, even after the leg has been amputated. The receptors are still active and 'ghost stimulators' wake him up screaming. Twins are even more like that. Our neurotransmitters send and receive through time and space. I know I'm receiving and I feel like he's still sending even though I know he's dead. How do we know twin language and ESP don't transcend death itself?"

"Either way, Dennis, it's not hard to see that you need to do something different. Find another way of honoring your brother, making his loss meaningful, and make sure the world is better for the effort. Confront others before they can confront you. Now, join me in the Lord's Prayer and we can ask God to bless you in whatever you decide to do. I'll be looking forward to your decision and I will support you in any revelation and any manner in which you decide to unveil it. Until then, you cannot be forgiven for something you are continuing to do."

Dennis thought about those words, prayed over the matter, and wrestled with his options in lieu of sleep. He knew he had to step up to the plate. When he went home, his twin was waiting for him in the mirror but refused to speak. Dennis knew his brother's look of disapproval over the conversation with the priest. The younger Wyllie recognized that the two might have different ways of handling trouble. He took two pills Dr. Herb's wife had given him to help him sleep and poured himself into bed.   Eventually, the glare of the sunrise pierced the morning mist and poured itself onto his half pillowed face. A Dennis personality pulled back the covers and slowly rolled off the mattress but it was a David type who strode down the hall with resolution. This person was in the melding mode. He picked up the phone, called the local news and alerted them that he had a 'major announcement' to make about himself, his brother's death and how he planned to 'come clean' and put to rest any questions about his own true identity."

CHAPTER TWENTY-EIGHT

Media Circus and Paparazzi Parade

Jumping forward to his present condition, Mack Barnes knew the Shark could do many things but, in the end, he couldn't quite keep the whole team out of jail. Sherri made her scheduled visit and Mack made the best of talking through a window to his wife. At the end of the hour Barnes returned to his enclosure and settled in for the night, alone and in custody for the time being. He was starting to get a little case of claustrophobia and longed for that backyard porch and meadow. Even Randy Halemano's Hawaiian beer sounded good right now. As he laid his head back on the bed he realized Bob had actually done an amazing job, particularly in front of the media that sweltering day in late August. He reflected on how the Shark came through in the clutch for Dennis.

At Wyllie's insistence, Bob Sarkasian had called a press conference for 8 A.M. Monday morning., "All the media vultures will have to get up early," Bob reckoned, "after their late night weekend chasing movie stars, rap singers and sports figures. Those guys live large over the weekend, and don't deserve a good night's slumber. They're such easy prey when they're sleep deprived."

Sarkasian walked into the prearranged room without a brief case, notebook, or even a piece of paper. Mack described it this way, "His empty hands showed he had nothing to hide. Karate means 'empty hand' and like Mr. Miyagi who also 'never used a weapon', Bob was about to 'wax on!'" The bigger than life lawyer greeted the crowd as he arrived on the stage, "Good afternoon ladies and gentleman of the press." He spoke from a podium garnished with a bouquet of microphones, "I'm going to make a short statement and then I'm going to take a few questions. Finally, I'm going to make one announcement that should send all of you off to whatever holes you crawled out of."

The gathering seemed somewhat collectively insulted. All of them, however, were more interested in all three parts of the plan so they shut up and listened. The vultures were perched and eyeing what they assumed was their prey.

"First off," Shark announced, "my client, David Wyllie and I are here because we need to clean up this carnival atmosphere most of you have created. We feel that wild accusations and misinformation, coupled with innuendos and half-truths have grown into a circus environment. If I can extend the comparison, most of you are more interested in the side shows and the clowns. Your ringmasters have directed your attention to the trapeze flyers; acrobatic pyramids of human interest; and a well choreographed collection of animal acts that have all of you jumping through hoops."

Completely exhausting the analogy, Bob went on without a script, "my client has been forced to walk a tightrope without a net and most people are more interested in the fall than the balance he has to exhibit to survive. David Wyllie is still in mourning over the loss of his twin brother. He is, at the same time, training for a poker world championship that he is favored to win. Because he is a twin, it's easy to accuse him. By the same token, it's hard for him to simply provide DNA which will only prove that he is a twin. I might also add that some of you have even suggested exhuming a body as part of the act. Before we propose a solution, let's see if we can answer a few questions from the peanut gallery. Please identify yourselves by name and who you represent."

Hands flew faster than 1st graders volunteering to be milk monitors. Bob pointed to a serious young man who looked more like a cop or firefighter than a reporter. Bob guessed he might start out with a serious question, "State your name and who you represent. Go!"

"Kasey Thomas, TMZ," he called out, "What about everything we hear about facial recognition?
Some people claim they have proof from images on television or in photographs. Doesn't the public have the right to know?"

"Facial algorithms," Shark responded, "identify similarities in faces, either geometrically or by utilizing a photometric approach. Both have been used, mostly in Germany, London and here in the U.S. where it originally involved the Department of State and now, I would imagine, the NSA. In London, for example, they had a 35% reduction in crime even though they never solved a crime based on either system. In most cases, the fact that the cameras and identification logs were in place, simply scared off the typically stupid criminal and caused them to go elsewhere. Boston Airport, Tampa Florida, and Russia all found that the system could be 'helpful in conjunction with other factors'. Most of you think of facial recognition as something from a Tom Cruise, futuristic movie. I might remind you all that, in that movie, criminals were identified *before* they actually committed the crime. That was a movie and it was science fiction, not science fact. Facial recognition goes back to the mid 1960's and has improved significantly. In one case, you might take special interest in, the most effective algorithms actually picked out identical twins in a large crowd. However, they could not tell which was which. The one question that twins hear consistently from classmates, friends, and even family, is the one that robs them of their unique identities: 'Which one are you?' Yes, their closest friends have trouble being sure. You might as well use skin texture, linear discriminate analysis, elastic bunch graph matching, the Hidden Markov Model or even some combination of multi linear subspace and neuronal motivated dynamic link matching. All of those are in the press packets I have for you. Most of the 'proof' I've seen has been photo shopped."

There was a collective sigh from most of the poor spellers and those who suffered from science 'allergies'. Bob went on, "We could even include retinal mapping, bone density scans and probably some form of rectal probe and we'd still never get more than a 40% level of confidence. I might suggest we increase that a little by just flipping a coin. At the end of the question period, David has a much more effective way of proving who he is, once and for all. Next question, please!"

"Parry Murphy, People Magazine," a voice shouted. "Why do you think someone broke into the boys' dentist office and why are their birth certificates missing? Dentists don't really keep any heavy drugs or gold around their office any more. The only things that disappeared were the Wyllie dental records. Why won't David's mother release her copies of the Wyllie twins' birth certificates? Any comment?"

"Did someone take it as a cover up on behalf of the twins? That's a question I can't answer," Bob stated as part of his 'true lie' strategy, "I think it's *just* as plausible that one of you broke in, hoping to expose a hoax and make money on the exclusive pictures and articles. If one of you did, I think it's just as plausible that, not finding what you wanted, you decided to keep quiet and make it look like one of us was hiding something. You have to admit, both stories make sense when you factor in 'the appearance of guilt'. You have us both ways. We can't be expected to defend both scenarios since neither can be proved."

"As to the birth certificates," Sarkasian surprised his audience, "if anyone wants to see them after next week, we will be glad to provide them....for a price. After all, most of you have made money already without any proof of anything whatsoever. This should be worth plenty. Are there any other questions?"

"Lavonne Beeson, The Inquirer," a voice piped from the left. "Is there any truth to the speculation that local police officials were told to falsify their reports so that the town of Temecula could still be represented at the World Series of Poker?"

"I'm so glad you asked that question," Shark said sarcastically, "Ms. Beeson…Lavonne is it? The answer, of course, is 'yes'. It was so important to the city of Temecula to be part of the poker world that people risked their jobs, imprisonment, their elected positions and outstanding community reputations. Everyone just lied to everyone else. It took coordination, a sense of adventure and a mutual disregard for the keen instincts of people like you and that rag you write for. Oh, and just to be perfectly clear, I'm being facetious and condescending. Ms. Beeson, I'm actually blatantly pissed off that you would even suggest those things about the fine city of Temecula and its people. On the plus side Lavonne, I might suggest that you look far too intelligent and sophisticated to earn a living by attacking people, like my client, with lies and innuendos. May I have the LAST question please?"

One lonely hand cautiously rose above the crowd. A tall man identified himself, "Russ Williams, Science Illustrated. I just wondered why David didn't just volunteer to take a lie detector test. It seems to be the most straight forward approach. I'm sure people would see the willingness to do so as an act of good faith and sincerity. Is there any chance of that happening, Mr. Sarkasian?"

Bob looked at the reporter in mild shock and awe, "Who let you into this place, Mr. Williams? I wasn't expecting sane and rational inquiries, much less a question that would steal a little of my last point's thunder. Thank you for setting us up. David Wyllie has not only agreed to take a polygraph test but the results will be revealed in a live nationally televised special. The show will be hosted by the network's rising star, Milano Pigmentel on his live, nationally syndicated show. Milano's people will insure that everything is absolutely above board. Both sides have agreed upon the questions we have submitted. A giant monitor will let everyone, in the audience, and at home, view how the machine reacted to David's response during the completed test. I can promise you all we will have answered media madness with an insane show of our own. We only ask to be left alone if he passes. See you all on Saturday. Thank you."

The new 'David' joined Bob as they walked off the stage. "Bob, that was sensational," the Coyote complimented. "You absolutely rocked and knocked them on their heels. Looks like I hired the right man, Shark. You're earning the money I'm paying you and then some. "I had no idea you knew so much about facial recognition. How many people did you interview? How many hours did you put into that dissertation and how did you do it without notes or a teleprompter?

"Don't tell anybody kid," Bob said as he walked, "Most of that was 40 minutes on Wikipedia! I just have a photographic memory so it was more like reading an invisible script." They both lowered their heads and smiled as they headed out of the studios.

Dennis, who was a little anxious about the polygraph, asked Sarkasian, "Why didn't we just go somewhere and have my name changed legally?"

"Already checked that one out, son," Sarkasian replied, "The paparazzi had that one covered and were waiting for us. Don't worry.

I'm sure you have an edge on any machine. Just in case, however, and to answer your question completely, I want you to have something as insurance. The Shark reached into his jacket pocket and pulled out an envelope. He handed it to Dennis, put his hand on the young Wyllie's shoulder and said, "I want you to open this envelope before the taking the test for the Milano show. It will definitely change your life. In fact, it might just give you a whole new outlook. I want to warn you, though. It might not be something you're prepared to deal with. It might leave you even more confused. It will definitely give you and your brother something to talk about the next time you two meet. You'll want to read it before the Polygraph but give yourself about 20 minutes to digest it. Without it, I would never have allowed you to test your ability to outwit the machine. I have to tell you that, when I showed it to Dottie and explained what it meant, she was as surprised as you'll be. She knelt down and prayed and asked to be alone. Have I got your interest yet? Sleep well until the show and cut back on the sleeping pills. Your eyes look deep set and dark. Relax and put a little time and effort into enjoying your REM time in bed. You might even want to open the envelope instead of taking a sleeping pill. I think it will work better for you."

CHAPTER TWENTY-NINE

The Envelope, Please!

Dennis tossed and turned all night, unable to relax and get the sleep he needed for the lie polygraph test and the live television show the next day. He rolled out of bed around midnight and deliberated his choices. Wyllie was showing the first signs of insecurity. He had always been confident through every challenge and test he had ever taken in the past. Yesterday, after he had taken days to prepare an act and bluff his way against a polygraph, he realized he might be overmatched. His research was not encouraging. Dennis reached over and grabbed the sealed envelope Sarkasian had given him. He decided he might want to know the contents. It didn't take much time for him to take the letter opener to it. He was shocked but totally relaxed after scanning the information inside. Wyllie slept the rest of the night like a breast fed baby nodding off to the sounds of an ocean wave synthesizer next to the bed.

The morning of the Milano Show Mack approached the Coyote backstage and asked, "Did Bob give you an envelope?"

Dennis responded, "He did. He told me to open it before I took the test and appeared on this show. He prepared me for a shocker but insisted I read the contents. I opened it late last night and called Shark. I felt 100% better about taking the polygraph this morning. I kept asking myself why Bob had agreed to let me take the test anyway. I would have assumed he thought it was an unnecessary risk."

Bob only told me the envelope contained the secret to beating the lie detector," Barnes shared, "is that true?"

"In a manner of speaking, it is," the young Wyllie replied, "In the best sense of the definition, it's the *only* way to beat the polygraph and Shark shared the secret with me."

Dennis told Barnes he had opened the envelope and pulled out three sheets of paper. He read the third page completely. He examined and inspected the other two, holding them up to the light and then started smiling.

"Mack, let's all find out who I am," Wyllie said with confidence. "I don't know the results and it'll be fun watching myself to see if I revealed any 'tells' under pressure. I'm confident that there is no way I failed and I'll prove it as we all watch the filmed test on stage. Even though the actual test won't be live, I was not given the results. I studied how the machine was made. I knew how it worked. The Shark and I eventually found a way to beat it. I never expected he could find something that would make it all so brilliantly simple."

Who would have thought the world of veracity could be commanded by a Geraldo Rivera wannabe? To be fair, Milano had a remarkable sense of entertainment under the guise of revelation.

Pigmentel could pull the 'pub' out of public and maximize the 'op' in opinion. No one donned a top hat or a tuxedo like Milano, with the possible exception of his hero, Geraldo. The Milano Show had certainly found a masterful way of charming the audience and making Milano, himself into an up and coming celebrity in a variety of settings. This was not a Dr. Phil moment. It required a protagonist with flare and someone who could combine entertainment and investigation. This arena would be in the center of Hollywood where family values and production values oft times counteract each other. In Tinsel Town, the three virtues are Lights, Cameras and Action'. In the movie capital of the world, Faith, Hope and Charity are three ex-cheerleaders. The first two went on to become actresses. In a best case scenario, Charity went from a starlet to the wife of a studio executive. In this town truth is constantly tested and Dennis Wyllie was about to be put on trial in a game show atmosphere.

After the opening intro and disclaimer from the network, Milano walked onto the stage in front of a hastily gathered studio audience. It was comprised primarily of tourists who had been walking down Hollywood Blvd. when a bus pulled up and asked them if they'd like a free buffet and a chance to witness a live, national Milano Show. It is not a new practice. When Mack was in college, he once told the twins, he and his roommates would wait for a similar bus on Friday nights. They'd sit in the studio for live interviews. They would ask questions, sign a release and meet back at the apartment with their dates the next night when the show was aired. The roomies didn't have much of a life back then. Combined with a shortage of funds, appearing on television seemed to impress the ladies at a discount price. Nowadays, you tube is so much easier.   Pigmentel opened the pageantry, "Tonight we have a very special show. David Wyllie, the young star crossed poker player who has been relentlessly accused of masquerading as his deceased brother is here to clear his name. Our producers here at the show were approached by Mr. Wyllie and his attorney. David and Bob did so without any request for compensation. Their only requirement was to limit questions to one's approved by both sides. We are not delving into anything other than those dealing with his true identity. We also agreed upon control questions designed to establish a validity baseline."

Milano twisted the end of his handle bar moustache and went on, "The complete test and security procedures were administered over a two hour period in a sanitized and scientifically based environment. The actual questioning took less than twenty minutes. David was drug tested before and after the test. He is a great poker player but I have been told by our experts that even the ultimate yogi could not control his blood pressure, galvanic skin response, sweat, and respiratory elements enough to fool the machine in the correct setting. He has a thespian background but even Sir Lawrence Olivier would have a tough time acting his way through a 'polygraph probe'. David is also an accomplished magician but we have our own representative from the Magic Castle in Hollywood. Mr. Wyllie let himself be monitored and inspected before, after and during the test. This master magician could find nothing deceptive or illusionary in David or the machinery used during the test."

"Finally," Milano took a deep breath and shifted gears, "without further explanation, I would like to introduce to you a fine young man, David Wyllie, and his lawyer and friend, Bob Sarkasion.

"Gentlemen, come on out here on the stage, Pigmentel invited them. "I have the test results in this manila envelope."

"Glad to meet you both," Milano said as he shook their hands.

"I'm glad to meet you too, sir." Dennis said.

"'Sir' is a little old and formal, David. Just call me Milano," the host offered. "Most people don't need a last name to recognize me."

"Whatever you say, Sir...or rather, Milano" Dennis nervously responded.

The host looked into the audience and pointed at a man in the first row. "I'd like you to meet our polygraph expert, Mr. Daryl Jorgenson, who has worked for the FBI, the NSA and the numerous law enforcement agencies across the nation." A brief applause of acknowledgement echoed through the audience who had just finished a well deserved, complimentary meal after arriving by bus.

Milano added, "Mr. Jorgenson, are you confident about the results of this test?"

"I'm extremely confident," Milano, "In fact, I would stake my reputation on the results."

"In that case, David and Mr. Sarkasian, "I told you we might have a special surprise for you. Are you ready to do our own little 'Finder's Test' LIVE?"

"What do you mean LIVE?" the lawyer asked.

"We plan on showing the tape of the entire interview, as planned," Milano said, turning to Dennis and his lawyer, "but we would rather substitute a little surprise of our own."

"We agreed to the format and 'little surprises' were not part of the deal," Shark answered.

Milano continued, "This change of plans is purely voluntary on your client's part before we give the results of this morning's session. Call it dramatic license. Call it intrigue. I call it 'something my famous hero might have done'. We thought we would show the audience how the test works, LIVE!"

The Shark exploded, "This is just the kind of horseplay I was afraid might happen. We're out of here unless you go back to our original agreement and terms!"

"Don't worry, Bob," the Coyote assured his lawyer, "I'm fine with live action. In fact, I thought we were getting off easy and I prepared for this and several other scenarios. Why should today be any less confrontational than everything else that's led up to this? I just have to request that the pertinent questions remain the same and only involve issues of identity. I assume the control questions will be similar, if not exact." Dennis looked at the audience, pointed his finger at them like a showman and asked, "what do *YOU* out there want?" The well fed onlookers stood up applauding and urged Dennis and Milano on. Everybody wants to see a success story but they'd all rather see a train wreck. Either way, they could all say the same thing in the morning, "I was there!"

"You're either a brave man or you're ready to get it over with.

Let's light this candle," the giddy host agreed with a sudden pulse of excitement. "Gentlemen, set the stage."

Pigmentel motioned to the stage hands for the props. They proceeded to wheel out a huge machine and a giant screen TV monitor. Also on the stage were a couple of chairs and one of those 'lovely assistants.' As Mack would later recount, "She was obviously 'eye candy' on the set, dressed in very little that covered even less."

"We'd like to invite you all to witness an abbreviated re-creation of the polygraph test LIVE on national television," the anxious personality said to his guests. "It might be a little over the top but we just thought it would be better show biz. Any TV host could open an envelope. This is the Milano Show and I'm, well, its namesake. We thought we'd let everybody here and out there, at home watch the monitor as it reveals the results. They should certainly replicate the results found in this envelope. Remember, even I haven't seen what's inside. Are there any objections?"

Dennis, as unflappable as always, responded, "It couldn't be any more of a carnival than the one I've been living recently, don't you agree, Bob?" Sarkasian nodded. The Coyote then turned to Milano, on LIVE national television and said, "I don't think it could be any worse than Al Capone's Vaults, do you, Milano? Let's do it Piggy!"

Milano seemed somewhat stunned at the young Wyllie's counterpunch but he was even more relieved that the stunt had been agreed upon so he continued, "Come on up here, Daryl and let's get David strapped in and the monitor activated."

The giant screen was turned on. Dennis was hooked up and

the examiner started his questions.

"Usually," Mr. Jorgenson noted, "we start by asking your name but that would seem to be the finale we're building up to. I might add that, with the audience, the lights, cameras, and national TV, this test will be even harder to pass than the one you took with me earlier today in my office. Are you sure you want to go on?"

"Let's get it on," Dennis replied, "Question One!"

"The first few are just for control purposes," Jorgenson reminded his subject.

"We want to make sure the equipment is still working like we did in your earlier exam," the interrogator explained. "Question One: Are you a human being?"

"I am and always have been," Dennis answered.

The huge monitor showed a straight line as the examiner reminded his subject, "just answer 'yes' or 'no' if you can."

"Of course, I'll do that," Dennis agreed.

"Next question," Jorgenson alerted. "Have you ever lived on Mars? Go ahead and lie."

"Yes" Dennis answered

The audience's eyes shifted to the monitor, as though they were hoping that they had just stumbled upon a space traveler. The line jumped up suddenly as if recording seismic movement in the Los Angeles area.

The questions went back and forth until the examiner felt confident enough in the machinery to ask that all important question, "Are you David Wyllie?"

Wyllie gave a long, dramatic pause reflecting on how everything could have possibly come down to one simple question and then said clearly, "Yes!"

The monitor remained perfectly flat denoting a truthful answer. No further questions were needed.

The Coyote was who he said he was or he had found a way to completely beat the test. Was this really David Wyllie or had the world found a new McGyver? Either way, he had passed the test and a somewhat disappointed Milano came over, opening the envelope with results as he added, "the results here were the same as the results of the complete test. David Wyllie, we wish you well and congratulate you on putting all the rumors, attacks and false accusations to rest."

The host looked Wyllie directly in the eyes and said, "I bet you will always be a huge fan in the future of the Milano Show, won't you?"

"Yes, I will!" the Coyote said with a smile.

At that point, he had forgotten he was still hooked up to the polygraph and the monitor. The line spiked higher than a 7.2 earthquake. At that, Pigmentel went instantly into damage control mode. "Just a quick reminder," he said as he picked out the live camera for a close up, "all of you at home can watch Tuesday night when our show will attempt to answer the question 'Zombies, Vampires, Ghouls and Werewolves: Which are based in fact'. I'm Milano in Hollywood. Good Night and thanks for watching."

Some things in life are, for some reason, generally accepted by the public without question. Somebody put locks on places that are open 24 hours a day. Gravity is not visible, even at an electron level.

It can, however, be measured. Proof on national television, even when it comes in the form of Milano Pigmentel, is enough to win people over. Once the polygraph vindicated David in front of a live audience and the cameras, he and his team were suddenly the sane ones and their detractors had become the new, as Bob described them, 'crazy sonsabitches'. This is how we do it in America. Public opinion is only satisfied in the court of public opinion.

Mack greeted the Coyote as he came off the stage, "Bob must have been right on," he said, "What was in the envelope and how did it help you beat the lie detector? Hell, you didn't just *beat* it; you **destroyed** it!"

The proven David handed the envelope to Mack and explained, "There is no way to beat a polygraph. It's not 100% dependable but you certainly can use it to your own advantage." Inside that envelope just happens to be two birth certificates complete with footprints and hand prints, In addition, there's a note from one of Bob's henchman who compared it to our own fingerprints. My brother and I were born at Poolin Hospital, outside of Fairbanks, Alaska. I don't know how Bob got the originals and I'm sure it involved something illegal. In any case, the nurse either mixed up the babies or mixed up the forms. David's prints were on my certificate and vice versa. I *am* David Wyllie! I have always been David Wyllie. I just never knew it until last night. I guess Shark thought that I might not want to know the truth. Both of us had the same birth weight but my hand, foot and finger prints match the certificate with the name, David Wyllie. Poolin was one of just of a small number of hospitals that inserted hand prints between the two footprints. There is no doubt that I should have been David my entire life. Dennis *did* die tragically as if fate had put the correct wallet in the correct car the night of the accident. In Shakespearian terms, a classic tragedy just became a comedy of errors. Let's hope it has a happy ending like the plays. After all, I can be David without lying about who I am. In point of fact, the only way to beat the polygraph is to tell the truth. That's what I did."

"This is incredible news, Dennis…I mean, David," Mack said, flabbergasted with the explanation.

"David is now playing at the final table the way it should be," Wyllie explained, "the way it has already been announced. Outside of the folks at the Rio and the Nevada Gaming Commission, I'm clear. Tonight should be enough to eliminate Plan B forever. I'll be able to continue and intensify my training for the Main Event with Annie Duke under a clear conscience and a completely refreshed personality."

"Mack," the young Wyllie pointed out, "I'm a 'New Man', I'm David Wyllie!"

It appeared, for all intents and purposes, he had only one hurdle to clear before he could break the tape and win.

This, however, was not your ordinary sprint. The hurdles would be irregular and force some to catapult over each rather than simply clear them. It would be more of a steeplechase. Every lap would include a hazard. Maybe he could go home and finally get second consecutive night of uninterrupted sleep without libation or medication.

CHAPTER THIRTY

Binding Arbitration

When David got home he noticed the door was unlocked. He feared that someone might have broken in, knowing he was appearing on the show. He was right in the worst way. Nothing seemed to be missing or disheveled so he concluded that his distracted departure had accounted for the unlocked entrance. Wyllie headed for the bedroom. The boys were about to share one more thing: Delta. Standing against the wall and in the shadows of the dimly lit room was an imposing figure. Positioning herself between David and the door was the leather and vinyl clad super woman his brother had never mentioned. This time she was wearing 6 inch heals. Delta was slapping a long riding crop against one palm and carrying a set of straps.

"I thought I'd show you that negotiations aren't always in black and white," the uninvited guest declared, "We have some shades of gray areas to explore in our relationship, my dear."

David wanted to yell but he quickly deduced that this was

simply a case of mistaken identity or possibly someone who could actually be dangerous. "This might be a tougher beat than the polygraph," he told himself, suddenly realizing that 'beat' might be an operative sign if said aloud. "My brother must have had some type of dealings with this beast. I might have to pretend to like this," he concluded. He had to admit that thought was one David, most men, and a good number of women would never have worded quite that way. This time he was about to enter someone else's fantasy and try to make it part of his own reality. The trouble was: he had no idea why.

"If this is about money, we can work something out," he offered.

"Oh, this is about the money but I didn't think it would be that easy or that you'd fold without a little coaxing. The costume is one I use in my Dominatrix gigs. It's a great way to meet powerful men after work. They have to tell other people what to do all day. After hours, they like relinquishing control and doing what they're told to do. It's not about sex. It's about giving up and submitting. I make all the decisions. Now it's time for the two of us to come to terms. I like to call it 'dickering'. Let me check your bargaining stick." With that, she grabbed his package and David made a huge mistake. He swung at her face. Delta punched back….and hard. When he woke up he was tied to the bedposts and naked. He still had no idea what this was all about.

"Was this a stalker? Was this a set up?" he asked himself as he scanned the room for cameras, "Surely there were more subtle ways of getting him to cooperate." He felt the pain of the crop against his thighs and looked up at, what he could only compare to as some sort of comic book villainess. Whatever it was, he knew he had to maintain his David image.

"What does it take to move you from flaccid to firm, David," she asked as she leaned over in his face and buried her black suited body into his, "You were certainly more aroused the last time we started to play."

"Ah! A clue!" he realized, "My brother and this Amazon had a previous physical relationship. This helps with the understanding but still doesn't present a solution."

"I don't have time for this now," he bluffed, "why don't you untie me and we can come to some mutual arrangement that can satisfy all our needs without either of us having to role play. What do you want me to do?"

"I want you to just cooperate with me and maybe join us by signing that agreement. Did I tell you one of your coyotes is already working for us? We're just scratching the surface," she said as she ran her fingers down his chest.

"Oh!" He quickly screamed silently, "Scratching must be one of her operative words! She has claws, I mean long nails! Maybe I could picture another partner and go along with the act. Maybe she'd untie me and we could discuss some financial arrangement." He still wasn't, as some say in similar situations, 'up for the moment'.

"What's wrong with you? It's like you're not the same person." It wasn't Delta's first rodeo. She had an epiphany. She backed off a bit and decided to explore her instincts. Reaching into her own bag of tricks, she pulled out a vibrator and turned it on."

"Relax, David, I'm going to untie you and turn you over. I think I know why you haven't been acting like yourself. Did I tell you I knew you could convince your gay twin without a visit from me? I never met Dennis." She pressed the buzzing instrument against his legs. Suddenly, in the way she had expected, she had his full attention. Wyllie switched from disinterested and fearful to interested and terrified. The combined images of being turned over and threatened with that stimulation initiated mixed feelings. Delta's actions had activated sensual reactions too intense to control. She had confirmed her own suspicions. This wasn't the same twin! She continued with her verification.

"Tell me my name and I'll let you go right now." Of course he couldn't.

"I don't have time to play Rumpelstiltskin," David countered as he tried to bluff his way out of his situation. In poker it might sound like, "You really don't want to call. I'm just warning you."

"You took your brother's place, didn't you Dennis? You're gay. There's no other way this could happen to Delta." David wondered if she had shifted into talking about herself that way or did she actually become that 'third person' in the room?

"All you have to do, precious," Delta went on, "Is to admit to me that you took over for your brother when he died, sign the contract, and Delta will decide how to use that for her own best interest."

David decided this, was indeed, 'duress', and he had no other way of escaping her. He knew from the first whip and punch, this could only get worse before it got better. Since this wasn't really about sex, duress would be easier to prove with a few more whips, scratches, and bruises. He 'took one (or more) for the team'. Finally, with all the dramatic surrender of a veteran actor, he agreed to submit.

Delta untied him, gave him a towel, helped him redress and sat him up on the side of the bed facing his brother in the mirror on the vanity. She fluffed his hair and gussied him up like a mother does with her child on the first day of kindergarten. At that point she pulled something else out of her bag. It was something that almost made him reconsider his decision. She turned it on and pointed it at the young Wyllie.

"Go ahead darlin'," she said reassuringly, "Speak right into the camera."

"Maybe this is the way it all ends," he tried to convince himself. "Maybe no choice is the best choice."

He began to talk, "I am Dennis Wyllie and my brother, David died in an auto accident. I wanted to take his place in the WSOP. I've been deceiving everyone, ever since."

"Thank you, Mr. Coyote. I'm going to take this back to my people," Delta explained, "and they'll decide how to make money with it. I'd go ahead and sign, though. That way we have no reason to ever share our little secret at all."

He decided to sign the paper. Wyllie hoped one of his neighbors would catch a glimpse of 'cat woman' as she left his place. "One man's pleasure is another man's duress," he argued." The Coyote smiled when he concluded Delta hadn't viewed the Milano show. Suddenly, David remembered that, at the insistence of Sarkasian, he had recently installed security cameras in the hallway. He locked the front door and double bolted it. The entire break in had been captured on tape.

"Just one more complication for an underpaid lawyer," David tried to convince himself. He took pictures of his injuries and texted a full report to Sarkasian with a time stamp and reasons for not filing a police report for now.

"Some day," David compartmentalized, "after the tournament, Delta would have to be, well, 'dealt with'."

CHAPTER THIRTY-ONE

Leading Out/First to Act

David had managed to dispel all questions of identity in public and plead guilty a few hours later in private. He had left the show ready to finally prepare for the Final Table. He looked forward to his first innocent sound sleep since Big Bear. Wyllie suddenly concluded the whole world was out to get him. David, as Mack used to describe it was 'going from Camelot to the parking lot.' Part of his newly found poker shifted from dominated victim to master of his own face. He told himself, "Delta is a hand to be played on another day. I have to play the cards in front of me and let the chips fall in my favor." He slowly, once again, removed his clothes and let them fall on the floor as he staggered across the room. The young Coyote downed a couple of quick shots from the Yukon Jack bottle. Mack was a YJ drinker and warned the boys: 'the Black Sheep of Canadian Liqueurs' can 'flock' you up." David looked over his shoulder to see shoes, socks, pants, and shirt in an ordered line behind him on the floor.

"It looks like I just walked out of someone else's clothes or some lifeless body is ready to step back into them," he said to himself. He was emotionally drained and felt a sudden need to release. He seemed to sense footlights in the room and a shouted an impromptu stage line that gushed from his soul: "I have cast off the throws of another to stand naked in front of the world. I'm tired enough to be a character on *The Walking Dead*," he thought, "and I'm starting to sound like a poor man's Shakespeare." David turned as he spoke and came face to face, once again, with his mirror image. "Today, my departed brother, I have thought as you. Tonight I choose to dream as me." He was still ripping off the master. He downed his third shot.

Mack had once told the boys that the most obnoxious drunks were 'thinker drinkers'. "When unusually intelligent, well-educated, people get extremely sleepy or 'on their ass blitzed," Barnes had cautioned the twins, "they have been known to quote or even paraphrase Shakespeare. Sometimes they move on to Sartre, Nietzsche or Tolstoy. Take back Leo. Nobody has *that* kind of time or energy when they're wasted. A person would have to be a 'Crimea River' drunk for that to happen." Barnes thought he had impressed the twins with a Russian literary play on words. Without hesitation, however, Dennis had shot back, "and that's only 'just in Timber Lake.'" (the Crimea River's source, Mack found out after researching the boy's repartee). Barnes decided never again to try to outmatch the boys with trivial facts or puns based on classic novels.

David was reenacting dramatic roles from high school classics when he had shared the stage with the now correctly identified Dennis. He continued his diatribe in front of his reflective image. "Some day in that great somewhere, unlike most people who dream of being reunited with a loved one, I will long for the day we can pull ourselves apart. We were closer, my brother, when we were unique to each other and more than friends in a mirror." The twin in the mirror stared and remained silent.

"We were never intended to be twins," David lamented, "We were one person for more than a week after inception. A week more coupled and we would have had to be cut apart or spend our entire lives conjoined. We share much more than DNA, my reversed image friend. We share a combined consciousness and connectivity. You and I know that everyone searches for the things that make them stand out as individuals. We have had the benefit of being able to find that and appreciate it in each other." He was still remembering his acting skills and he was becoming a 'legend in his own mind'. His recollections grew by leaps and bounds. He approached total blackout. When he looked up into the mirror, the new Dennis looked back in total agreement and seemed just as confused. "Did you really die?" David questioned. "Was that the other half of me? I do know that I now have to look to others to understand myself. When you die, is it like that in heaven? Do you finally know who you are? Have you discovered who I am? Can I do that here without you?" His reflection seemed to mimic David and even asked the same questions in synchronic harmony. "Next month," David added as his words began to slur a bit. "We go to the Final Table. I have an idea of how to incorporate more than your memory into my entrance. I think you will not only approve, but howl in appreciation. I'm going to wear something that builds unity between brothers. It'll be one of those 'in your face…or faces' moments. I know you'll be there with me but Annie and the other pro coaches gave me every strategy I'll need to dominate and the humility and class to deal with the rest of the table."

Dennis remained inside the mirror but seemed to approve and look forward to the game of a lifetime. "You'd like Annie, brother," David added, leaning and pointing at the mirror, "She's taught me more about game theory and 'follow through' than I could have ever imagined. I really didn't know how much of a novice I was technically until that woman helped me to grow. She talks about controlled studies, modified behavior, built-in irrationality, money management and something called 'heart'. Did you know that what we call poker, she calls 'Decision Making under Conditions of Uncertainty'? Uncertainty, is that where we are, brother?" David and his brother were both starting to look, sound and wave their arms like drunks in the alley or castaway customers when the bar closes. "I mean I know how to narrow down the range of hands my opponent has," David continued. "I know how to evaluate equity of betting. Did you know, Dennis, I need to develop a 'brand?' Did you know my ego shouldn't be in play? Did you know Annie Duke is the cutest teacher I've ever had? That even includes that black special education teacher who used to dance like Tina Turner at assemblies back at Chaparral."

Actually he was dying out as he got to the last few words but, luckily, he passed out on the floor for the evening. Dennis, almost simultaneously, did the same.

CHAPTER THIRTY-TWO

When You Know It All: Start Learning

Because of Annie Duke's own hectic schedule that included motivational speaking to corporate leaders and private poker lessons, David had made weekly trips to Vegas for his training sessions. Like all young poker players with skill and confidence, he was only there to steal a few hands with the inside scoop.

Annie was one of the best because she read people, understood situations, calculated the odds, and played the percentages. In the long haul, that's what separates professionals from amateurs.

If Leonardo was the Renaissance man, then Annie Duke was the poker equivalent of a Renaissance woman. She played regularly, of course; had taught at the Poker Tour (WPT) Academy; put in months of work with her charities and fund-raisers; and still managed to excel as a mom. Duke treated David like he was a professional. He was not. Wyllie had the intelligence, mathematical understanding, and feel for the game but he lacked the experience and knowledge of what to look for at the table. As alluded to earlier in his late night conversation in the hotel, David had become a quick and humble learner. Besides the obvious, Annie had helped him lose his brother's inflated ego. At one point Duke made an understated observation, "Most people," Duke said, "are living on a high just getting to the November Nine. I don't sense any of that with you. It's like you'll be sitting down for the first day of the Main Event. I like that! I've studied your tendencies and you seem to have studied them too. Some of your most obvious physical movements and strategic reactions have all but disappeared. Don't get me wrong, though. You've developed some new ones and we'll work on those in the next few weeks." She had discovered more than she knew.

"Annie," David shared with her as a way of soothing his conscience and recognizing the part 'luck' had played, "I know you should be at the table and I should be home in Temecula. The world might have been quite different if I hadn't sucked out with that fourth Queen. I have to say, though, that I've never seen you talk about that hand with anything other than class and dignity. I hope you can impart a little of that to me in case I blow it."

David silently voiced his biggest fear, not willing to share it with his coach, "If that happened to me, I'd probably have another family melt down. I'm glad I have the Duchess as my inspiration."

It was obvious that the young Wyllie had a gay male, intellectual, poker-loving crush on his coach. Why not? She understood the subtleties of the game. She came from rough, tough Montana where men were men, and women weren't. In recent interviews, Duke had shared some early verbal attacks and how she handled those onslaughts. She had to deal with misogynistic men who couldn't stand losing to a female. She also had plenty of ways of taking advantage of the ones who thought they were being flirtatious. Sexual harassment, to paraphrase Annie, was always a distraction for the male players and motivation for the woman to use to their advantage. David was not going to be distracted by a beautiful woman for obvious, if not shared, reasons. On the other hand, most young poker players' wardrobe consisted of pizza stained T-shirts, baseball caps worn off center and 'good luck' underwear not to be changed while their owner was on a winning streak. David had gone from early imitation costumes to hard core Coyote. He had just devised a sensational twist for an outfit to wear the night of the November Nine. When he announced his idea to Annie and how he wanted his deceased brother to be part of the action, his coach made one strong suggestion.

"David, you've shared how close you two were and how involved you still are with Dennis. I'm not a licensed psychologist but I am a good judge of people and emotions. Don't take this the wrong way but you are in serious need of some emotional support by a professional when this is over. You, at least, need some counseling. I worry about how you would handle it if you didn't win it all and maybe even if you did. You've been driving on a long road to get here and I don't know what will happen when you have to get out of the vehicle and go it alone on foot. You will be without your purpose. People without purpose are people with nothing to lose." The two shared the same concerns. Maybe she read his tells automatically. They were on the same page. He wished he and Delta could have been on the same page sexually. He needed an outlet and he started 'Delta talk' to himself, "I know I can finish off the ones who finish off the rest." He silently self diagnosed, "But who's going to finish me off? I hope there's such a thing as a poker orgasm. His internal humor was becoming darker and in need of a physical partner. The loss of his twin was shaded in troubling insights and gilded foreshadowing. The loss of his best friend was steeped in emotional frustration and loneliness. He missed his old life.

"Are you with me? Annie asked, "You seemed to have wandered off there for a moment. Let's get back to poker theory and gaming." Dennis took a long sigh and redirected his focus on the lesson. "Life goes on for the living," he told himself. That was then and this is now."

"You have a huge lead but that doesn't guarantee anything when it comes to the bracelet," Duke reminded him. "Even if it gets down to heads up between you and one other person, one all-in loss might be enough to shift the balance of power."

"I know," David admitted, "but I'm smart enough to do this and I didn't travel this far not to finish. I just want to do it as a team: You, me and Dennis."

"When you filled out that form that made me your coach and mentor, I took the mentor role just as seriously as the coaching," Annie explained. "You're fragile emotionally after the loss of your twin. You understandably haven't let go of him. It's great that you want him at the table with you but that's a mega distraction. It's also one more person inside your head. You need to be an individual who makes decisions without second guessing himself."

"I would have been there for him," David reasoned, "and he'll be there for me."

"From what you've told me, your twin brother was a special person," Duke explained and increased her concerns, "but he seems a little angry that you might be doing this alone and getting all the accolades without him. I know this would sound ridiculous to most people out there but, sometimes, we use our alter egos to do things we wouldn't dare do on our own. You're a good person, David. Go with the good. I almost see your recent brotherly conversations becoming more 'good cop/bad cop' arguments."

"Is this some way of telling me I'm going off the deep end?" Wyllie asked.

"All I'm saying," Annie pleaded with her student, "is that, when this is all over, win or lose, promise me you'll find someone to help you decompress psychologically and not let this go the way of your family history. I know about your dad and how suddenly and devastatingly it all went wrong. I'm serious. There really is a dark side to each of us and you've let it get concentrated in your brother. You could use him as an excuse to make bad decisions. Do you think that could ever happen?"

David put his head down and broke into a whimpering sob, "Sometimes I wonder, Annie. Sometimes I think he's the one taking charge. Sometimes I agree. I think he's a trouble maker and I'm just here to get in his way or do his bidding. That's getting harder and harder to deal with each day. What if he ever decides to do something crazy?"

"David, this is critical," the Duchess clarified, "Exactly *what* do you mean by 'doing something crazy'?"

"I'm just asking you to keep an eye on me at the table," Wyllie implored her, "on the outside and in the game I'll be fine. Watch him for me. He'll be on my right. I'll try to ignore him as long as I can. I know he's planning something and I can promise you that it wouldn't be pretty if he ever totally got his way."

Annie wrapped her arms around her young charge. She sensed there was much more than poker to be played at the Final Table.

"No big deal," David told himself without conviction, "or would it be the biggest deal of the tournament?"

Neither could or would admit to their fears of how far things could get 'out of hand'.

CHAPTER THIRTY-THREE

A Wild Card Missing

Two days before the Final Table, T.R. Ricky and Dick Galliano rented an entertainment suite near the pool at the Tropicana. Dick called it a "Batch Lore" party. Most of the original, surviving Coyotes were there. The group was there, ostensibly, to honor their Wyllie Coyote and wish him well with the November Nine on Tuesday night. Even a contrite Angel Vasquez showed up. He and his wife had been investigated, charged, and then cleared of all wrong doing in the sad and sudden death of Domingo Fernandez. As a show of good faith toward Mack and the boys, Angel had hired the 'dancers' that showed up as 'entertainment'. It was obvious from the start that T.R. was looking for action and maybe another 'trophy' wife. His ring finger was naked and he was ready to coordinate the rest of his outfit to match. Money was just around the corner and he reasoned, "There are more than enough ladies in Vegas to help me spend it."

Ruby was still in a wheelchair from her fall. She could only turn in circles because there was always a tall, mixed drink in one hand. She was a poker wonder, herself, and advised David, "When you feel you're beaten or outgunned, surrender. There will be a time and place to call all bluffs no matter what they have on you!"

David flashed back, "She couldn't possibly know about Delta. Boudreau was a woman with instincts who, somehow, read his dilemma. Nobody ever went wrong trusting the advice of Ruby, at the table or in the middle of a life challenge."

"You have no idea how much that helps," he told Boudreau."

"Of course I do." Ruby replied. "It's all over your face and it needs to be dismissed before someone else reads it at the table. Now, leave an old lady alone with her drink and visit with the others."

Father Jinks showed up in his priestly suit and collar to make everyone else feel that this was a blessed event. He had been expecting another call from David to explain the TV show. He kept checking his phone but there were no messages. Certainly David was even more confused in the present than he had been back in Temecula.

Jake Wayland, accompanied by his facial-haired flock, was standing waist deep in the pool with a floating bucket of beer for his friends and a well-hidden flask of single malt for himself. Mack had commented, "Everybody stands around in the pool drinking beer and no one ever leaves for the restroom. Makes you wonder, doesn't it?"

Joy, Dr. Herb's widow, looked radiant and was doing a good job mingling. Her smile and gestures were there but her heart wasn't in it. She brought the good doctor to the festivities in that heart; with her soul; and on her mind.

"Herb would have loved this," she said to Sherri as she mixed, "and I would have loved him loving it."

"He's here tonight," Sherri reassured her, "and he's standing there right next to you. It's very obvious to everyone here."

Domingo, of course, wasn't there but he was mentioned in the opening speech David offered, welcoming the whole group. A toast was made in his honor, followed by a moment of silence. A full autopsy had investigated the rumors. The findings revealed that Fernandez had died 'in good health' as the result of a congenital coronary birth defect.

Coach Buck, Kahlid, and even Bryce, 'Jacks Twice' Tanner attended. Everybody seemed to find a fine balance of drinking. Each drank only enough to recover in time to view the poker contest ahead and still stay intoxicated enough to forget how much money was at stake.

Katy and Tom Knight showed up but the school superintendent seemed more interested in avoiding the picture taking all around him. Katy was as outrageous as ever and relayed all the images to her children and grandchildren in Texas and Florida while texting the details of the whole soirée.

Calvin Moffett, the off-duty jailer, and his wife came directly from a wedding so they were overdressed for this collection of characters. Calvin was in a tuxedo and his wife, the boys' aunt, was already tipsy in the first hour of the reception. She loved roulette. Her numbers were calling her name. Calvin had been an NFL football player but he had no way of blocking her from the casino.

Jonny Collison was there with a lovely young lady. They seemed to be close friends, at least.

Bob Sarkasian turned to Mack and a few Coyotes and asked, "Where's Steve Purcell? I didn't think he'd ever miss a chance to party." Mack asked around. Nobody had seen him in weeks. Somebody remembered him coming by their place with a knockout redhead. A couple of others chimed in with the same story.

"He told me," Kahlid volunteered, "that this bombshell, Delta, was taking him on a plane ride to Chicago. That was a couple of weeks ago. I went by his mobile home park for a real estate viewing. I asked around and nobody had any idea where he was. His mom had moved out suddenly without any farewells."

"A plane ride to Chicago? Never been seen since?" Bob asked with the look of 'been there'. I don't like the sound of that. Didn't he tell some of the Coyotes that he was offered a job with Delta's group?"

"I think he was going to take the job," Bryce offered, "he told me he sold his share of the winnings and had big plans with what to do with the money."

"Still doesn't sound like Steve," Mack assessed, "I'd better give him a call to make sure he's alright."

Mack pulled out his phone, checked contacts, and pressed Purcell. The number was not in service. "Did the guy pull one 'fast one' too many?" he thought, "Did he get in over his head this time?" With a 'Chicago' group, you certainly don't want to ever get in 'over your head'," Mack thought to himself. He always figured

Steve would be the one who would end up behind bars. Certainly Barnes couldn't have pegged himself as the one who would end up with mug shots. Mack remembered better times with Purcell whom he had encountered in the most unusual way. Maybe it was an unwitting glimpse into the old musician's past and future. They certainly travelled in circles that would never have intersected in anybody's Venn diagram. Barnes recalled the first time he met Steve. "He should have known this was one crazy bastard who not only lived life on his own terms." Mack reflected, "He dictated them when someone pissed him off enough to make it worth shit." Almost thirty years ago, Barnes had to locate Purcell to do some work for a friend. The address took him to a bar in old Murrieta once owned by Babs, a woman of exceptional reputation. She told stories about the Wild West atmosphere of the valley in the 1960's. She was there, not so long ago, when cowboys and Indians joined forces under the leadership of a Samoan sheriff. Those strangest of bedfellows slugged it out with the Hell's Angels on Main Street, Temecula. The unlikely posse ran the bikers clean out of town. You could still ride your horse into town as late as the 1980's. When Mack asked for Steve, he was directed to an old barnlike building next to the back parking lot. He knocked on the door and introduced himself.

"My name is Barnes and I have some work for you, if you're interested," Mack announced.

"Isn't that just dandy," an obviously hung over Purcell replied, "You are a Barnes and looking for a worker; I'm a worker who lives in a barn. Guess we're starting off near even." Barnes tried not to show how much he liked that one. Mack later learned that Steve made his money off an old car that didn't run. Every Friday and Saturday night, he'd roll it into a special place in the bar parking lot next to his bedroom window where he slept lightly. At least one person a night, intoxicated, would hit the car. Steve would hurry out and offer 'not to call the police' if the customer would just give him $100 or whatever they had on them. This time with the Chicago group, Barnes feared in his thoughts, "Purcell might have played loose with the rules and crossed the wrong people." Steve, the group would later learn, had done something in Chicago alright. Always living on the edge, he made an unpredictable and gutsy deal with the 'dark side'. The 'seat of the pants' ex-drummer would never visit Temecula again. In fact, Steve Purcell was never seen or heard from again. That, however, would not an end to his story. In stark contrast, in many ways, it would be a new beginning.

Back at the party, things hit a snag. "Mack," Bryce Tanner said, "the dancing girls aren't dancing. I asked Angel and he just laughed and told me to ask them to get started. I'm a little shy, you know, and a Christian, so I thought you might be better at it. I'll go *with* you."

Mack, realizing he must appear bold and heathen to Bryce, approached the two women who he later found out had arrived on the back of Angel's motorcycle. "Shouldn't you two be dancing?" Mack asked politely.

"We don't dance," the older, more 'experienced' of the two women ardently announced. At this point even the worldly Mack, distracted by the crowd and thoughts of his friend, Steve Purcell, followed up without evaluating his inquiry, "If you don't dance, what *do* you do?"

"Oh God, Sherri immediately realized, "that was the wrong question to ask these two."

The younger girl proudly advertised, "She gives a mean hand job, and I'm the quickest tongue in the West."

Bryce Tanner blushed, turned quickly, and left in shock. Thanks to years of dealing with troubled teens and unpredictable outbursts, Mack composed himself quickly and softened his reply, "so….you work for tips, do you?"

T.R., who had wandered over, offered to take care of the situation and disappeared with the two ladies for the evening. Mack looked at his wife and purged his soul, "Who put Angel in charge of entertainment? Dick should have put him in charge of something like appetizers."

Sherri interlocked arms with her husband as they walked away and sagely suggested, "Maybe Dick did just that, Mack, and maybe Angel misinterpreted the meaning of 'appetizers.'" Mack remembered why he married Sherri in the first place. He knew then what he had always known. She was a keeper.

CHAPTER THIRTY-FOUR

On Tilt: Moral/Ethical/Religious Dilemmas

With the disappearance of Steve Purcell, David began to question whether he had caused, or at least incited, things that had befallen some of the Coyotes. He didn't believe in the concept of karma but it seemed to be manifesting itself in too many instances to be coincidental. Joe Halemano had called and asked about it from another of his dreams. "Is karma working for us, David?" Halemano asked and went on, "I hope so. I noticed one of the 'November Nine' is an Indian. He's the real kind, you know, he might even wear a turban." David lied and reassured Joe he had nothing mystical to worry about.

"Would Domingo be dead? Would Herb have lived longer? Would Steve be missing?" Wyllie questioned himself silently. Who's next? Me?"

After sneaking out of the party in his honor, David drove alone away from the flashing lights of Vegas proper. He needed to get as far away as possible from the glitz and glamour. He didn't have to go far off the strip to realize his dream. David drove by pawn shops, massage parlors, pool halls, and a string of 'special interest' spots that cater to the desperate and the disillusioned. A large vocabulary, a Mensa membership and a kind but innocent heart can, generously, turn 'poor people' into 'currently disenfranchised.' By any standard, though, David seemed to be wrestling with his soul and conscience.

California Dreamin' by the Mamas and Papas, played on the radio. When he heard the lyrics: 'stopped into a church I found along the way', he suddenly knew he had to talk to his parish priest one last time. He turned the car around just as he was entering the next circle of Vegas Hell. It was the land of Big Lots, Laundromats, psychics, and 'pay day loans'. He hurried back to his hotel room. Once there, he felt comfortable enough to call Father Jinks who had come to Vegas for the tournament and was staying at the Tropicana.

"Father, this is David Wyllie," he said. "Can you hear another confession over the phone?"

"Hello my son. I have been hoping you'd get back to me. I think we'll just call it a post script to the one we had after your brother died, if that's okay with you?" Jinks replied.

"That's fine, Father." David agreed, "I just want to know if I need to come clean on everything we talked about. I just want to know what I need to do to feel like the old me," David explained. I have to tell you. It's more complicated than before. The birth certificates were backwards. I really am David. Dennis really did die in the accident. Does that change anything?"

"Thank you for explaining the Milano Show, David," the confessor said, "I'm glad you don't have to lie about your identity anymore and it does change some things. The only person who can exact the correct pathway is the person who chose to travel in that direction in the first place. Do you know what I mean, my son?"

"I do. What would you do if you were in this situation, Father?" David offered.

"I would hope that my limited poker skills and over active religious training would have precluded me from being where you are now, David." Jinks said, then added, "As a priest, the only answer, religiously and morally is to tell the truth. One truth can rid a person of a thousand lies. Remember, as a benefactor in the spoils of the tournament, my money is already spoken for. Despite the many ways I utilized the hubbub over your success and my winnings, the Archbishop has already scolded me on my gambling misadventures. The Bishop's Relief Fund for the foreign indigent will benefit as atonement for my indiscretions and excitement.

"Don't I owe something to someone at this point," Wyllie asked, "isn't it too late to turn back?"

"As an insider and confidante under the sanctity of the confessional, I am following your incredible road to riches as it plays out," Jinks told David, "I can completely understand why it seems to have gone too far and involved too many to simply quit."

"If I wanted to stop the madness, how would I even attempt such a revelation?" the Coyote asked.

"Officially," Jinks proposed, "I would look for the right moment and pray to God for the wisdom to know when, where, and how to come clean. There is no right way to do the wrong thing, my son. There is no wrong way to do the right thing, either. Pray on the matter and ask for divine intervention to guide you."

"Wow! You really don't know what the hell to do either, do you?" David said, "I *will* pray and ask for all that wisdom and strength but I'll probably go more with the brain on this one, Father. Dennis is more and more in my life. He was in the back seat of the car on the way over here. I tried not to look in the rear view mirror but, when I did, he was not happy. Sometimes, I think he's really there and other times, I think I'm going down that path my dad found himself travelling just before he finally came unglued, gave up, and took the ultimate way out."

"Then the answer is simple, David," the priest replied, "You have to keep your sanity no matter how crazy that sounds," Father instructed. "Good luck and let me know if I need to meet with you, in person."

CHAPTER THIRTY-FIVE

The Antes are Up

David went downstairs to the casino and played slots because he needed some mindless entertainment.

"How do people do this all day?" Wyllie asked himself. "At least, in the old days, you got exercise pulling down on the side lever or handle or whatever they call it.
Looks like the one-arm bandits are still robbing people, hands free. Push a button to bet, push a button to start and pull out a paper to 'cash in' to a faceless machine. Where's the social interaction of poker?" David wondered, "Where's the drama, the calculations, the reads, the dealers and so many more human factors?" One thing David liked was that the machine didn't care who you were, how you played or why you chose to be there.

"It's just a machine, damn it, and it has all those lights, characters, colors and sounds," he tried to explain to himself, "It's all so clear cut and such a win or lose proposition." It was a mindless distraction for Wyllie who was avoiding his room and a follow-up talk with his brother who would have his own advice to contribute.

"Looks like I won a mini-jackpot," David told himself, "I won $34.32. Aright! Glad I don't have to split that 20 ways when I get home. Maybe I can just pour it all back into the machine and hope it tells me I'm a 'WINNER!' ten more times before it takes all my money." The woman on his right had a plate of Chinese noodles on her lap, tucked between her mid section and the buttons. She and the screen had an obvious relationship. She kept rubbing one hand across the win line while she held the chow mien with the other. She called the slot by reputation, "Come on, you devil, 777, 777!" After finishing her dinner, she tried 'making up' with the screen, "I'm sorry," she apologized, "I only want some love." It worked. She won some money and left satisfied.

"In an hour, she'll be hungry again," David guessed. He decided he couldn't bring himself to take on the pleading approach even though he had been doing the same thing with his priest. Finally, after going up and down for over two hours, David had coaxed the machine to show four rows of penguins and the 'Ice Bonus.' He cashed in his winnings of $11.33 and caught the next elevator to the 22nd floor. When he walked into the bathroom, he was shocked by what he *didn't* see. There was no reflection at all. Had his brother used up his time on this earthly plain?

"In Shakespearian terms," he reasoned, "this whole tragedy really has become that **Comedy of Errors** which was the last play the two had performed in high school. That plot revolved around two sets of identical twins. He thought more about the similarities in story lines. He remembered that one brother had mistakenly received a gold bracelet that the other brother had paid for.

"How freaky is that? Wyllie told himself, "My brother earned his way to a WSOP Main Event. Now I could take his bracelet without paying for it." David knew that there still should be some sort of image in the mirror when he entered the room. He had to pinch himself to make sure he wasn't dreaming when he found himself looking into empty, normally reflective glass. Remembering the role his brother played in that school production, he decided to call after him, sarcastically, with spliced lines from two different plays, "Domeo, Domeo, where for art thou?"

"I'm over here on the bed, fool," a voice called from behind him in the darkened room, "It's time we figured out what to do and how you're going to make sure you don't rob me of my jewelry!" David was angry. He turned to find his brother lying on his back across the bed. He seemed so cocky with his head on the pillow and the TV remote in his hand. Dennis had come out of the mirror.

"That can't be good," David reasoned. "That can't be good, at all!" What a time to come to that realization.

"Ouch!" he said with a pinch to his own cheek, "No, I'm not dreaming. That can't be good either."

David and Dennis were now sitting side by side for the first time since before the accident.

"Are you actually somehow here?" asked David. "Could I finally be losing it like Dad?"

"I am most certainly here, and I just found out we switched names again. Are you sure this is the last time we play musical chairs with our identities?" Dennis questioned. "Reality doesn't preclude the explanation of insanity" Dennis continued, "With all you've been through, neurotic is a given. It's a not a long stretch to psychotic. People have actually been 'out to get you' so I think you have a free pass exception on paranoia as well."

"Tell you what I'm going to do;" Dennis told his living brother, "We need to formulate a Plan B of our own."

"Here are your choices:

a. You come clean. You live/I die happily ever after

b. You win and you bury the bracelet with me

c. You lose and I get to 'make a scene' at the final table

d. You win and *you* get to make that scene"

e. All of the above"

"Did I mention that I won't be around after the final table?" Dennis explained, "So any consequences that may come about from your or my bad behavior will be left for you, as they say in the poker world, 'deal with it, man.'"

"I'm making an announcement in the morning and you'll know my decision then," David declared. "I still don't know what I'm going to say but I know it will be based on what friends who support me have advised me to consider. Everything is crazy right now. Night is Day and Black is White. You try living this life. You couldn't. You think you're going to live it through me! Live it with me and we can make it happen, together."

"You have your choices, brother," Dennis reminded his twin, "I have every confidence that you'll make the wrong one."

"Part of me wants to come clean and deal with the backlash of honesty." David started to rant, "We live in that kind of world today. Honesty has its own backlash. Truth has its own ramifications. 'Telling it like it is' destroys what people want to hear and then have to come to grips with. I absolutely know that part of you wants me to call a news conference and burst everybody's bubble. No one will be happy: the Casino, the Coyotes, the paparazzi, the social media. "Even the town we live in will disown us."   Dennis answered. "People say the truth will set you free. In this case, although we are certainly prisoners of our own fabrication, lying seems to be in the best interest of the game we are playing. Drama is real life. Subterfuge aligns itself with transparency. 'Standing up for one's self' is blurred with 'looking out for others." Our own integrity depends on living a lie. The people who sent us here think we're working for them. In truth, that's just the mumbo jumbo of this media-hyped whirlwind. Every day, I feel less like a poker player and more like a goddamn congressman."

Mack would have disagreed. He probably would have added something like, "Unlike Congress, David, you have to set individual issues aside and take some positive and, in this case, bipartisan action."

"Did I even mention, my brother," Dennis added, "You usually seem to talk a lot more when I'm *not* around. You just went off on a rant. I never thought you had it in you."

David had no way of arguing with a good observation so he decided to go for the jugular, "Oh! and thanks a million for never mentioning a creature called Delta!"

At least they got off the subject of poker and identity for the next two hours. One was full of curiosity and laughter. The other one was packed with anger and gay expletives. Finally one went to sleep and the other jumped back in the mirror.

CHAPTER THIRTY-SIX

Beat the Bullies; Share the Wealth

"Finally," David thought, "I get a chance to talk on my own behalf. Hopefully, the whole team of Mack and Sherri, Bob, my mom and Fr. Jinks will be proud of me."

Again, this was a bright young man who was only naïve, it seems, when it came to pretty good ideas that involved awfully ugly plots. Dennis, on the other hand, had recently hatched a 'plot' of his own. He would give his living brother a chance to come clean but he had reservations about what his twin was about to reveal.

The Barnes family and Bob met him in the wings of a simple meeting room at the Rio to view the young Wyllie.

"David or Dennis," Sherri told the Coyote backstage, "whatever you've decided to do, Mack, Bob, and I have agreed we support your decision and we'll be there to explain it to the home players."

"Thanks Mrs. Barnes," David said sincerely, "I really do

appreciate that vote of confidence."

Because of the short notice and travel time, only a few of the local Vegas TV stations sent reporters. They were joined by some of the press corps in town for the Final Table. Since the Milano Show, everything seemed to be dialed down at least a few notches and people were starting to find new stories with fresher casts. Still, something 'revealing', 'unexpected' or a 'game changer' could be a story to latch onto. Father Jinks, relieved that his advice looked influential, watched on his lap top in the local rectory he dropped into to get away from the casino. Mom Wyllie had already been apprised by her son as to the content of his speech and found it 'uniquely Wyllie twin'. Moreover, she knew that both her sons were involved, somehow, in the decision. In fact, Dottie felt David was about to take a huge step in dealing with his detractors. He was about to take command of the situation and make it his own.

David stepped up to the rostrum and leaned into speaker. "I guess you all know who I am by now," he announced, knowing there was more than enough sarcastic irony in that statement alone. "I want to make a short announcement and I hope you will all have something to talk about. I will take no questions at this time and the details of my decision are included in the press release that will be handed out as I disappear backstage." Interest grew in the room.

"As you all know, my brother Dennis was killed in a tragic accident," David's voice cracked, "and I am still trying to deal with that. Many of you have fueled the fires of intrigue and imagination that currently simmer in the public melting pot. People were sympathetic but anxious to move onto 'the discovery phase of his case', as David the lawyer would refer to it. They needed a 'news worthy' story.

"I am slowly reentering that same 'public' from my own self imposed fortress of solitude," Wyllie went on, "I will be more visible soon but I will do it slowly and at my own pace. Please do not confuse my privacy with avoidance of issues. Right now I have to make that announcement."

The crowd seemed to be put off by Wyllie's circumlocution. They were losing interest in his words.

"Today I am honoring my brother's honesty," David said, "by making sure that people everywhere are not afraid to stop living lies." The room bustled with enthusiasm and waited with baited breath.

"Dennis waited 15 years to even share with me that he was gay. Today, my mother and I are donating his share of the winnings at the Final Table to GALA, the Gay and Lesbian Alliance. We hope to fund high school programs for teens dealing with their own sexuality, especially those who suffer from depression and are at risk mentally and emotionally. As you know, the suicide rate among homosexual teens is incredibly high and the vulnerability of these young people requires support, education, and hopefully acceptance of all people for one another. The primary target areas this money will be used to help are those directly related to access counseling and mental health services and those programs that specifically fight bullying in schools. A grant program will be set up to evaluate services based on those criteria. This amount will be somewhere between $150,000 and $1.4 million if I am fortunate enough to win the WSOP Main Event. Many of my home tournament players out there gladly invite all people to join most of our pack of Coyotes in the support of these issues which focus on the mental and emotional health of the very vulnerable. GALA and the teens they embrace, along with a few poker pros I've enlisted, are asking all gay teens and their friends to join us at the final table with our newly formed support group. You can contribute to in any way you choose by donating at **Deal Us In @gmail.com**. We only hope you all will take a seat at our table with us on this one. Thank you."

David had decided to go outside the choices Dennis had presented to him. He decided to go with 'none of the above'. He hoped that Dennis would accept his decision. The news people didn't have the story they had hoped for but, like any other day, they had *a* story and they could embellish it from a human interest point of view. It was good copy, if not the headline they hoped for. Only Jinks, a Catholic priest, was mildly put off.

CHAPTER THIRTY-SEVEN

Aces Cracked

The clock struck high noon. The Wyllie entourage was gathered in the luxury suite David was given complimentary use of the week of the Final Table. The tournament was a day away. He and Mack were sharing stories of 'what to do with the money' if they won. David went first, "I'd like to buy a place near Laughlin where I could feel close to Arizona *and* California. It would give me that sense of a 'meeting of the minds' with Dennis. It's still so strange to *be* David and talk about Dennis in the past tense."

"How about you, Mack?" David asked.

Mack sensed that David needed some of his old fashioned twisted humor and he could always fill that bill. "I told Sherri I had a wild idea that might save some people money and everybody some long hours of putting on. We've attended funerals this month for very special people. It made me think, though. I've gone to funerals for people at work who were morons, jerks, bullies, creeps, etc. In general, they were people I either couldn't care less about or hated with every bit of my heart and soul. I now firmly believe we can make money and serve a purpose at the same time.'

"And…," David egged him on.

"First, we buy fifty acres in the middle of the nowhere in a southwest desert for practically nothing," Mack proposed, "then we buy a ton of giant soup cans.

"Giant soup cans?" David queried with mock interest.

"Yes," Barnes continued, "Finally, we advertise unmarked gravesites for all those aforementioned people that nobody ever wants to bury, visit, or even think about again. The cost would be minimal. People would provide the ashes. We would provide the desert land and we wouldn't even have to pay for upkeep or landscaping or headstones. Nobody cares! We could just have one employee who drives out there once a month. He would fill the cans with the ashes; dig the holes; bury the containers; and cover them with sand. An optional certificate, suitable for framing, would certify that their not-so-loved one is interred there. Best of all I have the perfect name for the place."

"What's that? I'm afraid to ask," David cringed at the set up and dreaded the rim shot.

Mack put him out of his misery quickly, "It would be called "**Ash Holes Are Us!**"

David hung his head and let it bob a little, "Now ***that*** sounds like something I could invest in. In fact, I know of at least a dozen potential customers. Do we have to wait until they die?"

"At this point, yes." Mack could see his plan to relieve David's stress was working. His godchild was starting to unwind and relax.

He continued to exaggerate the fictitious business arrangement,

"But we can always expand and add a "To Go" section and maybe some "Early Bird Rates".

By the time the two had exchanged 'punmanship' on the subject and every 'dead', 'stiff', 'grave', and corpse related joke had been exhausted, both were holding their sides and totally exhausted. The Coyote seemed devoid of serious thought. That, Mack hoped, would last until the next day's play for the bracelet as a member of the November Nine. Everything seemed to be falling into place. Gone was the constant scrutiny of the media. Far away was the threat of being discovered. No one but David knew anything about the filmed confession with Delta and he felt he had 'outs' on that one, anyway. The time had come to drink, share a few more laughs and then nod off in their recliners. They felt like firefighters sitting back in satisfaction and exhaustion when they return to the station after responding to a serious 911 call. They both could have laid there until early next morning if left uninterrupted.

Unfortunately, in what seemed to David to be no more than a blink of an eye, Bob Sarkasian was banging on the door and bursting into the room. The whole game had been turned turn upside down.

"Gentlemen, what we feared most has happened," Bob exclaimed, "the Casino Management has contacted me and wants the three of us and Annie at a hearing in less than an hour. I want you to remember that we prepared for this in the hopes we would never have to present Plan B. Does everyone remember their arguments? I have copies with me"

"Slow down," Mack said, at once trying to clarify and calm the situation, "Did they say what the meeting was supposed to be about?"

"I don't know," Bob lamented, but they sounded more resolute than if they were just fishing. I don't think they'd even bring this up the day before the big show if they weren't absolutely sure. We have a defense for that but they claim to have other evidence that's irrefutable. It's time to go to Plan B directly. "Call Annie and have her meet us in the executive board room ASAP!" the Shark commanded. We can win this and clear the air without going into yet another 'cloak and dagger' scenario. It's time to man-up!"

The action zipped fast forward to the board room. Bob, Mack, and Annie were all seated across from the Rio and WSOP officials. Surprisingly, many of the paparazzi were there and the media cameras were in position. A handful of poker players were in the crowd and so were a few Coyotes. Everyone, it appeared, had been tipped off. "Someone must have planned this for more than the last two hours. Somebody knew something. That's for sure," David thought to himself, 'They all must know."

The Chairman of the Board for the Casino/WSOP Management team stood in command position behind the curved table elevated at one end of the room. "We have uncovered indisputable evidence that, once and for all, confirms that the Wyllie brother about to play at the final table tomorrow is NOT the same brother who played the previous days qualifying sessions held months ago," the Chairman sounded, "and furthermore, there has been a concerted effort by many here today to collude and defraud the Casino and the World Series Main Event. We have met and are ready to rule on the fate of those involved. As part of due process, however, we will hear from any or all of you before making our ruling. Please do not insult us by denying your actions," the speaker explained, "You are each entitled to speak in your own defense or as a group through one party. When you are finished we will issue our decision and outline the consequences." Camera lights were flashing. The crowd was in stunned disbelief. Could this be true?

Annie leaned into David loud enough to be heard by Bob, "His eyes blinked on the last half. He's not totally bluffing but I sense he feels pressured to raise the ante. He really wants to fold. Did you pick up on his high heart beat and the vein in his neck, David? I think we have a chance at this one."

As everyone took their seats, the serious mood of the committee alerted the team that they were suddenly in dire straits. It was time to pull out the big guns whose rapid fire justifications would, hopefully, both answer and explain the rationale for the group's actions. Maybe because Dennis had recently walked out of the looking glass, David reflected on observations of Lewis Carroll. He recalled an appropriate line. "The time had come, the walrus said, to talk of many things: 'Of shoes and ships and ceiling wax; of cabbages and kings."

David's mind continued to wander, "The next hour," he reasoned, "would be filled with the counter logic of the Jabberwocky and the justification of an inherited, yet unexpected title through the untimely death of an older brother. It was Richard II all over again!" Bob had drafted, penned and assigned a series of independent and vaguely related arguments in search of sympathy from the panel at the Rio. It was time for David, his team, the Coyotes, and, incredibly the WSOP, to swim with The Shark.

CHAPTER THIRTY-EIGHT

Plan B

What had been escalating chatter in the audience went silent when the speaker pounded his gavel and raised his voice.

"Do any of you want to speak to this matter?"

"I'll go first," Mr. Sarkasian stated. "I'll be covering the first of four defenses, any of which, could probably stand on its own merit in finding for my client's exoneration."

Sarkasian handed each of the members of the presiding table, a sheet of paper marked "Exhibit A". He then proceeded to read the statement loudly so that the people in the cheap seats could follow along.

"My client," Bob extolled, "received, in an envelope, a copy of his baby footprints and fingerprints. Along with those documents was an expert finding that exposed a hospital error. The nurse responsible for the prints on the birth certificates simply placed the feet and hands of each baby on incorrect sheets. Neither David nor Dennis was aware that they had, in essence, been legally living their lives under each other's name."

"Therefore," Shark submitted, we present a defense we are referring to as:

'ACTUS EMENDABILI'"

"Like the 'correctable error' situation in basketball, a wrong can be corrected if no actual action has taken place in the interim. For example, a technical foul shot at the wrong basket can be corrected by retaking the shot at the correct basket if no time has expired. Once the clock moves, the opportunity is lost and the action stands. No time has expired in the Main Event. The error is correctable.

"When he saw the evidence," Sarkasian continued, "David realized that Dennis had signed up 'thinking' he was David. He had to move quickly and 'before the action resumed.' He, in fact, *was* David and had every right to amend a correctible wrong. In hindsight, he might have come forward with the information but, I submit, 'acting in what he considered to be ACTUS EMENDABILI, or amendable action, the decision he made to 'keep the ball rolling' was understandable and he asks you now to understand and appreciate his course of least resistance to correct a correctable wrong. Thank You."

"That's an interesting argument, Mr. Sarkasian. Unusual, but one the board will take under consideration but we can't promise anything more at this time."

"That's an interesting argument?" David whispered to Bob as he returned to the table, "that sounds good."

"That sounds like something I tell people when I have already made up my mind," Sarkasian shared.

The Duchess asked David, "How fast would you say his heart is beating? I can't really say he's bluffing but I know he'd rather fold than call. You count his blinks and I'll monitor his neck, veins and body touches."

You said you had FOUR defenses? Do you want to present another?" the stage questioned.

"I'll go next," David volunteered as he also had a prepared hand out and began to read, "This defense is based on previously verified documentation and we have entitled:

'INNOCENCE BY INTENT and CONVICTION'"

"Dennis committed no deception. He unknowingly registered as the wrong brother. He did so, believing himself, in good faith, to be David, the only name he had ever known. He registered incorrectly and played honestly as me. He died thinking he had played fairly. In fact, he did play entirely fair. He should not be penalized for acting on his own convictions and doing so with purity of intent. There can be no collusion either because each brother acted independently and each of the people who were privy to the information were bound to privacy by either the seal of the confessional, lawyer/client privilege, or as part of a signed and witnessed employer/employee letter of confidentiality.

Sometimes innocence is simply the absence of guilt. We submit that neither my brother nor I have ever, in truth, been anyone other than who we actually were or who we believed ourselves to be. Every action should be measured in acting on one's convictions and intent. Thank You."

"Again," the chairperson replied, "something to consider that we haven't considered to this point. Anyone else have anything else to add?"

"Mind made up!" Bob said as he turned to David upon Wyllie's return.

"The Chairman is starting to sweat," Annie whispered to the rest of the team. He looks nervous and he's sounding stronger. Weak hands always try to look invincible. We're getting an edge and I don't think he was expecting us to call their bluff. Look confident but not cocky. Look cool, calm and collected."

"I'll give it a crack," Mack volunteered, "here's my own papers and I actually have a two part defense for David." The first part is vital to the nature of competition in the poker world. Please let this defense fall under the heading of:

'LACK OF BOTH DECEPTION AND CHEATING TO GAIN AN ADVANTAGE'"

"David and Dennis were as close to even as is humanly possible. Whether it was online poker or the home tournament where they finished 1st and 2nd, they demonstrated their relative equality of play. Tomorrow, no advantage would be gained by David. If anything, this David ranked lower than the 'previous' David Wyllie who was registered by the unknowing Dennis. This 'real' David couldn't even beat his brother in a home tournament. This David earned far less in the world of computerized poker last year than the brother he replaces. No skill, no chips, no action put anyone at a disadvantage at or before the final table. That is, with the possible exception of David Wyllie, himself.

The second part of my proposed defense points the finger back at the Casino, itself. This would, then be referred to as:

'LACK OF OVERSITE BY THE RIO AND FAILURE TO FORESEE THIS SCENARIO'"

"There is no procedure in place," Barnes informed the group, "that guarantees that any other player has played hands in this or any other WSOP event for another player. No structure exists to find out if look-alike friends, not to mention twins, have ever played hands or even days for each other? If we bring up the Steinberg brothers, would it surprise you to know they 'may have' played the tournament on alternate days in 2013 to keep rested?

I want to show you all a little film clip from late in that tournament that shows that even one of the announcers, Norman Chad, humorously points out the refreshed personality of 'one' of the twins and poses a question to his broadcast partner as to whether they are playing on alternative days and/or sessions."

(At that point, a short video was played revealing the exact moment of the announcer's observation.)

"There are not even records to indicate how many twins have played in the tournament or whether they might even have switched tables on a break. Nowhere in the rules are there even conditions for the death of a player. He or she would just miss rounds until their hands were also dead. I might suggest this possibility should be addressed by the group in front of me right now. Thank You."

The Chair seemed weary, if not understandably surprised by the onslaught of defenses. "Is there a final point? Surely, Ms. Duke, a woman of your prestige and reputation wouldn't dignify this procedure by getting involved with this, would you?"

"I think I'll do just that," she said, "and I have some documents for you all as well. I was as fooled as you all were during training," Annie confessed, "but I can't sit by here and not mention the one line that appears over and over again in your contract that each player signs. You certainly stipulate repeatedly that the Rio Casino will have 'sole power to rule in any matter' but you back that up with exactly what the basis for taking action will be based upon. This, then, is a defense based within your own stated parameters:

'IN THE BEST INTEREST OF THE GAME'"

"The rules and regulations that were signed by participants cite on many occasions that the RIO will take actions when they deem them 'in the best interest of the game'. An argument can be made that the 'best interest of the game' dictates that, if you rule that either twin played illegally, every hand they were involved in should be 'null and void'. In fact, the whole tournament should be replayed from the start. This would not only be implausible, it would be impossible.

Not only is there no advantage in replacing one twin with the other, there is a consistency and a structure of single entity that presents itself uniquely in this case. David is simply making an obvious correction which satisfies the 'the best interest of the game' clause in your own manifesto. One might argue that the only thing David planned on doing was making sure the game was 'made whole' by sitting down at the final table when his name was announced.

If the RIO had questions about his identity, they should have raised them in a timely manner. Even if they did, David would have passed the test the same way he did with a polygraph on national television. He told the truth. At the very least, the final table could have been delayed for several weeks to pursue the process and it would have upset countless workers, players and those who rely on the action being played on schedule. It would NOT have been 'in the best interest of the game'. Thank you."

"Thank *you*, Ms. Duke. I can assure you that we will take time to weigh all the arguments. The board will recess in private and promises to take each of them into consideration."

The administrators, realizing some film crews had devices that can pick up whispers in the distance, removed themselves from the room to meet in private.

"If they come back in 20 minutes or less, they went with the original," Mack advised.

"If they don't come back at all," Bob added, "We won."

A half hour later the chairman approached the podium and read a short, prepared statement:

"Thank you for meeting with us today," the Chairman started. "We, as a group and organization, are satisfied, if not thoroughly convinced, that your rationales have merit. In our opinion, this matter has been settled. We are closing the file on this aspect of the tournament without any future consideration. We find that there was more awkward innocence than coordinated guilt involved. You have generated a great deal of interest in the World Series Main Event this year and we are not about to distract the entrants; detract from the Main Event; or delay the action when there appears to be a noticeable lack of victims. Congratulations and good luck to all. Now, unless someone out there has any argument to the contrary, we will find this matter officially closed. Are there any objections?"

The team was hugging and shaking hands with each other and were about to exit in celebration when the meeting was unceremoniously crashed by a newly arrived guest. The sound of oversized doors being thrown open startled the entire board room. Everyone turned in total disbelief. The press was too stunned to even raise a camera. The board took a huge gasp and the entire defense team looked at the young man who had stormed into the meeting.

"I object! I totally object." No one could believe who or what they were witnessing with their own eyes.

"I'm David Wyllie" "I'm NOT dead! I'm here to play tomorrow and no one can stop me."

"How could this be?" David told himself. I saw him buried."

The intruder kept repeating,

"I'm DAVID…..DAVID…..DAVID!"

"David, David, David!" called Mack as he shook the young Wyllie's shoulder, "You need to get up out of that recliner and go to bed. You were really tossing and turning in your sleep."

David took a deep breath and realized his body was in full lather, "I was just thinking that my life couldn't get any more complicated or staged. I guess I saw too many cheesy soap operas as a kid. With everything else in this unbelievable story, I had to add a ridiculous dream sequence to my own real life. I always hated those things when I came across them in books. I always felt like the writer was pulling the legs out from under me as a reader. Dream sequences make me feel a little unclean. I've just never had such a vivid nightmare in real life. In this case, the whole thing was just a combination of good wine, bad salsa, a lack of sleep and playing Mack's imagination games. That's what happens when the fairly intelligent me and extremely guilty me combine to fill in the blanks on tomorrow and beyond. I guess this is what they call defragging. For Freud, it was a private theater. For me, it was a packed board room. Some people have called it 'little slices of death' or 'rehearsal living.' Whatever it was, it worked. I do feel a sudden, glorious relief. I'm tired of trying to defeat the unpredictable aspects of life. Bring on the unpredictable, but understandable, game of poker!"

CHAPTER THIRTY-NINE

The Final Table

For most of the players in the November Nine, the drama was about to unfold center stage at the Penn and Teller Theatre, Rio Casino, Las Vegas Nevada. For one young man who had lost his twin brother and been subjected to incredible scrutiny from every direction, the drama seemed to be winding down a bit. David gathered himself backstage before being introduced and heading out to that Final Table. Of course, Dennis was waiting for him with an opinion, "Okay, little brother, looks like you have to win or one of us is going to have a shocker for the evening news." David didn't seem sure of himself at all, "The fact that we are even having this conversation makes me extremely uncomfortable. It would appear I'm coming apart emotionally. I have one night to maintain my sanity and make sure neither of us does anything crazy. Do you hear me?"

"The fact that I hear you is irrelevant in this whole matter," Dennis noted, "The fact that you hear me is the important thing. If you win, as expected, you're fine. If you lose, everybody out there will turn their backs on you. Have you ever seen a pack of coyotes attack? They have even been known to eat their own in the process. Win and it all comes together. Lose, and it all comes apart. Don't fret, brother, you'll know it was you who lost it. Everyone else will think it was me. David refocused and tried to distract his brother with a mixture of humor and strategy. It worked for Mack, maybe it would work for him.

"You can sit behind me because I'm the only one who can see and hear you," David instructed his twin, "I'd actually rather have you walk around the table and tell me what cards my opponents are holding. No, that would be cheating, and we wouldn't want to be accused of that, would we?"

As the other players were being introduced, the twins had one last conversation between the man of the moment and the man in the mirror. They listened to the names of their competitors at the table as they were introduced to the full house crowd.

"Our first finalist tonight," the announcer trumpeted, *"is from Mumbai, India. This 21 year old has been dubbed 'Slum Dog' because, simply by making the final table with a huge stack of chips, he is a favorite to become a millionaire tonight. Ladies and gentlemen, may I present Rahjid Gandhi."*

There was, the boys understood, no relation to the Mahatma. Gandhi is a common surname in his neck of the subcontinent. Of course, Rahjid never made the British Empire fold its hand utilizing bluff, guile, and passive resistance. The two Gandhis shared plenty of personal but non-familial traits like patience, certitude of action, and the ability to use their adversaries' strengths against them.

"Are you sure you're ready to go out there tonight?" asked Dennis, "I wouldn't go out there without protection. Just to be safe, I'd make sure I had a weapon if I were you. Oh wait, I *am* you. Where's the gun we bought at the pawn shop the other day?"

"I'm just fine without being armed. I think I'm just stressed and a little shaky in the hands and feet" replied David, "I saw the automatic pistol you left for me. I put it in the ACME bag but I put it there to make sure only I have access to it. I wouldn't want it in your possession." When David uttered the words 'your possession', the two realized how close he was to describing their crumbling and dying relationship. The introductions continued.

"He enjoys being called the 'Beast from the East'. Born 30 years ago in Viet Nam and raised for 20 years of his life in Southern California, the always formidable, C.J. Pham."

The two brothers seemed to be avoiding an all out confrontation. David felt his brother taking control of the situation and he had been getting steadily stronger daily since he left the mirror.

Another player appeared and took his seat at the table.

"Coming to the stage is a 42 year old finalist, Josef Velnokov, "Cold War" is the poker tag most of his victims have hung on him. He hails from Moscow, Russia. Please help me welcome him to the table."

"I told you to bring a weapon with you," Dennis said, in case they turn on you. You helped me pick it out. Did you forget that important piece of the puzzle?"

"I brought it just to keep you quiet." David snapped back, "I'd never use it. I'm not a violent person. Never have been; never will be." The numbers on stage were growing.

"Our next player at the table is from right here in Las Vegas. Please give a great big hand for The Rio's own 'young gun' the 22 year old David Cash. With a last name like that, no nickname is required. Give it up for local talent, folks."

The twins continued their conversation backstage.

"You've been through too much, David," his brother reminded him, think about everyone who's been out to get you recently. They're all out there and they'd love to see you lose. If you don't win I'm afraid to think what that crowd might do to you. Of course, you could just win and you'd never have to look for that hand gun."

"I have a great support team out there," David insisted, "Annie has my back and has given me great insights. The Coyotes can't stop hootin' and hollerin'. Our godparents, Mack and Sherri have been incredible mentors. My lawyer found every strategy he could muster to get me through the tough stuff I've had to face, and, of course, I have you. Can I count on you?"

"This next 'young man' is our only senior citizen at the Final Table. Please help me welcome "Cannonball Holland" who is 56 years young today. Cannonball was playing poker long before some of tonight's competitors were even born."

"Annie knows I sucked out on the river when I knocked her out of the tournament," Dennis said, trying to inflame the situation, "I cost the Duchess a chance to win the only thing she hasn't won: the ultimate poker bracelet. She's setting you up to get back at me. Those 'fans' of yours will turn on you if you mess things up. You **pay** your lawyer. Mack and Sherri were never that close until we made that little game of theirs famous. They don't care about you. NOBODY HONESTLY CARES ABOUT YOU! They're all just waiting for a payday or for you to fuck it up." Both scripts have them coming after you en masse the minute you win or lose! Look for the signs. There'll be people there to take you away if you don't win. Look around. If you don't, I will. I'll be your wingman. I owe you at least that, little bro." David and Dennis exchanged silent stares as the announcer brought on the other last three opponents in the 'November Nine'.

"*From the Pampas of Argentina, please welcome Pablo 'El Toro' Torrealba. The 44 year old Pablo has certainly earned 'the bull' tag with his charging table talk. This is the second top 20 finish for Torrealba and he tells me he plans on winning it all this time.*"

"*Right behind "El Toro" is 33 year old Englishman, Richard Kingslyl. No nickname. No expression. He's English. He's 'proper'. What else would you expect from the London upper class? Please, people, a proper welcome to the only bona fide gentleman in the group.*"

The master of ceremonies continued.

"*From the land down under is the leader of the only group that can yell as loud as Coyotes. Put your hands together for the 'Aussie with the Posse', Jonas McKenzie.*"

With that, an immediate and somewhat obnoxious chant bellowed from the Land Down Under section: "Aussie, Aussie, Aussie, Oi!, Oi!, Oi!"

The color commentator, Norman Chad pleaded, "I never thought I'd say this but, Can I get a Coyote Howl?"……please, someone, anyone? I thought we heard the last of that when Joe

Hachem won the Main Event"

"We'd better get ready. What's that you're holding in your hand?" Dennis asked David.

"It's a special jersey. I was saving it as a surprise. Remember I told you it was an 'in your face', or should I say, 'in *our faces* theme?" David reminded his counterpart. "I'll put it on while they call my name. I'm beginning to wonder if I subconsciously picked it up for some other, more sinister, reason," he said under his breath, hoping his brother didn't hear him." Lately, David realized that Dennis had become the one who was starting their conversations. Dennis was the one who seemed in control. Dennis seemed desperate to make his mark on the Main Event since he felt robbed of his opportunity to play in it and finish his triumphant march. Dennis, he surmised, would not accept even a 2nd place finish because would have felt that should have won it all. David looked down into his bag of tricks. There was no rabbit in there this time. The only things he could see were snacks, that infamous tangerine, and a fully loaded, semi-automatic handgun the twins had bought and placed there just this morning. David knew he would never have put it in there on his own.

"And finally, the young man you've all heard so much about recently. He's been through a terrible tragedy in his personal life; added color and excitement to this year's tournament almost every day; and comes in with over half the chips on the table. Here he is. I think we need to show him that we are all glad to have him here with us this evening: David 'The Coyote' Wyllie. What do you have in that Acme 'bag of tricks' for us tonight, young man?"

The man with the microphone didn't realize just how big that question was. Luckily, for David, it was meant rhetorically. Both brothers walked out onto the stage to resounding applause and coyote howls. One was invisible to the crowd.

Dennis was wearing the current Phoenix Coyote jersey with a howling mascot head on the front. In what was seen by many as a gesture of brotherly support, the chip leader was wearing the old, long since replaced uniform of the Phoenix Coyotes. It was now just an 'alternate jersey' worn for special occasions and 'throw back' nights. The logo was a stylized, part Indian kachina doll and part cave drawing coyote image with a hockey stick in its hands. Most of the National Hockey League hated the old jersey because it looked like a coyote with either two heads or one head that seemed to be splitting in two. It had been bizarre to most of the hockey world, confusing to many others, and a bit troubling in a nightmarish way to the rest.

For David, it represented his divided personas. Annie Duke hoped it was a sign of support but she feared it was a clue that something might be brewing deep inside her student, her apprentice. She kept looking at the split head or heads and wondered if it signaled trouble. She knew that, in David's mind, the two were inseparable but seemed to be coming apart at absolutely the worst possible time. Her concerns were legitimate and, after the tournament, win or lose, she promised herself to get him to a rehab center she trusted.

"Let's just get through the final table," the Duchess told herself. "Let's just make it through the night!"

After everything he had faced in the last two months, she suddenly felt more like a big sister than a coach. Annie had come to care about the boy. His mental health was deteriorating. Thank God this was the last time he'd have to perform. Maybe tomorrow he could just live his life and get away. It was a new Coyote who took his seat. He seemed a little nervous. Although no one but David could see his brother, Dennis was smiling from ear to ear. It was if he knew he was in control. David suddenly realized that even the last conversation *in front* of the mirror had been ignored by his dead sibling and that was before his 'coming out party'.

The final table had a 15-minute delay before it was televised. That allowed each team of coaches to let their players know when someone had been bluffing, slow playing, or doing things by the book. It also, obviously, prevented anyone from seeing the cards as they were played and relaying that information to another player. Some final tables lasted for 24 hours or more and could be more than a little boring for the audience. It seemed most of the crowd was just interested in which one of these players would gather enough of everyone else's chips to duel Wyllie head-to-head.

David's job was simple. He reviewed his strategies, "Play only the hands you know you can win. Don't risk your huge stack. Let the others devour each other until the final two remain. "Oh, and if you can, make sure you have more chips that they do," Annie had advised him.

One by one, each of the small stacks were forced to play all their chips. The increasingly expensive blinds they were required to post were slowly eating away their money, hand by hand. After more than an hour, the first to go was the Englishman. It was the horrible scene players all dread: the 'ace on the river'. Some victims curse, scream, or fall to the ground in frustration. Kingsly simply put on his blazer and shook everyone's hand at the table. It was an upper crust, chin up, tally ho scene right out of Masterpiece Theatre. "Good show old boy!" Mack would have said.

Two more hours went by before the Russian bluffed, the old pro called and the Argentine saw a chance to triple up. The 'bull' pushed his whole pile into the center. The other two followed suit. When the dust had settled, one blew a goodbye kiss to his grandkids and grandma; one hugged his little bovine card marker; and the other stacked his chips while humming 'Somewhere My Love', the theme from **Dr. Zhivago**. Only six were left in the barnyard but the Russian had moved up in the pecking order. He still had to worry about the Coyote but he had his sights on the kid. During the dinner break, David went over to Annie and told her that Dennis was upsetting him.

"He has me confused. He wants me to fight back if I lose. He's sure that I'm in trouble and he's getting a little scary. I don't know if he's 'on the brink' or not. He seems a little paranoid and not in contact with reality. I'm not sure what he has planned but I don't know if I can stop him. Maybe the fact that he's dead is affecting his judgment. I'm worried he might do harm to someone, maybe even me, if we lose." Annie really didn't have to rely on her degree in Psychology at this point. She knew David had never really grieved the way he should have. She had seen the accelerated split with his brother. He had been taking prescriptive drugs since the Milano

Show and the pressure was getting to him. She wondered if this mild-mannered, gentle soul had reached his breaking point.

"David," Duke instructed him, "I want you to know we all love you and that, when this is over, you'll need to see a friend of mine who has a place for you to get some help. You need to get away from all the attention and just work it out. You can deal with this, David. I have total confidence in you." Of course, that was a lie. Now she had to worry that David might actually do harm to *himself*. When David left, Annie immediately went to security. Duke let them know she had reason to believe that more of a presence in numbers and a closer collective proximity to the table would be a good idea. She told them that she could be overreacting but they still should play it safe. They respected her and trusted her instincts. The chief of security decided they'd rather err on the side of caution. There would be increased presence on the stage. After the break, it was obvious that the talented but chip poor Pham and the veteran Cash were running on empty and went out on consecutive hands to the Coyote, who had little to lose by making calls on both. Not long after that, Mckenzie and his Aussie Posse were silenced once and for all by the Slum Dog. This Final Table was averaging one casualty per hour…very fast in 'poker years'. The fact that the Coyote had such deep pockets was definitely the prime factor. David counted his chips and knew he could let Velnokov and the Indian decide who got the 7 million and who would go home with the 4 million. It would be one of those *win/win even bigger* dilemmas. The Russian played his hands a little like the old Kenny Rogers song. He knew when to hold 'em and he forced 'you' to fold 'em. He gradually built a sizeable lead on the young Asian. At one point, Slumdog played through the flop by checking with a King high flush. Rahjid min-raised his way to trap the Russian. Gandhi knew he couldn't lose. The only Ace that could beat him was on the board. He decided to make it look like he was making a bully bluff and wagered his entire stack. The Russian bought was he determined was an over bet 'bluff' and called with three of a kind. After that, it only took a few hands for the Gandhi to send his crippled Russian opponent home in third place. In the end, flushes beat straights and the only movie theme being hummed was Ballywood.

We live in a dog-eat-dog world and this time, stretching it a bit for its advertising value, it was a canine classic. The Coyote was taking on the Slum Dog with the same questions that would be asked if the two had a confrontation in nature. How wild and vicious is your Coyote? How big is your Dog?

Four armed guards brought brief cases of money and dumped them on the table while casino models placed the sacred bracelet center stage. Ten Million dollars were on the table and even more guards carefully positioned themselves behind the dealer and the players on stage.

David didn't even notice them.

Dennis did!

CHAPTER FORTY

Under the Gun

Some years the classic 'heads up' would last for hours. Some years it would end sooner. The whole matter seemed to come down to one player having a great hand and his opponent having a better one. Both players had guaranteed themselves a multimillion dollar payoff but bragging rights, poker immortality and that priceless bracelet were still on the line. Each year, when the final two come out of their corners, it's more like a battle for the world heavyweight boxing championship. The audience called for left hooks, short jabs, counter punches, haymakers, upper cuts, combinations, and crosses. Mack, the consummate coach, wanted defense. The combatants were timid in the early 'rounds'. Both started slowly with each feeling the other out. They bobbed and weaved; feigned punches with minor bluffs and short leads. When one was on the ropes, he seemed to sidestep traps with the instincts that had helped him survive the week long tourney to this point. The fans sat back and prepared for this one to 'go the distance'. In the world of pugilism they often refer to the sport of boxing as 'the gentlemen's art of self defense'. Sometimes, however, one, or both parties throw caution to the wind and run amok of the rules. Sometimes, people go to a boxing match and a fight ensues. When that happens, it might only take one punch before one is lying on the canvas looking up at the lights and the other is raising his arms to the heavens. In that scenario, the crowd swoops in and lifts the champion up and onto their shoulders. This was one such story but the winner would be carried off in a manner no one saw coming. The end was about to come swiftly in the next hand or two. Maybe the both players were just exhausted. Maybe neither one really cared about the extra three million dollars.

In any event, Slum Dog looked at his cards and bet three million. David called. The dealer buried one card and then spread three cards on the flop: Ace/King/8, with two hearts. Both players checked when the turn was a Queen of diamonds. When the last card was the Ten of hearts, it made both the chances of a flush and straight possible. There was always the possibility one of them had three of a kind but not probable because of the checks. The Slum Dog put all his chips at risk. The crowd hummed with excitement as they rose to their feet. The Indian could take his first big lead or the whole tourney was about to come to an end. David turned to his brother who was sitting just behind him on his right. To the other players it appeared he leaned back with outstretched arms and looked to the heavens.

"What would YOU do?" David asked his brother almost silently, showing him the two cards in his hand.

Dennis had a solution for a win and a solution for a loss. He got up and walked around the table to get a look at the Indian's hand but the cards were flat on the felt. Dennis knew, win or lose, David would be all over the news the next day. If David lost, Dennis would win. If David won, they'd BOTH win. The deceased Wyllie sat down in a position just above the ACME bag and was posed for action. He looked down at the pistol. In fact, he had already decided who he would shoot first if he lost. That scene would get more than a little dicey.

Dennis went back to his brother. "I can't tell you what to do but I know what I'd do!"

David glanced into the ACME bag Sherri had made for his brother. He took a long look at the automatic weapon next to a tangerine and partially concealed by a top hat. He knew that, if he failed to win the bracelet, Dennis would reach in and grab the gun. He couldn't let that happen but he felt powerless against his late brother. Somehow, he knew he would take all the blame and everyone would think he had fired the shot. "After all, the two of us look so much alike," he realized.

"Lots of people have tried but failed to tell one of us from the other," David told himself, "They'll think I acted alone whether I shoot the dealer, Gandhi, the whole place or just myself."

"Call Time and think about the story Mack told us about the 'omen' and what it means," Dennis suggested.

Both brothers were calm, almost too calm. The crowd was in stun mode. Sherri turned to Mack and asked, "What's he waiting for? Does he know what he's doing?"

Mack wrapped his right arm around his wife's shoulder with a firm hug and told her, "If I know the boys, and I do, this will be a team decision. He's talking to Dennis and probably doesn't know we're even here."

Quite the opposite, they were talking about a story Barnes told them once. Since this was such a monumental decision, his Indian opponent would give him as much time as he needed to make up his mind. Calling 'Time!' on your opponent can send the message that you are impatient and nervous, even weak. After all, he was a Gandhi. Even the Mahatma knew that 'doing nothing' could be the ultimate sign of strength. Passive resistance is a calm power that puts pressure on your opponent without expending any risk or energy. In the end, it sent the British Empire packing.

The boys were still talking. It wasn't exactly the time for a 'Mack Attack' but David remembered the story his brother was referring to. Mack had said that he woke up on the 6th day of the 6th month, 1966 and looked at the clock. The time read 6:06! He got up, ran to the paper on his porch and checked the 6th race at Santa Anita. There was a long shot named Route 66. He called his bookie, and bet his last $500 on that horse. When the boys asked him if the horse won, Mack fired back, "No, the son of a bitch finished 6th!"

"So don't bet on omens?" they asked.

"Always bet on omens," Barnes replied, "You just have to think them out before you go off half-cocked!" "They always work," Mack added, "just not always the way you thought they would!"

David called 'Time!" on himself. Everyone, including the dealer, the Slum Dog, the live audience, and, even Norman Chad were flabbergasted he had called, 'Time!'.

"No one in this situation ever calls time on themselves," said Chad. Under strict rules, another player at the table has to make that call. When the floor man pointed this out, Slum Dog offered to make the call as a gesture of chivalry, if David agreed. David agreed. He had one minute to act or his hand would be folded. He would be in second place for the first time in the finals.

"I think the pressure's gotten to him. The lad has given himself one minute to make up his mind," Chad's partner Len explained to the television fans at home.

In fact, David had one minute to make up two minds. He looked at his cards again and wondered what omen his identical twin was talking about. The floor man walked over and said, "I will count down from 10 and then, if you haven't acted, your hand is dead"

"My hand is 'dead'?" David said to himself, "That's it! That's what Dennis was trying to tell me. The omen is real!" How could I have missed it?"

"I CALL!" said the Coyote.

Everyone was still on their feet but now they were leaning forward, waiting to see cards. Slum Dog, having been called, had to show his cards first. He threw down his two pair: Kings and 8's. All eyes and cameras shifted to Wyllie. David knew the media would have a field day replaying this reveal. He had to, just this ONE TIME, slow roll each card separately. First he also revealed an 8. Then to the yells and a few jeers from the crowd, he turned over the Ace: Aces and Eights. A higher two pair. He had his bracelet. He was king of the poker world.

What his brother had tried to point out, in a twist of fate, was an omen that let David play Dennis' hand and vice versa. Historically speaking, 'Aces and Eights', is the hand Wild Bill Hickok was holding when he was shot in the back and killed during a poker game in Deadwood, Dakota Territory. From that day forward, 'Aces and Eights' had been known to all poker aficionados as "The Dead Man's Hand." This time it was all too apropos. This time it was literal. This time the omen worked. "This time the 'son of a bitch' finished first," Mack would later tell his wife, the Coyotes, and anyone else who listen.

The Champaign popped, the announcers made their way to the table in front of all the cameras. The Indian shook Wyllie's hand and both raised their arms together. The bracelet was presented and the money, after being photographed to death, was being picked up by a team of guards for transport to the vaults and safe keeping.

The young Coyote ran from the table. He was trying to find Dennis. Annie knew she had to run after him. Grabbing the ACME bag he had left under his chair, Duke was careless and all hell broke loose. As she went to pick up the satchel, she bumped against the table and lost her hold on one of the two straps. As she did, the bag tipped and the automatic weapon fell to the ground. Someone yelled, "Gun!" The crowd either fell to the floor or retreated toward the exits. Annie found herself with raised arms and instructed by security to go down on her knees. Photographers caught the action and that gave David a chance to make his way away backstage in pursuit of his twin. He was still looking around when Annie finally convinced casino police that the bag and gun were not hers. Two officers confiscated the weapon and accompanied her to stage wings.

"What are you doing back here?" the Duchess asked David.

"I had to find my brother," the Coyote told her.

"Did you bring a gun to the table tonight, David?" Annie asked as security grabbed the arms of the champion.

Tears were streaming down his face. He kept looking back at the empty hallway.

"What did your brother say to you, David?" Annie asked, concerned about his state of mind. "Why did you have a pistol in your bag?"

"I was afraid Dennis would use it if we lost, Annie," Wyllie admitted, "I wanted to make sure it was in my possession and not his."

"These officers are going to have to take you for questioning," Annie told him, "but I'll be right there with you and, later, I'll be taking you to someone I know. Did you have a chance to talk to your brother a final time?"

"Annie, he said good-bye and told me I was now on my own. He said that he almost stayed too long. He told me I was going be just fine."

"That's a *good* thing, David," his mentor assured him.

"I know," agreed the champ, "but I've never been alone before. I think I'll need help. You'll never believe what he, what we, what I, almost did."

"I think you got help from your brother," Annie went on,

"and I think you just need a little extra help from someone I know. Dennis decided to leave. That, alone, was a major milestone in your recovery. You just have to relax and let this whole thing calm down. It's only a poker game. You won twice tonight and you're going be better for both. You'll find a way to be okay. Come along now with these officers and me. Let me do the talking. You're going to be fine now. You'll, most certainly, be just fine."

The WSOP Main Event Champion didn't stay for interviews, at least not on camera. He was accompanied by police who stood behind him and placed handcuffs on his wrists just minutes after the Rio had presented him with the bracelet. He was led off to jail after having been escorted to the podium. Not exactly raised on shoulders and carried off in victory, but certainly 'in the arms of security'. David was being booked downtown as his name was engraved on the perpetual plaque along with the legends. His interviews that night took the form of a lengthy interrogation.

Finally, friends posted his bail while his Coyotes calculated their shares. Mack, Annie, Dottie and Sherri accompanied him to the hospital where he spent the night diagnosed with total exhaustion. Two days later he took a break from his treatment and appeared with his mentor and coach on the Today Show via satellite. David announced that he "was suffering from depression and a sort of 'post traumatic stress disorder.'" In actuality, David Wyllie had every right to suffer from PTSD. His brother was killed. He went to and spoke at his own funeral. He had beaten a polygraph on national television and he had made a deal with the devil through his brother. Delta, the confession and her 'consortium' were still hanging over his head. Finally, he had just won the Main Event, even though he only played poker in Vegas for just less than 8 hours. Of course he had been traumatized. He lived for months in a state of complete disorder. Finally, "Who ever heard of someone suffering from 'Pre' Traumatic Stress Disorder?" Mack would add, "That's just called nerves."

CHAPTER FORTY-ONE

Mo Power to You

Mack had observed, "Lawyers only have to pass the bar once and then they visit it regularly to meet with others of the same breed." In this case, the Coyotes survived the wolves. They also overcame a Slum Dog, a Duchess, A Raisen' Asian, a Giant, Milano, and the rest of the November Nine.

Father Jinks, Sherry, Dottie, Bob and, surprisingly, a fully recovered Ruby had saved a table at Hennesy's, a local bar across from the hospital.

"You didn't think I'd live almost 90 years without being in Vegas for all the marbles, did you?" Ruby asked.

All of the inner circle team gathered to celebrate their unbelievable journey.

"It was a bit much for all of us but none of us completely understood what the boy was experiencing," Father Jinks commented, "I knew about the conversations with his brother but I attributed them to conscience."

"I knew about how David worried about acting out if he didn't win," Annie added, "but I'm afraid to speculate on what other issues he was dealing with. I think I know but it sounds like you guys know a hell of a lot more." She was till reading everyone's tells more than their 'don't tells'. She decided it was better *not* to know some things.

"I knew the two were inseparable, "Mack admitted, "I thought he just had to self-diagnose and self-prescribe treatment. He always seemed to be capable of just about anything he took on and competent enough to survive."

Dottie summarized, "We all had strategies, Plan B's, scripted press interviews, and poker advice. None of us, including me, saw the danger he was in. We never took the time to sit down, as a team, and share our concerns and observations. We almost lost him the way we lost his father. We didn't recognize the signs. In fact, we ignored the obvious markers. I'm most to blame, having lost a family member once before. We all, David included, got caught up in the excitement, the spectacle, and the effort David was making on behalf of his twin."

"Let us all join hands and say a prayer of thanks that the Lord was looking out for David," the good Father said, looking forward and redirecting the room's energy."

"Amen," the team chimed in.

After an awkward moment of silence, Mack slapped his hands together and offered, "So much for this year. What about keeping the team together for next year's home game?" No one seemed to use words in retaliation. Instead, they released their emotions and condiments on Mack. They dowsed him with ketchup, mustard, relish, cokes and beer until he looked more like a Jackson Pollack canvas. The tension had been cracked and Barnes had it coming.

"He's being released as we speak and will be joining us in a few minutes before he checks back into rehab," Annie announced.

The priest had one more suggestion, "how about some wings, taters skins and some zucchini?"

"Here's to one hell of a roller coaster ride these past months with a wild band of wonderful people!" Sarkasian barked.

"Here's to the people who didn't make it back to the station," David added soberly as he walked into the bar. There was a chorus of 'here, here' and at least one "Amen" from the priest who had already gulped half the frosted schooner he had raised above his head.

Amid the hugs and tears, Sherri's eyes were zeroing in on the television set in the center of the room. "Why is David's picture on the screen?" she asked. Everyone looked up and Sherri ran to the bar, trying to hear what was being said.

"Turn it up, turn it up, bartender…..this is important!" Sherri pleaded.

It was the Monique Power Show or 'Mo Power to You', as it was billed.

"She's the first female to have a paternity show of her own," Sherri explained, "before this it was either Jerry or Maury.

"And she's not afraid to call a whore a whore," Ruby added, "She doesn't coddle those girls. After all, when I was young, there were a lot of names to call women who didn't know which of three men were their baby's father. None of those names was 'victim'. The whole group was momentarily stunned by Ruby's blatant opinion but quickly turned back to the screen. Mo was engaged with a couple. On the monitor behind them was a picture of David Wyllie and a scrawny little baby boy who looked just like the man who just won the World Series of Poker. A husky fella named, Donnie, was facing the hostess. Donnie made no bones about what he thought or why he thought that way, "Does that child look like he's mine, Miss Power? Well, does he?" The man made a point and the audience seemed to agree. Mack agreed, "Unless that baby is planning to overeat for the next twenty years and get a red neck buzz cut hairdo with a red dyed mullet along the way, that baby looks more like the Coyote than that lady's boyfriend." It was unanimous. Almost everyone could make a case that the child in the picture actually looked more like a David than it looked like Donnie.

"I tried to get David Wyllie to take a DNA test when my wife told me she had cheated on me when she was a cruise ship dancer. His people put me off. That's why I decided to go a whole 'nother direction," the good old boy went on, "Miss Power, I don't want his money. I love little Justin and I hope he loves me. I'll stand up for the kid and treat him like my own." The crowd sympathetically applauded as Donnie raised his hand to stop the tears.

"Will you still continue to be a husband if he's not yours?" Power asked.

"I don't know mam," Donnie softly acknowledged and then wiped a tear from his cheek, "I don't know. I hope it doesn't come to that, but that there picture just don't lie."

Mo Power picked up the envelope and said, "when it comes to little Justin, Donnie… …."

"Why the hell do they have to go to commercial when you can't fast forward to the answer?" asked Ruth.

After a series of commercials, the show finally came back on. The rest of the patrons at the bar had joined the team in front of the monitor. One intoxicated customer walked in and asked, "Does anyone object if we switch to the hockey game?"

A resounding "YES, We ALL Do" blasted in his face. T h a t was followed by 'Shushes' and 'Quiets' before the camera rejoined Monique, who slowly repeated "when it comes to little Justin, Donnie….. Power gave the entire audience and everyone watching at home a chance to mouth their guesses…..

You….ARE the father!

Tears, hugs, and kisses filled the bar. People who didn't know Donnie or Justin or even David grabbed each other and celebrated the announcement.

The same thing happened back at the television studio. The Coyote team had just made it to what they saw as the finish line. There were no other hurdles, they thought, in their way. They could finally go back to Temecula in peace.

"One last thing," David said as he motioned the group to settle down and listen, "I have one more announcement that I will be making when I'm permanently out of rehab and feeling like myself. It's something I just have to do. I don't want any of you to worry about it and I'd like you all to be there. It's my way of saying goodbye to Dennis and I mean that in so many ways. No questions. Trust me on this one. "Is anyone up for a group hug?" David offered. They were all up for anything at this point.

CHAPTER FORTY-TWO

The Pack is Back!

What happened to the Coyotes? Each one proudly wore their adventure like a Boy Scout would. Each one would have a different badge to sew onto their sash.

Bryce Tanner, the man who will forever be remembered as the guy who showed people how *not* to play a pair of Jacks, parlayed his one-hand loss into his dream improvements on his new house in Austin, Texas. He already had the land and he didn't quite have enough money to make it into 'Bear Country'. He did, however, have enough ($100,000) to finish his house and barn. When Mack and Sherri finally got a chance to visit the Tanners they were wowed. Bryce had a magnificent pool, a 3300 sq. ft. house and barn on over 5 acres. Mack and Sherri had to laugh and shake their heads as they walked into the foyer. Over the two story river rock fire place was a 5 by 8 foot painting of his had-to-have bears….playing poker! Good to see he got the last laugh on being 'first out'.

As promised, Father Jinks turned his money over the

Archbishop's Relief Fund. The pastor had played the game; shared the tribulations of David in the confessional; and, true to his vocation, given him sound religious, moral and ethical advice. In spite of trying to do the right thing, he was actually glad everything turned out the way it did. Next year he had an open invitation from the Barnes family to attend the Kentucky Derby in person. For a pony loving priest, 'Church'hill Downs, with its legendary 'steeples' sounded almost sanctified. Jinks knew it would be a pilgrimage he would be willing to make. Mack and Sherri were picking up the tab. Jinks was in demand for guest speaking and he always had a great homily based on one of the Wyllie Coyotes stories to captivate his congregation.

Jonny Collison bought a customized minivan. He was able to get in and out of places in his wheelchair that he could never have imagined before. With some of his winnings he was able to put people to work. The friends who 'pimped his ride' started a little garage with Jon's help. They've been able to grow the business of converting Kia Souls for the disabled. Anyone in a wheelchair could now slide in through the rear door and right into the driver's seat. Some of their most cherished clients are injured veterans of Afghanistan and Iraq. They've been able to partner with the Wounded Warrior Program to help facilitate the normalization of those who sacrificed for their country. Against Mack's advice, Jon did buy that racehorse. Collison named him *Poker Prophet* but everyone around the stables called him *Card Dead* behind Jonny's back. The horse ran three times as two year old and finished 5th once. Jonny finally sold the equine at a drastic loss and never went back to the track again. He had attracted an admirer from his only Coyote TV interview and she moved in with him. They're talking wedding. That can be a good thing for a lifelong bachelor. As Mack always said, "I feel sorry for single men. They can each go through their whole life without ever realizing they're making mistakes." That remark usually earned him a punch in the arm from Sherri.

Katy Knight renewed her wine club membership and used most of her money to better the lives of others. Her husband made sure of that. Charity work was not a new thing for Kay but it's still a great place to make up for family secrets and insure a return to marital harmony.

In this case she picked a good one. She and her husband, along with Mack and Sherri formed an organization that facilitates the access of family members to their deceased relatives who happen to be undocumented immigrants like Domingo. Hernandez' body had remained at the mortuary for two weeks until his father could travel by truck to make a 'legal' identification. His common law wife and kids didn't qualify. The organization provides confidential legal advice, financial aid for travelling relatives from other countries, and provides post mortem shortcuts to insure that the proper respect and services are afforded families in a timely manner. Katy also wants to use $10,000 of her winnings to travel to Vegas for the Main Event next year. Husband Tom said 'maybe'.

Calvin Moffett had a couple of girls heading for college on partial scholarships so some of the money went for their education. He and his wife had always wanted to check out the wonderful world of time shares. Calvin started his own computer business and retired as a jailer. His wife hired a housekeeper and a pool boy. Moffett replaced the Oakland Raider T-shirt he always wore with a Coyote jersey. There would always be some extra bucks for 'bling' around the collar.

Ahmed Kahlid invested most of his money at the poker table. Ahmed parlayed his little bit of fame into 'local hero' status. He wears a Wile E. Coyote T-shirt at the casino and certainly gets the most out of it. He gets free drinks, free lunches and 40% off the Lobster Buffet on Fridays. Life is sweet. God is good. Ahmed knows gambling money and gaming fame are fleeting but, for Kahlid, every week is 'fleet week.'

Randy Halemano went right on teaching. He and wife, Nancy, threw a well-deserved luau for the group a couple of months ago. During the invocation, Randy raised a Mai Tai in a toast. He asked the gods to make sure Herb, Domingo and Dennis would 'find their way back to the earth, the fire, the sea, and their own god who created them." He also reminded the crowd that Pele's curse had been negated. Halemano didn't know why, but David could never have been the gay virgin father of Dennis' shipboard love child. Randy reminded the Coyotes of how 'The Hawaiian Entourage' had 'let off steam' near the lava tube and found a way to rekindle the family spirit of Ohana. It would, forever, bind together David, Dennis, and Coyote Nation. Somehow the Kailua pork and banana leave wrapped fish brought flavor to the message. Mack was so inspired by the speech that he had a plaque put outside the cabin at Big Bear. It reads, "When trouble erupts like a volcano, go with the flow, bro." At present, Randy and his wife are in the process of buying land with Mack and Sherri for that upscale manufactured home retirement park they plan on calling "Rainbow Villages". They are counting on investments from some of the other Coyotes.

Big Jake Wayland bought a case of the very best Scotch and each of his sponsoring co-workers collected a half year's salary. He built his mother-in-law a separate 'casita' where they visit her any time she remembers their phone number or Sunday mornings, whichever occurs first. Karly got a trip to Palm Springs that included matching robes. Jake snuck in and put chocolate candies on their pillows. Wayland shaved his beard and looks forty again. Okay, the beard stayed, but the bounce in his step from having money in the bank made him seem at least a dozen years younger.

Dr. Herb's widow, Joy, used most of their money on things the insurance hadn't paid for during the cancer battle. She got enough money to buy her own place near the beach in San Diego. She has been given honorary Coyote status by the group and posed for the home game photo at tourney's end. Joy went right on playing poker in the appropriate 'Survivor' tourney each week in the Pechanga Poker Room where she and Herb had been a cherished couple.

T.R. is now a bachelor with a BIG dog. He might be serious this time. He and Dick started a consulting firm that concentrates on making the two of them rich. The company minors in helping struggling businesses. Together, they're a hoot. T.R. presented each of the Coyotes and David trophies at the Luau. Dick sang a medley of songs that dealt with poker during an impromptu karaoke session. He stretched the envelope with songs like, "Little *Deuce Coupe*", "*Call* Me", and "Jumpin' *Jack* Flash". He dedicated the last one to Bryce Tanner.

Coach Buck put most of his million plus in the bank. He donated new uniforms to his high school team and set up a youth camp in town. Stan also initiated camping scholarships for talented kids who didn't have the money. He paid for their parents to travel with them and, just maybe, allow them to fall in love with the town of Temecula. The question, Mack proposed was: "Is that recruiting or just home spun hospitality?"

Domingo's money was the most contentious. He didn't pay anything to enter and promised to 'settle up' with Angel after the tournament. One new auto shop arrived in town, though, and Domingo's wife and kids will be well taken care of. Maria Fernandez was undocumented, as was Angel and the late Domingo. Each would have had a hard time pressing legal and financial issues since none of them had any written contract and 'settle up' as a verbal agreement is weak at best. Here's how the whole thing shook out. Bob Sarkasian and Mack brokered a signed agreement and all parties were amenable. Joe received $3000 or ten times his entry. Mack would received the same, which he gave to Maria 'under the table' in honor of her late husband's method of payment for most of his handy work. Angel received $150,000 and used it to start that auto shop. Maria received $150,000; and a trust fund was set up for the Fernandez children who, hopefully, would find success following in the footsteps of their father.

Bob, for acting pro bono, got a huge prime rib dinner down at Rainbow Oaks Restaurant along the I-15 Freeway.

Speaking of Bob, he managed to play the role of legal team

leader to perfection. The national spotlight was kind to him. Sarkasian remains in constant demand. The $400,000 was a nice little bonus but he has been asked to join Annie on her crusade to make on-line poker legal and honestly monitored. Bob lost some weight, found a way to understand his daughter, and realized that success is not measured in dollars alone. He has become more human, but is still a lawyer and hustler. The last two terms just might be redundant. He will always be Bob. He still gambles, drinks, and tells dirty jokes. The Shark lives life large. To his credit, he gave his daughter enough money to open her own pet retreat. She wanted to call it, "Good Dog Stay" complete with hotel, spa, outdoor swimming pool and "wreck" room. Ironically, she found out the name was cute but already owned by some other groomer. Her daddy offered to buy the rights.

Ruby resumed playing poker and gave a large portion of her $1.2 million in winnings to her grandchildren in the form of college funds. She also started a Women's Tournament. If men play and are knocked out, they each receive lovely parting gifts chock-full of female hygiene items. As Ruby put it, "Some of them can use it and all of them can find a place to spray it, wear it, or stick it!"

That was just Ruby. She invited dealer Washington Evans to join her as a travelling companion on a cruise around the Mediterranean. They enjoy each other's wit and conversation as friends, nothing more. Sherri asked her, "Don't you worry people will talk about you sharing a large suite with a good looking, charming, younger man?"

Ruby, as only she could, stepped back, feigning surprise and answered, "Good God, I HOPE so. In fact, I'm *counting* on it!"

Probably the wildest story revolved around the M.I.A, Steve Purcell. His mom is staying with his brother who receives a mystery stipend for care giving. "Steve," Mack explained to the group at the luau, "appears to have played both ends against the middle." Mack went on, "He must have been pissed off when Delta and her consortium tried to rip him off, along with the rest of the Coyotes. He joined up with the Chicago group and was hired to, basically, take over the process. Sorry, that's why none of you ever saw Delta again. I heard a few of you discussing her visits. Turns out, state and federal agents had been out to get those guys for years. All they needed was somebody on the inside. Steve was that man. He worked as a double agent, collecting pay from both. He accepting mob money for the Coyote's interests with phony papers; got Delta to testify with him; and then became part of the witness protection plan where he also got a bonus and that 'start over' he was looking for." Purcell became a new man in a new town with a new wife. It wasn't Delta. Steve paid his brother handsomely to be their mom's caregiver, using his $850,000 he collected through the feds. With the money he got from the Chicago group and never returned, Steve is just another millionaire."

"Not a bad gig for the old guitar man. Hopefully, he can stay off the booze and drugs. He should be high enough on life," Mack added.

David fully recovered from his 'close to' meltdown. He was recently named 'Man of the Year' by one of the largest Gay and Lesbian organizations. When presented with the award, he took the opportunity to honor his dead brother with what turned out to be more than just the contribution of $1.4 million. With tears in his eyes, days after his win, in front of a huge audience of admiring fans, he told the crowd, "My brother, Dennis, was a man of immeasurable integrity. When he told me he was gay, I was shocked. I'm his twin brother and we shared almost everything. We had the 'twin radar' most people confuse with 'two bodies, one mind'. I have to admit that he was the better brother." I want to thank you all for the honor you have bestowed on me. I want to do more to honor my brother today. I want to share a secret with all of you. I have been living a lie for quite some time. It is now time to reveal the truth to the world."

The crowd leaned forward in anticipation. Mack and Sherri were in the stands. The media suddenly shifted from their human interest story to 'breaking news' and 'sports follow-up'. Mack turned to Sherri and said, "This should be interesting." Sherri looked Mack in the eye and replied, "Did you know he was going to do this?"

"The boy has to do what he has to do. He's been lying for so long that he might not want to face another day without truth. At the risk of being obvious, he might want to protect someone's good name."

David backed away from the microphone and looked down at the stage. He took a moment to gather himself. With a tear in his eye and a breaking voice he raised his head resolutely.

"Today, I join my brother and hope that I can live up to his courage when he admitted he was gay. Today, I admit what I can no longer deny. Like my brother, I am also a gay man."

Some of the fans were stunned. Many applauded and screamed their support but most took time to digest the reveal. Slowly the people stood and shouted their support. Now they understood why he had pledged Dennis' share to this particular charity. It was either out of guilt, or admiration or a mixture of the two. They had come to honor an outsider and ended up welcoming one of their own. What else did he have to say? They sat back down.

David continued, "I will proudly live my life openly for the rest of my days. My biggest regret is that Dennis and I never shared the biggest secret of all. We both chose to deal with our sexuality utilizing a game day strategy. He was on the offense and I was on the defense. Thanks to the winnings and contributions from fans and friends. We have established a program that will actively support bullied, confused, and isolated teens that may be in need of psychological, mental and emotional help in high school. We were, you should know by now, 'mirror twins.' I only wish you knew how hard it was to look into the mirror and face up to reality. From this day forward, I will live my life the way my brother chose to live his and do my best to help young people who need support at a critical time in their lives. I couldn't be a true advocate without acknowledging my genuine motivation. I feel free today and I know Dennis is looking down and understands."

Mack understood, "I didn't give him that advice, Sherri. He came up with that one on his own."

"Mack, I think David realized," Sherri added, "that the only way to live the rest of his life honestly was by telling one last, huge lie."

"No reason to lie any more!" Mack shot back, "The people who do know the truth: You and I, Pastor Jinks, Bob and Dottie will just have to file this one under 'keep our mouths shut'."

"Or 'memoirs nobody will care about in another year or two,'" Sherri summarized.

In the meantime, David was exchanging hugs with his many fans. He had the look of an innocent for the first time in nine months. He finally worked his way through the crowd to find his mentor. He and Mack grabbed each other in a bear hug.

"Where you gonna live, David? Will it be Temecula or Phoenix?" Mack asked.

"I've given it a lot of thought and WE are going to live, at least for the time being, in Laughlin."

"When you say 'WE,'" Mack asked, "does that mean you and Dennis are still together? Still having trouble letting him go?"

I've had the right treatment. He will always be part of me but I know he's gone. When I said 'WE', David clarified, "I was referring to the fact that the house in Laughlin and has separate quarters for my mom. She can stay there part time or full time if she wants to sell her house in the valley."

"Good," Barnes answered with a sigh of relief, "Have you got a place in mind?"

"David said, proudly, "I've had my eye on a waterfront bungalow near the casinos. It has a private dock and I just put a down payment on a very fast little watercraft for skiing."

Mack couldn't resist the obvious, "A 'boat on the river'? Is that what you're telling me?" Even the corniest poker story-teller would have hard time swallowing that one.

"If everybody comes over for the housewarming," Mack continued, "You'd have a full……" Even Mack couldn't bring himself to add the word 'house' out loud.

The two gave each other one final hug before saying their good-byes and went their separate ways out of the arena.

"Mack," Sherri said with her arm clamped around her husband's, "I think we'll have that boy in our lives for a long time."

Mack lamented, "We'll have both boys in our lives, Sherri. Just like Dottie, "we're all just family."

CHAPTER FORTY-THREE

Back on the Meadow

Did you wonder how Mack got a 'get out of jail card'? He didn't. He served his entire sentence. The judge had given him the minimum fine and the minimum sentence required by California law: one day from New Year's Eve to New Year's Day, 24 hours. In the morning, Mack was released from his stay in jail. The judge had given him solitude at Barnes' own request. He had accepted the sentence for 'organizing private gambling and/or gaming without proper permission or license'. As fellow Coyote Calvin Moffett unlocked the cell, Mack put the last of his 24 marks on the wall. He had paid the $1000 fine and was finally going to 'see the light of day' once more.

"The first twenty hours went by fast," he told his wife in the parking lot, "I spent most of the time reliving and reflecting on the past six months."

Sherri was just glad to have her husband back and Mack was quick to turn the scene into an overplayed and somewhat pathetic attempt to be romantic in front of a small crowd of supporters.

"The last four hours sucked," Barnes told his wife, "When a man is denied his carnal lusts, he becomes an animal in there." A few of their friends and onlookers turned to go.

Carrying on with his "not so mellow" dramatic soliloquy, he continued, "When I look into your eyes and hold you in my arms, I want to take you in this place, at this hour and share with you every part of my being." The 'old people being gross' display had most of the crowd somewhat ill and sent even more packing and heading home. It was a bit much for most.

Sherri loved the way her husband could exaggerate his feelings, even to the point of being ridiculous. She decided to empty the lot completely by responding with an 'over the top', tongue in cheek, passion of her own.

"Two things you have to do for me," Sherri pleaded.

"You name it, I'll do it," Barnes told his wife.

"First of all, Mack, when we get home, rip off my clothes and make mad, crazy, love to me until I can't remember my name or how to walk." Obviously they were already alone by now and the playful was starting to sound more ridiculous, if not pathetic.

"Of course I will," Barnes told his wife as he held her in a way that was physically inappropriate for their ages. "You mentioned a second thing," Mack reminded her, "Whatever could that be? Say it and I'll make it so."

Sherri knew her husband and pulled him close against her chest and lips, "If you ever decide to write a book about poker, Temecula and the WSOP," she said with even more passion, "Make sure this conversation makes the final editing cut and if it ever becomes a movie, I want Kevin Spacey to play you, Mack."

Mack softened his hold on Sherri, drew back his head and asked, "Who can we get to play you?"

"Mack," his wife assured him, "If Kevin Spacey plays you, I'll play myself."

It was the reason they had laughed their way through thirty years of marriage. They were 'mature' but they still liked to think young. They never lost their senses of humor. Thank God! Mack and Sherri still live on the meadow in Temecula. Besides the park model trailer in Big Bear, they bought a little condo in Hawaii Kai by Diamond Head on Oahu. They spend the holidays in the islands from Thanksgiving to Christmas and beyond.

Their combined earnings of $1.2 million pay for their weekly poker tournaments at Pechanga Casino. She knew that, if she hadn't challenged her husband to follow his dream, the world would have been a more peaceful place. They'd still have a home equity loan to pay off. Domingo and Dennis might still be alive, of course, but the whole adventure comes back to her every time she sees Mack out on the back porch looking out over the meadow. On New Year's Day, after his release and drive home, he found his favorite chair in the back yard.

"Sherri, bring me one of those Long Board Beers Randy sent us," Mack yelled. "You, know the one's with the Don Ho Bubbles."

Mack looked out over the meadow through the ever darkening dusk. He heard the sound of a whimpering animal. Barnes had heard that sound before and he knew what was about to happen.

A pack of critters had assembled to attract and then attack their helpless prey. The rest of the group sent their best candidate out into the hills alone. When he got there he cowered down in a fetal position and pretended to be something he was not. He mimicked the cries of an injured animal. Out of a hole popped the ears, the head and then the complete body of a rabbit who followed the sounds out of curiosity. Sometimes it might be a lost dog or stray cat. When close enough, the actor magically recovered to attack its prey. This performer/imitator was joined by the rest of the pack and the horrible sounds of vicious growls and helpless cries filled the evening. The worst part would be the sudden silence as the onslaught ended. This was a nightly occurrence in the meadow, in the valley. It was all part of an animal plan and the pack mentality, including the post victory howling.

As Sherri handed Mack his beer, he had to stop and realize wildlife was not always without its moments of natural selection and survival of the fittest. He had to admire how the whole group had worked together as a team, using one of its own to act on the group's behalf. Barnes appreciated how they all seemed to share in the spoils, albeit, unevenly. Some got more and some got less but they all seemed better off for the adventure.

"Oh, those wily coyotes," Mack said softly as he gently smiled, looking up at his understanding wife.

"Oh, those Wyllie Coyotes!" he whispered under his breath.

Post Script

By the way, remember the question Mack stumped the home poker group with before the game?

Nobody won the $100 that night. They all got distracted by Angel's arrival and the start of the tournament. Nobody remembered to research it or bring it up in the action that followed. I'll give you the original set up and the Mack version of the answer.

He told the home game crowd that he had two boys in his first class, at the first school where he had taught. The two looked exactly alike and they had the same mother and father. They were born in the same hospital in the same room and were delivered by the same doctor only minutes apart. They were the same age and they shared the same DNA. They grew up together and differed only in first names, yet they *WEREN'T* twins. How was that possible?

Did any of you figure it out? Mack didn't find out for several weeks. The boys originally had him scratching his head, too.

One day, while Mack was talking in front of the class, I appeared at the door and asked to talk to the brothers in question. I, too, looked exactly like my siblings. The reason they *weren't* 'twins' is because we were 'triplets'. Maybe, now you know how I got involved in Mack's life. He taught all us to be writers and we're all former students and have been best of friends for nearly 50 years. Some of Mack rubbed off on each one of us and it probably came through in my story telling as your narrator.

Sorry, too late to collect the $100. Good night!